DISRUPTED

WHEN THE INTERNET OF THINGS TAKES OVER

D1438176

"I do not think that the radio waves I have discovered will have any practical application." - *Heinrich Hertz*

Part 1 - The Opportunity

DISAPPOINTMENT

THE BEDROOM DOOR slammed, making the entire flat shake as Katheryn marched out on her half-naked boyfriend.

"Kat wait," Paul called after her through his closed bedroom door and stumbled out of bed with only his boxers on. It was nearly 6 am in Amsterdam, and he'd only just come to bed after a wild and crazy night with his computer. Katheryn had reached her limit a moment ago when she'd told Paul she was too exhausted to get 'cosy' with him and he'd complained they never spent time together.

"No," Katheryn yelled back at him as she stood by the front door, already shoving on her brown boots, "I've had enough. This is getting ridiculous." Paul came out to stand in front of her. "First of all," she seethed at him, "I can't believe you have the guts to say we don't spend time together. You're the one that's always on that damn thing!" Katheryn's eyes cut over to the laptop on a table in front of the living room sofa.

Paul's gaze followed and his mind automatically flicked to the comet-detection algorithm he was working on – the reason he'd come to bed so late. Katheryn took in her boyfriend's dishevelled dark hair with his dazed expression and let out a sigh.

"Look Paul," she spoke in a softer tone, "How can we have a proper relationship if we never spend time together – never talk?"

"Okay, let's do something today then. We'll go have a picnic at the park this afternoon or something, I promise." Kat regarded him for a moment, about to relent, but then her face hardened, hurt and resolve flickering in her golden brown eyes.

"I'll believe that when I see it," she said wryly, "Do you know how many times you've promised to go out with me, or get dinner with friends or even just watch TV, and then you came too late or forgot all-together?" Paul thought about this and opened his mouth to respond, but Katheryn wasn't finished.

"It's *all* the time Paul. Then you say you're sorry, yet it happens again and again. I don't need apologies, I need you to *do* something about it. But now it's clear - I don't think you ever will. I think you love your precious games and programmes more than me. I'm almost jealous." She let out a bitter laugh and crossed her arms over her chest. Paul crossed his own arms.

"That's simply not true," Paul retorted, his apologetic demeanor replaced with a defensive frown, "You're exaggerating." Apparently, this was the wrong thing to say. Katheryn's face drained of all colour then turned a deep shade of red as she levelled him with a scowl.

"Exaggerating?" she hissed, "Are you kidding me?" Paul swallowed hard, but stood his ground since she was, in his mind, over-dramatizing the situation. "Well, then, that's it Paul. I'm done. Here!" She was almost at the point of hysteria, tears streaming down her cheeks as she pulled out her keychain and took off a silver key with trembling fingers.

"Here, you can keep your stupid flat key along with your stupid computer. I hope you two are very happy together!" She then proceeded to throw the key straight at Paul's chest.

"Ow!" He stepped back in surprise and the key clattered to

the floor. Before he could react further, Katheryn yanked open the door, nearly hitting his face, strode partially out, then stopped and looked at him.

"We're over Paul - completely over."

Perhaps a little too late, Paul felt regret at not being more understanding, now that she was running down the two flights of stairs and leaving him for good. "Hold on," he called down as he raced after her all the way to the sidewalk. "Will you wait just a minute, please Kat!" Paul stood there, still in his boxers as Katheryn paused and turned around from five feet away. She sighed, wiped at her teary eyes and gave him a look full of pain, but still with utter resolve etched into her expression.

"Sorry Paul," she said simply, "I won't wait for you any longer. Goodbye." Then she turned and walked down the street, boots clicking with each step. Paul watched, still too stunned by it all to cry or scream or do much of anything.

When an older couple walked by, presumably on their way for an early coffee, and gave the barefooted young man a strange look, Paul decided it was time to go back in and sort through the storm of emotions raging inside.

* * *

Rafael Silva hit the gas-pedal of his silver car and smiled at the silent hum of its electro-motor as his new 'gadget' accelerated on the highway. There was nothing quite like the thrill of adrenaline pumping through his veins while smoothly flying along the road. It was almost midnight that Friday and Rafael was headed home after a great time with some old friends at Dugans, his favourite Atlanta sportsbar.

While he was born in a southern Brazilian city, Curitiba, Rafael had moved with his family to the States when he was just five. So these friends were from both grade school as well as college right around Atlanta.

As head of sales at Idrel Toys Inc., Rafael was the odd man out among his buddies who were mostly in finance and banking. "You guys are just selling air bubbles," he'd stated while he sipped a frothy ale.

"At least we get to wear a decent suit," one of his pals had smirked as he glanced at Rafael's jeans and casual tee-shirt. Rafael had shrugged with a grin. He loved not having to wear one of those stuffy suits and besides, it'd been a really good year for him. The company board was happy, which in turn made him happy. Due to their deal with a super popular Korean TV series, Rafael's salary had gone well into six-figures over the last two years. In his mid-forties, he was at the top of his game.

Though at the height of his work-world, Rafael had this unsettled feeling inside, a yearning to try something new and more innovative. He felt this restless sense now as he turned up the car radio's volume, pressed his foot down on the accelerator and sped off into the night.

* * *

Rafael woke up late the next day to the sound of his fourteen-year-old daughter's whiny complaints. "Dad, my phone is totally broken, and won't get fixed 'til Monday! You know what that means?" She sounded near tears. Rafael pulled a weary hand over his face and grunted. He and his wife had divorced four years ago, and Rafael had the kids every other weekend, which he usually loved. But at this exact moment, he just wished he could sleep in a bit more.

Unfortunately, his daughter wasn't done, and answered her own question with, "It means that I can't contact any of my friends *all* weekend and it completely sucks, that's what it means! What am I supposed to do?" Carolina could be a major drama-queen sometimes.

"Calm down, sweetie," Rafael told her with a sigh, "You'll be fine. It's not the end of the world, it's only one weekend. And look at it this way, you can really focus on your homework."

"Are you serious," Carolina's voice became even higher-pitched, "Only a weekend? All my photos and music are on there. Plus how am I going to keep up with my friends without texting? And homework? Ugh." With that she turned on her foot and marched out of the bedroom in a huff.

When Rafael was more awake, a cup of coffee and a scone in hand, his more rational and thankfully lower-pitched seventeen-year-old son, Jackson, came in. He wanted to show off the modifications on the remote-controlled car he'd been working on with his friends.

"Dad, check it out," Jackson tilted his RC-car so Rafael could see, "We've adapted the software to get more power from the motors." His son's eyes shone with excitement as he pointed out the changes. "And here, see? We've drilled holes in the body to make it lighter and lowered the battery for higher stability in turns."

"Cool," Rafael nodded with approval, feeling a wash of pride for his son, "Very cool indeed."

LIFE

PAUL'S GRANDMA, EMMA, decided to throw a party to celebrate life, and everyone was invited. A mixture of heat and a light
summer breeze created the perfect atmosphere. Although her
husband had passed away three years ago, Emma van Dijk was
happy to be surrounded by her children and grandchildren, all
running, talking and laughing in the garden of her flat's complex.

Today was August 27, the anniversary of Emma's wedding
and the reason she thought it was especially important to revel in
life with her entire family. Despite the fact that, due to her age,
she'd lost a bit of her eyesight, she watched as everyone enjoyed
their drinks and talked animatedly over her favourite light clas-
sical music.

Emma's grandson Paul sat next to her, happily eating one of
her specialties - smoked chicken salad. As she watched her lively
party guests, Emma noticed that some of the kids simply sat off in
the shadows, immersed in their electrical devices. With a shake of
her head, Emma leaned towards Paul. "I think children should get
away from those tiny screens and play with each other, like in the
old days when they ran around all day. It's so much healthier."

Paul nodded, though he wasn't one to talk, especially since

Kat had broken up with him a week ago due to him being glued to his own electrical device – his laptop. His stomach twisted at the thought of his ex-girlfriend's angry yet sad expression, and the chicken salad suddenly tasted a bit sour. He hadn't told his Grams about the break-up yet. "Oh Paul," she said, as if on cue, "You should bring that nice young lady with you next time you visit. How is she doing?"

"We, uh," Paul stammered, swallowing the lump in his throat, "Actually, Grams, we aren't together anymore. It's okay though, just wasn't meant to be." He added the last part with a forced smile when he saw Grams' concerned frown.

"Oh, sweetie, I'm so sorry," she sympathized with a kind pat on her grandson's shoulder, "I guess young love can be hard. You'll find someone else though, and soon. I can feel it." She looked intently into his eyes and gave a mysterious smile. Paul tried to hide the scepticism in his expression.

"Really? Well, I guess we'll see. Right now I'm good with being single. It leaves more time for my programming, you know." He gave another tight smile, as if he was trying to convince himself as well as Grams. Paul had suffered quite a lot over the last week, since Kat had left him.

Before Emma could respond, her other grandson, Chris held up a beer from across the garden and beckoned for Paul to head over. "Looks like I'm being summoned, I'll be back, Grams." With a kiss on her soft, wrinkled cheek, Paul walked over to his brother. "How's it going?" Chris asked, giving his brother a firm pat on the back along with a half-hug.

"I'm alright, uh, nothing new," Paul shrugged, not wanting to tell his recently married older brother about the break-up, "How's married life?"

"It's different, but Valentina's great. And work keeps me busy." Chris was running a dozen trendy clothing pop-up stores in the region and drove an Alfa Romeo. Though he was now a married man, Chris had been something of a hot-shot playboy before meeting his Italian wife, who'd been a student in Amsterdam.

"So, I have some news," Chris' dark blue eyes glittered, "I'm going to be a dad." Paul almost choked on his beer, and blinked incredulously at Chris.

"You *what* now?" he asked, "Are you joking? Man, never expected that from you of all people."

"Don't worry," Chris said, looking down at his shoes then back up, "I've accepted it. Valentina and I are moving from my flat to this crazy country house near the river. But, it's just twenty minutes from here which Grams is excited about, especially with her great grandchild on the way."

"Wow," Paul broke into a grin, "That's a huge change, Chris - sure you can handle it?"

"I think so," Chris chortled nervously, then shrugged, "It's kind of like a new adventure." They both took another long draught of beer and turned to look at Valentina who was now chatting with Grams and proudly showing her four-month pregnant belly.

Emma was positively beaming, and couldn't have asked for more joyous news at her life-celebration party.

* * *

Paul felt a rush of excitement as he worked on a new algorithm in his programme. It was by far the best he'd ever created, and he hadn't even been looking for the idea – it had come to him as if in a dream. The gist was that tiny smart pieces of software would duplicate themselves and share information. They would run on smart devices which were all connected to the internet. "Pure genius," Paul told himself as his fingers tapped away at the keys.

These smart pieces would collaborate with each other, like self-creating 'life' on cyber space - computer 'bacteria' that would grow into adaptive organisms. 'Turchaea,' is what Paul typed as the file name while saving it. The name was a concoction of the founding father of computers, Alan Turing, and the primordial bacteria, Archaea. "This is way too big for just me," Paul said to himself, "Definitely needs to go on the open source community."

And after five days of in-depth work on Turchea, where he virtually disappeared from friends and family, it finally happened – the code ran beautifully. Waves of pride washed through Paul along with muscle-cramp pain in his fingers and sheer exhaustion. But it was all worth it. He smiled as he felt the rush from being a part of the new technological movement - the Internet of Things, or IoT - which was about to spread through the world like wild-fire.

After a microwaved chicken and potato dinner, he tested and added examples to Turchaea. Thus, Thursday evening of September 23rd, Paul van Dijk posted the getTurchaea.zip version 0.1 on his open source community. He switched his monitor off and his phone back on. Hello again friends, family - world.

* * *

Everyone in China went crazy. As always, they discovered Paul's open source posting in lightning speed and, though some of their software code was a little dirty, they jumped on the Turchaea source code. The forums exploded with feedback and within two days Paul's Chinese RC-racer friend, Bruce, messaged him.

"*Paul, it's incredible,*" he wrote, "*The improvements from my Chinese friends make Turchaea smaller!*" Paul grinned as he read the whole message where Bruce went on and on about the brilliance of this algorithm and all the developments and twists that had been made to the original Turchaea. And within a few days Turchaea was used in a variety of beta-released Smartphone apps and cloud services. Paul was on top of the world.

That Monday night, he woke with a start, a new idea had struck him like lightning. He could incorporate Turchea into the RC cars he loved to race. Paul was so excited that he signed onto skype at 7 am and started chatting with his German hardware friend, Thomas. "Listen," his friend said with a tired grin, "If you get the money, we can do it easily." Paul's eyes sparked with excitement, though still heavy with sleep as Thomas continued,

"We'll just use existing components and downscale everything. Um, can I go back to bed now?" Paul ignored this last remark and adjusted his glasses as he responded.

"I'm gonna grab a cup of coffee - you wanna get one too and meet back in two minutes?" Thomas stifled a yawn and sighed.

"Fine – no sleep for me. Let's do it then." Coffee in hand, Thomas delved right back in moments later, talking details. Paul listened then asked,

"How much money do we need and when can we have it done?" Paul now wore his Bluetooth and was in action-mode while he paced through his messy bedroom and took sips of straight black coffee.

"Hold on, Paul," Thomas laughed, "One thing at a time. Let me sleep on this first, okay?" Before Paul could respond, Thomas had ended the call.

SHARING

"THAT'S NEVER GOING to fit in a remote controlled RC-racer," Paul told Thomas as he threw his hands in the air in disbelief. It was two weeks after their skype-chat and the two friends were in the lobby of a youth hostel in Berlin.

At the moment Paul was gaping down at all the hardware his German friend had brought with him. Thomas held up a hand. "Paul wait, this is just a prototype. When the design is finished, I'll downscale it to fit in an RC car, I swear." Paul arched an eyebrow, not fully convinced. But Thomas pointed at him and declared, "Believe me buddy, it will all fit in a single chip - don't you worry about that."

Though they didn't have any money to miniaturize it into a single chip yet, a business loan wasn't their first priority. They wanted to get the idea itself to work. "Come on, grumpy," Thomas urged, "Get your laptop connected and show me your Turchaea babies and I'll get some proper coffee to fuel our brains."

The next few days, Paul and Thomas practically lived in the corner of the hostel lobby. The receptionists were used to all kinds of strange people, but they'd never seen two young men sit there, never leaving to go and party. The only drinking these guys did involved caffeinated beverages and the occasional dark German beer.

Finally, after three days, their hard work paid off, Turchaea was successfully integrated into the prototype. It didn't look like a racing car at all, just a wired suitcase, but it was in fact a very sophisticated piece of mobile-internet connected IoT machinery.

Once powering the prototype, they put it online through Paul's home network server. Now that Turchaea was online and connected to the suitcase, the prototype woke up, created an internet cloud storage and began to replicate itself. After their baby's 'awakening', a green LED blinked and a robotic voice sounded. "Hello world."

Paul and Thomas exchanged eager grins. "Looks like our baby's alive and kicking," Paul said with a gleeful gleam in his dark blue eyes. Then, just like that, the mobile internet connection dropped and the robotic voice said, "Sorry, no network."

"You know," Thomas said jokingly, "I prefer the sound of a burp over this 'no-network' robot voice crap."

"Well," Paul replied with a laugh, "In that case..." And he quickly used his phone to record his own deep burp, easily triggered from the beer he currently held. Chuckling like schoolboys, Paul and Thomas rebooted using the factory defaults. Paul then deactivated the mobile connection, restarted the suitcase prototype and the green LED appeared yet again.

Much to their amusement, as well as that of the current hostel receptionist, a low burp echoed through the room. Paul and Thomas exchanged a look and burst into laughter. Paul held up his beer bottle. "Cheers to the cheap beer burp!" Thomas clinked his bottle with Paul's and they drank to the birth of their new baby.

* * *

"Perhaps you drilled too many holes," Rafael gently suggested to his son, Jackson, as they stood in the test zone of the RC Club.

Jackson's car had just crashed and he was desperately trying to repair it with carbon rods and ty raps.

"Yeah, yeah – I know," Jackson snapped irritably, "Can you just bring me the duct tape?" A moment later Jackson's RC friends came over and explained how they'd just upgraded their cars using an innovative new software that caused their special-tuned firmware to push the cars to their limits. Rafael looked at the group of Jackson's friends and asked, "Where do you get all your components from?"

"Different places," a teenage girl, one of the only females in the club, responded, "We swap and buy from a guy here at the club and sometimes get them through eBay. The software is open-source - top quality stuff!"

"Cool, thanks," Rafael smiled. While he watched Jackson and his friends continue to fix the car, Rafael wondered how this whole open-sourced software worked. Was it really all online, and for free? Who, if anyone, earned money from it - who owned the intellectual property rights?

Searching 'open source' on his phone, Rafael's eyes locked on a crowd-funding project by two students, one from Germany and one from The Netherlands. He motioned for his son to come over. "Jackson, come check this out."

* * *

As Rafael took a taxi to the Berlin youth hostel, he quickly scanned the printed document in his hands once more. He felt a wave of excitement at the thought of these remote controlled cars 'RCJoy Racers' that these two young men, Paul and Thomas, were working on. This was the innovative new project Rafael had been yearning for. It was perfect for the company and he was eager to, yet again, bring a successful new idea to Idrel Toys.

Ten minutes later Rafael paid the taxi, claimed a room in the hostel and grabbed a coffee from the lobby. He'd just poured in some creamer when a young man who he assumed was one of the many students approached.

"Are you Rafael?" the guy asked. Before Rafael could answer the student held out a hand, eyes bright with excitement, and said, "I'm Paul van Dijk." Rafael tried not to gape in surprise at the young man. This boy wasn't much older than his own son. His gaze went from Paul to another young guy who sat in the back, busy with some kind of electronics in a suitcase.

"Did I really fly all the way for these guys – they're practically teenagers," Rafael thought. The guy with the mess of wires looked up and called out a simple, "Hello, I'm Thomas." Then he promptly went back to work on the suitcase.

As Paul energetically told Rafael all about the RCJoy Racer idea and Turchaea, they sat near Thomas who studiously tested the prototype hardware. The three of them made for a nice, well-rounded team – Thomas was clearly the hardware guy, Paul was the software brains and Rafael had money as well as the brand and sales channels.

"So - today, why don't we first discuss what we want, and tomorrow we'll talk about how to make it happen," Rafael suggested. Thomas, finally done with his repairs, joined the conversation by launching into a twenty minute explanation about how they wanted low-cost, high volume chipsets and miniaturization.

Once Thomas was done, Paul added, "Our idea is based on a distributed open source IoT-system."

"Sorry guys," Rafael said with a furrowed brow, "I might sound like some naïve old guy, but what's IoT?" Thomas raised both of his eyebrows and exchanged a look with Paul. Did this guy really not know?

"IoT is an abbreviation for 'Internet of Things'," Paul began, "Every day, new devices all over the world can communicate with each other by using the internet. When they're equipped with sensors and connected to algorithms they become 'smart'. Whether it's a connected car, a thermostat or a smart-watch, in the end the Internet of Things improves quality of life."

"Okay, I think I understand," Rafael nodded, "Sounds like IoT has potential in a lot of fields, including toy production like with my company. Well, I'm gonna get some rest for tonight, but let's talk tomorrow about all the details, okay?"

* * *

"So," Rafael looked from Thomas to Paul across the café table at 10:30 am the next morning, "If I remember correctly, you guys have a miniaturized computer in mind which can be used in all kinds of toys and you've already distributed the software code among RC-racers - for free. Is that right?" They both nodded and continued to eat breakfast as Rafael went on, "And your software named 'Turkey' is based on a smart algorithm which enables the toys to share learned behaviour and limits, and…"

"It's called 'Turchaea'," Paul interrupted, "And its open sourced." The young man then launched into a bunch of techy explanations as Rafael's head began to spin. After five minutes of tech-talk, Paul tried to explain how it wasn't fully their idea.

"See, it's really based on preceding open-source code and we've been working with hundreds of people online – everyone openly shares their codes."

"But who gets the money?" Rafael asked as his forehead creased. Thomas decided to chime in here, over a mouthful of scrambled egg.

"You see," he told Rafael, "Nobody gets paid for it, we just share software source code. When an individual or a company uses it, they'll post the improved version back to the community. This lets us all move full steam ahead, you know?"

"Software isn't the issue," Paul interjected, "The hardware is, well, the 'hard' part. We need to develop it properly, scaling way down from the suitcase to a single chip." Rafael looked from Paul to Thomas.

"What do you need to be able to do that?" he asked.

"To put it simply - money, time and a production partner," Thomas answered without looking up from his second cup of coffee. At this, Rafael leaned forward and lowered his voice, demanding their attention.

"Listen guys, RC cars are a niche in the market. If we want to make a good amount of volume, we should market to a wider range of customers. Would you guys be able to alter this project for children's dolls?"

"We can put it in anything," Thomas replied, "We just need the money and a production partner." Rafael looked out the window, thinking for several moments.

"Okay," he finally said, "I think we have a deal. Let's get the stuff on the market before Christmas, sound good?" Thomas and Paul both broke into wide smiles, eyes shining.

"Thank you, we'll definitely drink to that," Paul replied with a raised cup of orange juice. The three of them clinked their orange juice glasses and Rafael summarized their next step,

"Let's do this!"

* * *

"Really guys, trust me. Definitely keep up with your RC-racing and everything, but let's focus on the mass market. Children's dolls are much more interesting than remote controlled cars," Rafael spoke loud and clear on the conference call. If those young men really wanted to move forward they had to focus on mainstream toys.

"To be honest Rafael," Paul said as his eyebrows drew together, "I prefer cars over of dolls – by quite a bit. We really don't know anything about dolls, or kids for that matter."

"Look, Rafael," Thomas added, "We just want to make good hardware and software. We're definitely not going to decide what type of clothes these dolls wear or how they look or anything."

"Relax guys," Rafael assured them, "No one's going to make you chose doll outfits. Just give me two weeks, and I'll arrange the marketing part. You guys just focus on the technology. Could you please take RCJoy from the crowdsourcing platform for those two weeks, and I'll get some trustworthy people on board?" Paul and Thomas both looked worried. Rafael sensed their hesitation.

"Look, I'll figure the doll part of it out, I promise," he assured the two, "Next week we'll have a production expert meet with you to discuss the first steps. Please trust me, I really believe in your idea - in your dream." He seemed to speak with utter honesty. Thomas took a breath and said,

"Okay, two weeks is fine."

"Yeah," Paul agreed with a nod, "We'll focus on the improvements."

"Great. And remember, no worries," Rafael smiled, "Do whatever it is you need to do. Oh, and try to figure out what kind of behaviour you want to give the dolls, okay?"

"Can we collect some insights from internet forums?" Paul asked.

"However you want to get the information is fine with me," Rafael shrugged, "Let's talk again next Friday, same time."

As soon as the call ended Paul shook his head. "I'm not going to spend all my time on investigating doll behavior," he grumbled to Thomas, "Let's post something on a web forum to ask about it, then we'll be ready for Friday's call."

Minutes later, Thomas and Paul had found a specialized 'Children's Cognitive Development' forum and posted a message:

What Do You Think About an Educational,

Smart Doll for Children?

Summary - We're making a sophisticated, interactive smart doll that is both a friend and a teacher.

It looks like a normal doll but contains a miniaturized computer that enables it to learn and recognize children's behaviour.

When children meet, their dolls will interact and play together along with the children.

This smart doll is mobile-connected to the internet which enables it to use learning programmes from other sources such as SchoolForge, Open Source Schools, and so forth. Parents will have a smartphone app to monitor the learning progress of their children.

We're currently developing and are interested in your opinion. We would also appreciate it if you could respond to our questions:

1. Do you like this concept?
2. What functions should it have and which ones should be avoided?

Thanks in advance for your feedback!

T&P

CHANGE

"WE'RE A TRADITIONAL company and our business methods hail from the last millennium," Rafael started as he looked around at everyone that Monday in Idrel Toy's monthly board meeting. His gaze also included Jason Zhing on a video link from China. Rafael had passed out his 'Opportunities of the Internet of Things' and began the projected slideshow from his laptop. Once he was sure he had everyone's attention, he continued,

"We at Idrel Toys design, manufacture and sell products via retail and online channels. And we know exactly who our customers are, what they like, how they make purchasing decisions and how high they're willing to pay. We always keep track of market share and recommendation indicators from customers. In a nutshell, everything seems well and good." Now Rafael got to the interesting part.

"The only problem is…" Here Rafael paused for several beats and made solid eye-contact with each and every board member before he went on. "The only problem is that we only sell *products*." His colleagues looked at him as if he'd become slightly unhinged. Through the video, Jason was first to respond.

"Sounds like we're doing great to me, Rafael. And what else

would we sell besides products?" Rafael stood up and started to pace around as he went into full-on presentation mode.

"Idrel's brand is strong and our distribution channel is good for the moment, I agree," he replied, "But, the question is, how long will it stay like this? We face cheap competition that's slowly growing and taking over market share. We have to find a way to ensure that customers will return to us in this day and age. Is there maybe a way we can achieve this by incorporating the 'Internet of Things', or IoT, into our company? IoT enables us to make our toys smart and add value by offering content."

Though there was some throat-clearing and a few mumbled words, everyone listened attentively. Rafael sat down again, leaned forward and spoke in his most convincing voice, "I say we look at the future, move ahead, and keep our lead in the market by leaps and bounds. I say we shift from 'buying' customers to 'subscribing' customers. And how can we do that?"

The others could see that he was getting worked up over this one, but they weren't surprised. Rafael Silva was always the forward-thinker of the team, constantly vying for change. So they waited quietly as he answered his own question. "We can do this by using the Internet of Things. Let's put out some awesome pilots and give IoT a try." Maria, head of Idrel's finance department, interrupted him at this point.

"Good ideas Rafael, we hear you. But please give us a specific example of how we can embrace this 'Internet of Things', or IoT as you phrased it. We ship and sell products for children. We don't offer any service." Mutters erupted throughout the room at this 'show-down' of sorts. Rafael gave a tight smile – he'd anticipated the most resistance from Maria and was prepared.

"A very good question," he said, "Thank you Maria. Let me start here - we have a customer-focused goal to improve the life of each and every one of our loyal buyers. IoT fits into this vision perfectly, and I believe that we already offer a service. For example, with our dolls." Maria opened her mouth to question him, but Rafael beat her to it.

"In a way," he explained, "Idrel dolls offer children friendship - a life-time buddy to play with. Kids learn from engaging in pretend-play. I simply suggest we merge products like these dolls with a service." Ignoring whispers throughout the room, Rafael took a doll from the display case against the wall and held it up.

"We should put technology inside this doll, or maybe something more soft and cuddly like a teddy bear. And with a simple electronic chip and a mobile internet connection to our new Idrel Toy content platform, we can offer educational programmes in the teddy bears that teach young children new languages, counting, even reading. Parents can load new learning programmes into it when their kids get older – the possibilities are endless." Rafael was now in full-swing, but Maria forcefully interrupted.

"Rafael, hold on a moment," she said in her most authoritative voice, "This does *not* match our vision whatsoever. We offer life-time friends to children, not some crazy technological addiction. I've never heard of such a thing in my whole time with the company!" She took a deep, calming breath, and proceeded a little more gently. "It's an innovative idea for sure, but I think we shouldn't get involved with IoT at the present time. Let's keep it simple. Why don't we develop an Idrel partner programme and gain sales with our existing retail channels?"

Most of the other board members nodded and mumbled in agreement as Maria added, "I don't want to simply wave this away for good, but getting into IoT requires a dramatic strategy change. I suggest we ask our existing external consultants to work on it and come up with an IoT-market analysis in three months, okay?" Rafael let out a sigh. "*Sheep*," he thought.

After the board meeting, 'Idrel-IoT-Innovations' became a very small action item on the minutes of the meeting and was assigned to one of his marketing colleagues. Rafael now knew that the corporate culture of Idrel Toys Inc was not ready for IoT yet. If he wanted to move ahead, he'd have to find another way.

* * *

Out of the 46 responses to the 'Children's Cognitive Development' forum post, which included both good, bad, helpful and unhelpful feedback, one in particular stood out to Paul. It was from a guy with the screen-name "John1990" and his response was quite extraordinary. The message began,

> *"As a teacher in South Korea, I really like the idea of offering technology to kids as a way of learning. Along with being a part-time teacher while studying, I follow research in cognitive learning."*

The response spanned four more pages after that, including his data, theories and assumptions about children's learning strategies, source references and a bullet-wise analysis on the methods of how children play and learn in particular age groups. The message ended with,

> *"I'm fascinated by children's learning processes and try to assist parents and teachers by getting their kids interested in learning through robot-play. I'm convinced that we need more than just screen-based devices.*
> *Currently, I'm working on my thesis and writing a development programme for children. It's based on a pilot project I did over the last two months with 250 kids (aged 8-12) using a tablet app which contained in-game learning tasks. Although the results aren't published yet, I can assure you that I see significant*

learning improvements in the gaming kids compared to their peer group.

I would like to ask you for a short interview that I could use in my thesis. It enables me (as a non-tech person) to understand and explain the technical possibilities of toy robots for today and the future. I can assure you I won't take too much of your time!

Thanks in advance,
Best regards,
John.'

Paul turned to Thomas and said, "This is someone we absolutely have to talk to."

"Yeah," Thomas nodded, "It definitely seems like he's on the same track as us, and can add a different point a view. Let's drop him an email suggesting a morning Skype." Paul sent a quick response to John, made a copy, then forwarded it all to Rafael with the subject line, 'Em-Teaching Strategy'.

* * *

"Why can't the time-zones be reversed - ugh," Paul grumbled to himself as he got up at the ungodly hour of 9 am, which was afternoon in South Korea, to Skype with John. With a huge yawn, he pulled his fingers through his messy brown hair, put on his glasses and answered the Korean teacher's skype call.

Paul's eyes blinked in surprise at what he saw. He was, quite frankly, shocked. In place of the male Korean teacher he'd expected 'John1990' to be, was a young woman. A really, really attractive young woman with vivid green eyes and dark blond hair, right around his age. He felt suddenly very self-conscious and ran a hand over his hair again, hoping he didn't look too dishevelled.

"Hey, I'm Paul." He tried to sound casual.

"Hey there, Paul, I'm Jane. How's your morning going?" She had a really nice voice, with a cool accent.

"My morning's good, thanks. You're, uh, not Korean," he said with a blush. He was stating the obvious.

"Yeah, I know." Jane replied with a light laugh, "I'm from Christchurch, New Zealand. I moved here to South Korea two years ago after university. Just wanted to explore the world outside my little native island, you know?"

"That's really cool," Paul smiled shyly. He was about to ask about her screenname, when she said,

"Sorry, on top of thinking I was Korean you probably thought I was a guy too, right?" Before Paul could respond she explained, "I used to go by 'Jane1990', but got tons of these ridiculous fake private messages, so I changed to 'John1990'. And that did the trick." She smiled widely and Paul noticed how warm and down-to-earth her smile was.

A moment of pleasantries later and Paul, getting his head mostly together, finally asked about the project at hand. She answered, "I seriously think traditional schools are outdated these days. We really need to reach the next level of education, like the School-of-Clouds concept based on the idea that children are able to learn on their own and teach each other. The only thing we need to do is facilitate this process, you know?" Paul nodded, impressed with her enthusiasm.

"So, how do you think we can change the school system?" Paul asked. Jane considered this for a moment as she brushed her shoulder-length hair away from her cheeks.

"You know," she finally answered, "I was really inspired by Sugata Mitra on TED-Talks. He talked about how these kids, who were supposedly in 'learning slumps', taught themselves English and computer programming. If we offer kids robots filled with know-how, open questions and some emphatic behaviour, it'd be amazing."

Paul watched her continue, his mind in a half-mesmerized state as he stared at her sparkling eyes – this girl was incredible.

"If we could also hook these doll-computers up to a School-of-Clouds," she continued passionately, "And get them to collaborate, we could be a huge part of future schools. Children could do what comes so naturally to them, so intrinsically - learn through playing." Paul opened his mouth to agree, but Jane continued,

"And don't forget, three years ago the UN reported that 58 million primary school-aged children dropped out of school. With Em we can make learning accessible to kids all over the world. But the thing is, I programmed the children's lessons in Scratch and my possibilities are limited. So, when I read your forum post, I was intrigued. I'd like to start a pilot project using Em and, Paul, I need you guys to get me started on this."

Jane now sat back and looked a little shy from having opened up so much to a virtual stranger, who was pretty cute at that. "Absolutely." Paul responded after thinking a moment, "Of course we'll help you with a pilot learning system. It sounds fantastic." He grinned and nervously adjusted his glasses before continuing, "I think we can make Em so that it allows users to run Scratch programmes. The emphatic behaviour would be based on Turchaea's self-adaptive method. You see," he started, but Jane held up a hand and laughed.

"Please, Paul, hold off on all these techy terms. You're making my head spin," she grinned and added, "When do you plan to have Em working? I'd love to test it."

"Um, let me have a chat with the other guys to see about that, and I'll drop you a line as soon as I find out, okay?"

"Perfect, thanks Paul," she said with a little wave, "And nice to meet you."

"You too, John1990," Paul gave a playful smile before they signed off.

TEAMING-UP

"I THINK WE should team up with friends outside Idrel," Jason told Rafael, "And develop something new. I agree with you - we can pull it off if we don't get in too deep with the board members about our day-to-day involvement. Then, if it's a success, Idrel buys itself in. If it's a failure, nobody will notice. Let's go for it."

Rafael grinned at his colleague. "That's what I like to hear. Let's outsource the production of all electronic parts to a specialized production partner."

"Good call," Jason agreed, "So, how far are you with Em? Is it still just an idea or do you have a working prototype?" Rafael proceeded to tell him everything about Thomas, Paul, their suitcase and the initial talk with Jane they'd recently had.

"Plus," Rafael finished, "I've got some investment and banking friends and we can definitely get start-up funding from them."

"Perfect. Let's go ahead with these young guys and the teacher woman. Let me talk with the other board members and handle Maria," Jason concluded.

After ending the call, Rafael continued to drive through the beautiful, sunny day and thought about what the next steps should be. He was really getting excited – this new project was almost prepared for take-off.

* * *

"So, which one of you guys can answer my questions?" Jane asked Rafael, Paul and Thomas at once from her classroom. She was grading papers, Rafael was driving with his headset while both Paul and Thomas were barely awake as they all skype chatted.

"Well Jane," Rafael took the lead, "We all can, actually. I'll be switching every now and then between calls though, so Thomas and Paul are going to explain the tech stuff now. But, I must ask you to treat this information as highly confidential, and not share with anyone else, okay?"

"Wait a minute," Jane said as her eyebrows arched up, "You posted a request on a forum and now you want me to keep everything on the down-low? I thought you guys were more into the open source way of working?"

"Relax Jane," Rafael answered in a reassuring voice, "It's just that we're still not sure about some of the financial details. Feel free to chat openly." And with that, Rafael left the conversation to talk with his administrative staff about a meeting agenda. Jane tried to grasp all the tech stuff Paul and Thomas then launched into, though it was a bit overwhelming. In any case, she was impressed.

"So," she said after listening, "How far are you guys from a working product?" Paul and Thomas exchanged a look.

"Not too far," Paul hedged, "We just need to straighten out funding and stuff to get a working product."

"Okay, cool," Jane smiled, then held up a little robot, "I wanted to show you this little guy. I use him in my classes to help the kids learn. And it gives me more time to assist students with social skills like communication, behaviour, emotions and stuff. Also, the robot helps hyper active kids to pay attention."

She paused for a few moments as she shifted on her chair and looked at the camera. Paul smiled right back and felt as if it was just the two of them almost, like she was talking to him alone rather than him and Thomas. Suddenly loud crackling sounded and Rafael was back. He'd been eavesdropping a little on the conversation with his phone on mute while he drove.

"Jane," Rafael said confidently, "I want you to meet us all in Europe and see if we can collaborate somehow. I'll pay for your flight, hotel and any other expenses."

"Sorry Ishmael," she said, "I can't go anywhere - I have to teach class and won't have a break until the holidays. In fourteen days we'll have a couple of weeks off, but I'm going to Nepal with a friend to walk the Annapurna range."

"Actually," Rafael said with a laugh, "My name's Rafael, but, never mind. We really, really need your help with Em. Your input with case descriptions and Em's response behaviour would be invaluable. We want Em to become a little robotic Jane – cool huh?"

"To be honest," Jane answered, after mulling it over for several beats, "I thought you already had a working robot doll. The only thing I see is an old, wired suitcase. I'm not going to skip my vacation, which I've been planning for months, for that, Rafael. I just wanted to have an interview with you guys, which brings me to my last question - do you think children will ask their parents to buy Em as holiday or birthday gifts?"

"That's exactly what our objective is," Rafael answered eagerly, "We want Em to be attractive to both kids and parents alike. Em will be a part of the 'Internet of Things', and I'm convinced IoT will lead to a robot-supported society. It has possibilities we can't even imagine." As Jane processed this, Paul gazed at her, absently wondering if she was single.

"*Forget it Paul*," he told himself, "*She's probably engaged to some amazing guy who needed to work in South Korea, which is why she's there.*" Whether this was true or not, Paul felt a kind of release inside. Jane was the first woman he'd been interested in since that whole Kat break-up fiasco, and it was liberating to feel that kind of attraction again. He was emotionally ready to move on.

Suddenly, the shrill noise of a school bell sounded from Jane's end. "Okay guys, that's my cue," she said, "I gotta go. Thanks for the interview and, to me, the possibilities are very clear in the world of education. Paul, I'll send you more information on the School-of-Clouds concept and a draft paper of my project results, okay? Bye for now!" Paul, Rafael and Thomas all chorused their goodbyes and thanks and then she was gone.

* * *

The plane slowly started to descend towards Shanghai Pudong International Airport. Paul sat next to Thomas and finished reading the draft research paper Jane had sent. After some convincing from Rafael and Jason, they'd agreed to be flown into Idrel Toy's Chinese electronic production partner, FLQ-electronics to discuss the doll project.

Jane's paper was impressive, with a nice, simple concept. Her Scratch lessons were designed to pique children's curiosity, provide facts and then give positive reinforcement with praise and compliments. The problem Jane faced in her classes was that not all children had an interest in the same things at the same times, as well as the fact they all had different learning speeds. The thing all kids did have in common, her paper stated, was the fact that they wanted to play with each other and possessed an intuitive eagerness to learn.

After reading, Paul's mind started turning. *"Maybe I could hook Em up to a kind of kid's version of Wikipedia and add a teaching layer on top of it."* While the idea was still fresh in his mind, he typed it in an offline reply to Jane, then buckled his seatbelt and prepared for landing.

* * *

"It's not a single factory," Jason told Paul and Thomas as they rode in a minibus from the hotel towards FLQ-Electronics the following day. He continued, "It's a research and development campus combined with several production facilities. You could say it's like a city. And no need to be nervous," he added, noting how Paul kept running his hand through his messy brown hair and adjusting his glasses, "This is a low profile meeting with some engineers I know, and Rafael will join us for the factory tour."

The minibus now reached the city's border and drove on a newer portion of the highway that cut through the mountain. Hundreds of bulldozers busily flattened out parts of the mountain. Paul had never seen a manifestation of growth and power on such a scale before.

To pass time during the long trip, Paul pulled out his phone and browsed his social media pages. Maybe Jane was bored and he could message her. He saw that she'd posted numerous pictures of herself and a friend buying a Lonely Planet book at the store, both looking excited. Paul read the posts, and found that the two young ladies would leave in less than two weeks for the Himalayas.

This inspired Paul to post a picture of the grey industrial Chinese landscape out his window. He smirked after posting it, then suddenly realized something. His crush on this young woman had grown pretty serious, there was no mistaking it. With a sigh, he kept browsing through all of Jane's pics and really wished she'd ditch her trip so he could meet her in person after all.

One hour later, Paul sat next to Thomas at an oval table, facing the large window that overlooked the FLQ factories campus. The meeting definitely wasn't as low-profile as they'd expected and Paul suddenly felt under-dressed in just jeans and a tee-shirt, surrounded by fifteen formally dressed men and women.

After Jason explained their plans with Em, and Paul briefly

talked about how it would work on a software level, they shared the Turchaeas concept and their open source strategy. "The idea is," Paul finished, "That I hand over and explain the code, then you guys will be able to add some production testing software." The head engineer nodded, taking all of this in.

"So," a woman in a business suit turned towards Jason and asked, "What are your expected volumes?"

"You know," Jason responded, "I think it's time to give you a demonstration. Thomas?" He'd effectively avoided the question and shifted the focus to the product itself, exactly as planned.

Opening his demo suitcase, Thomas gave a detailed but quick explanation of the hardware. He'd noticed that Em was having trouble finding the mobile network and wasn't starting, so he explained even further to buy time. All the while Thomas panicked inside, thinking, "*Why the hell didn't I try this out on a test run at the hotel?*"

When Thomas ran out of things to say, thankfully, the lead engineer chimed in. "Why don't we show you our FLQ video while you sort the demo out?" They were only five minutes into the sleek media show when a loud burp echoed through the room. Em had woken up and everyone's eyes flew to the demo doll - one woman giggled. Thomas laughed and told them,

"That's what she always does when she wakes up for the first time."

After everyone quieted from the burping doll, they finished watching the presentation. It was clear that this company had all the production capabilities needed for Em.

* * *

As all of this was going on, the minibus had picked Rafael up from the airport. During his drive to FLQ-Electronics, he was on the phone with one of Idrel's supervisory board members. "I think we should also move our traditional dolls to the next level," Rafael said after a little small talk.

"What do you mean exactly?" the board member asked. After Rafael gave a brief run-down of his IoT idea and Em, the man responded, "Isn't this just another technology push? I mean, do people really need and want this?"

"Perhaps you're right," Rafael replied, smiling devilishly at himself and his brilliant convincing tactics, "In the early days, the first human beings didn't need a wheel. So, when one of them came up with it, I'm sure there were both sceptics and believers. IoT is the same thing. The question is, as a company, do we want to be early or late adaptors?" The other end of the phone was silent for a moment.

"You know," the board member said at last, "I think you're right, Rafael. It's time we move on as a company. Why don't you share your ideas with Maria first, and if she supports you, I'm sure everybody will agree to going along with a pilot of this doll project."

As Rafael walked into the FLQ boardroom twenty minutes later he thought, "*I'm already here, why not speed things up and sign a letter of intent with these guys?*"

CREATION

"*DEAR MS. SOLON, I understand that you feel responsible and we share your feelings. As one of the largest mobile operator networks, we've taken precautions to ensure that our networks are able to withstand severe threads. We would like to invite you as a representative of the European Party to visit one of our network operation centres and present our...*"

"*Blah, blah, blah, there they go again,*" Nikole thought. She didn't want to present anything, just to get her inter-operator emergency roaming to work. In case of a mobile network outage, mobile operators should be able to act as backups for each other. Whether to make a call or have internet access, society these days was too dependent on mobile connection to let it completely collapse without backup.

"These idiots only look at the average revenue per user. They're not interested in 100%, full-proof networks," Nikole muttered to herself as she shook her head in frustration. She knew what she had to do, and with a sigh she called her contact for GSMA, the worldwide organisation representing all mobile network operators.

The next day, Nikole shut the passenger door to the taxi in Brussels and walked along with her Swedish left-wing coalition partner, Bjorn. He turned to her as they stood outside the hotel entrance.

"Let's hit the bar and celebrate the success of your 'emergency-roaming', yeah?" Bjorn lit a cigarette and added, "Why are you not going to work in industry? I mean, you're poised and clever enough." He blew the smoke carefully aside.

"Listen Bjorn," she shook her head, ignoring his last question, "I know you laugh about it, but mobile networks are too interwoven with our society. We're completely dependent on them. Nobody leaves his or her house without a smartphone these days. Apart from you, nobody smokes cigarettes anymore, but smart devices? We simply don't know how to live without them."

As Bjorn thought about this and blew smoke rings, Nikole mused to herself, "*Who 'owns' who, actually? Do people own phones, or is it the other way around in a sense?*" She said out loud, "A mobile network outage for just a few days would put society on hold. We've seen it in several countries already, and people don't know how to drive anywhere, communicate with family or friends and, this is quite serious, they don't know how to reach emergency services."

"You're exaggerating again," Bjorn said with a sigh. She cut him a look.

"Don't forget all the network-connected machines, cars and devices," she reminded him, "Toll systems would stop billing, bus drivers wouldn't be able to download their daily schedules, car alarm systems wouldn't work – the list is endless. That's why we've got to plan ahead and protect our people."

"Nikole, relax," he dropped his cigarette on the pavement and tapped it out with his foot, "Let's hit the bar to celebrate."

A few minutes later, they sat at the hotel bar where Bjorn watched the football match that was showing on the flat-screen. Nikole glanced at the match then asked, "So, just out of curiosity, when was the last time you switched off your phone?"

"I can't remember," he said with a shrug, "Even when I sleep or fly I just leave it on." Though he wasn't going to come straight out and say it, Bjorn knew she was right. Nikole had done a great job for the party today. Using the left-wing, EU-coalition partners, she'd forced the European mobile operators to cooperate on emergency roaming. They'd just agreed to support a standardized emergency procedure that would be automatically activated if an operator was down for two or more days in any European country.

Nikole smiled proudly as she thought about her success and finished her glass of Merlot. Bjorn had joined a group of random young men and women that huddled around the bar closer to the TV, all watching and shouting comments about the match. Nikole passed them on her way out, smiled and shook her head. She didn't care about the game's outcome, she'd earned her own personal victory today.

***

Jason, Rafael, Thomas and Paul re-united in the FLQ meeting room after lunch. Rafael was clearly in a good mood and almost glowed as he sat at the oval table. After being introduced to the FLQ lead engineer, Chen, Rafael cut straight to the chase.

"You've seen our plans and prototype and I've had a chat with my colleagues," he started. Rafael glanced at Thomas and Paul before he turned his eyes back on Chen. "We're convinced of your technical capabilities and would like to go ahead with you guys." Chen nodded, and Rafael continued, "Can we sketch a project time-line with some milestones?"

"Well," Jason chimed in, "We've basically finished a proven concept and are ready to work towards a prototype." The FLQ team knocked their heads together while Thomas and Paul blinked in astonishment. Paul whispered to Thomas, "Uh, did you know anything about this? We only have this suitcase demo - a far cry from a working version."

"It's okay Paul," Thomas whispered back, "These business guys know their stuff. They're clearly just over-selling it a little to get a good price." Paul nodded, but still shifted uneasily in his seat. It was all happening so fast.

After a few moments where the room buzzed with talk and excitement, Chen turned to Paul. "So, Mr. van Dijk, when can you share the software code so our guys can have a look?"

"It's already on-line," Paul answered, "Available as open-source RC-racing software."

"Mr. Silva," Chen shifted his attention from Paul to Rafael, "I'll ensure that our best engineers take a look and give you a good proposal."

"Paul," Jason interjected here, "Would you be able to stay longer and help out the engineers? You know, get them on track with the code and everything?" Paul thought about it, then shook his head.

"Actually," Paul replied, "I think it's more efficient if they first have a look at the code and then contact our friend Bruce in Hong Kong. He's familiar with it and speaks your language." He addressed this last part to Chen. Jason's eyebrows drew together, but Chen nodded and gave a time-line for looking over the code. The meeting was soon wrapped up.

"We thank you for your time, and for your trust in FLQ, gentlemen," Chen told them all.

During the minibus drive back to the hotel, Thomas turned to Rafael and said, "This is crazy, I hope you know. We need at least nine months to develop a good code, and hardware development takes at least a year. Don't forget, we still have to find an experienced teacher to develop the content part, and…"

"No we don't," Paul interrupted, "I'll get in touch with Jane again. Maybe I can get her to change her mind."

"So," Rafael said after a pause, thoughts still focused on Idrel, "I had a chat with Idrel and they insist that we have the product ready by the end of autumn, so we're ready to go for the Christmas sales peak."

"What?" Thomas almost shouted, then shook his head vigorously,

"That's only three months from now and physically impossible. Chipset development takes at least six months – you're completely out of your mind!"

"Hold on," Rafael held up a hand, "Let me explain. I understand that the miniaturization takes time and I agree that we need to do that. So, we'll follow your special-chip approach, but in the meantime, I suggest we start with a simpler version of Em. Seeing your burping suitcase, I'm sure that you're able to squeeze it into a larger toy, say a teddy bear, with some assistance from FLQ engineers."

"Man," Paul said with a sigh, "It feels like we're all over the place and not focused anymore. We started with RC-racers, moved to dolls and now we're talking about a teddy bear. What's next?" Thomas nodded in agreement. But Rafael was undeterred by their doubts.

"I can imagine that it looks out-of-focus to you," Rafael told them, "The thing is, with completely new products or services, you never know exactly where you're headed. You simple have to create the awareness and the demand will follow. It's fuzzy now, but everything will clear up and come into focus as we move forward, I promise."

* * *

"This is not a handheld tablet or computer," she mumbled to herself as she stared at her laptop, sitting on her bed, "It looks like some kind of device that connects to a distributed cloud." It was Saturday afternoon and the teenage girl sat cross-legged as she watched the internet data packets by using an installed 'network-sniffer' on an unsecured server.

"The strange thing is, most of the time they're off-line and when they're on-line, they always return to the same geographical area," the girl muttered again to herself, a habit she often employed, "They also disappear mysteriously for about two hours, and mostly pop up over the weekend. What the hell kind of device does that? And why would they use secured hashing - are they hiding something?"

She leaned forward towards the blue glow of her laptop, more and more intrigued as she puzzled through all of this. It was an interesting break from the usual, monotonous computers she often saw through the unsecured server. She now put this new, very curious device on her wall's 'to-hit' list.

It was just for fun of course, and she always told the owners when she found a leak. She stopped watching, installed a notifier then activated a log. She was convinced that she just needed to collect logs and study it next week to look for patterns. "I don't care how hard it seems," she told herself confidently, "There's always a backdoor."

* * *

"This project is brilliant," Bruce told Paul as they strolled through a Hong Kong park two weeks after the FLQ-electronics meeting. Bruce went on, "Information and algorithm-tasks can hop from bear to bear when they're close to each other – short–range. This is so exciting, thanks for bringing me in on it." He looked from Paul to the gravel path ahead that now weaved through a small patch of bamboo. Paul glanced from the trail to Bruce.

"Who better to get help from than my old RC buddy?" Paul smiled, then grew serious, "We don't really have time to write the software code, but Jason said to just get the hardware now and write the software to support it later on." Bruce nodded, then Paul kicked lightly at a small stone in the path.

"I should go," Paul said, "I'm swamped with trying to prepare slides and software packs to get the FLQ team on track. We need to start testing software soon and give a proper 'end-of-production' test, as Rafael calls it."

* * *

"No, I don't want anything to do with you guys," Jane told Paul over skype after he tried to convince her to change her mind. She pursed her lips and continued, "You're just making products to get kids addicted, and your commercialized intentions don't match the way I view the world." Paul blushed, embarrassed that she grouped him with the business guys.

"Look Jane," he implored, "I'm not a commercial guy at all. Yeah, we have people like Rafael who want to make the technology available for a larger group, but I'm more like those MIT University and robot guys you've contacted during your first project. In this project we also freely publish and distribute the software and hardware." He ran a nervous hand through his hair and finished with,

"I'm not driven by profit, I swear. I just want to do this for the common good. We support the company because they have the money to invest and make this possible, and I'm sure it will generate useful spin-offs whether it's for my RC-racers or your school robots."

Jane turned her head away from the webcam, then looked back. "Paul, you guys don't specifically need *my* help. Why don't you have a chat with the robot team that supported me in the beginning? But, you can only use them as long as you share your improvements with the rest of the community for free." He opened his mouth to defend himself further, but she added.

"And remember, you have to make this teddy bear act friendly and encourage the kids to learn. A bit like a grandmother would do - giving positive feedback, acting interested and asking open-ended questions - stuff like that. This is what children want."

"See," Paul replied, looking desperate, "You're perfect for this project, Jane. Look how much you helped just now by saying that. We really need your help to, let's call it 'grandmotherize', the bears." As she watched and listened to Paul practically beg her to help, Jane's resolve weakened. Then he added,

"I'm sure I can persuade Idrel to give you several boxes of bears for your project – for free." Paul noticed the spark of interest in Jane's eyes and ended with, "Jane, these bears will be fantastic for your students – they'll be able to detect stuff like when the kid strokes their backs, recognize smiling faces, know their tone of voice and even have speech recognition."

Jane allowed a little smile. "Well, that does sound pretty cool. I'll sleep on it, okay? Bye Paul van Dijk, have fun in Hong Kong." She gave a little wave, a big smile and signed off. Paul sat there and wondered if, just maybe, Jane had a little crush on him too.

MEETING

"CAN YOU IMAGINE Paul?"Jane gushed a few days later over FaceTime as she sat at a park bench overlooking a small pond, "The United Nations is considering *me* to work on a project with them!" Several days ago she'd contacted a South Korean mobile network operator, KMO-Telecom and quickly had a meeting scheduled with a UN-representative, along with Rafael. She was over the moon and the first person she'd thought to tell was Paul.

"That's incredible," he grinned into his phone camera as he walked down a quiet sidewalk, "I can't believe it happened so fast." While Jane beamed at Paul and he asked more questions, she realized something. She was developing a massive crush on this guy, and had a feeling he liked her too.

* * *

"And we'll have the internet of cars, internet of home appliances, industrial plants, logistics and smart cities," the KMO representative explained excitedly at the online UN meeting. He went on, "I'm convinced that with IoT we can improve the quality of life for humanity." All was quiet for a moment as everyone on the conference call took this in.

"You know," Rafael added, "Jane and her bears are just one example - a first step if you will. I think it's not about the bears themselves, but the services they can offer."

"Well," the UN representative said after a long pause, "This project looks very interesting. Let me discuss it with my colleagues and get back to you. Oh, and everyone, please keep the fact that we're interested on a low profile to avoid any attention from the press."

* * *

It had finally happened. Paul had met Jane in person, and currently found it difficult to focus at the UN meeting with her sitting right next to him. She'd flown into Hong Kong late the previous night and would be there to discuss the UN project for a few weeks. Jane had decided her Nepal trek could wait for something as important as this.

While it felt like Paul had known Jane for years, there was also a strong sense of attraction that caused his stomach to churn with nerves. "*Damn, she smells good,*" Paul thought as his palms broke into a cold sweat. His attraction towards her grew as she told the group about the behavioural aspects of the bears – how they could re-use a lot of the methods she'd developed during her robot project. Her expertise on such complicated psychological aspects showed her intelligence and passion.

Paul turned towards Jane when the meeting ended just before lunch, and he began to explain more about how the bears stored data, but Jane was too distracted to really pay attention. Meeting him in person had only made her crush grow more intense.

Paul was especially cute when he talked about techy stuff - his dark blue eyes gleamed, his hand ran through his messy brown hair, and he occasionally adjusted his glasses. Jane felt this overwhelming connection to him and, before she could stop herself, she pressed an index finger to Paul's chest and interrupted him with a smile.

"What's wrong with you today Paul? You're not wearing your usual single-coloured t-shirt." Her tone was teasing, but Paul looked confused as he glanced down at his shirt and his cheeks turned pink.

"Eh, yeah. I got this shirt from the gym since all my others are at the laundry-mat – this one's a size too small, sorry." He leaned in closer, and whispered, "Is it really that bad?" Jane blinked in surprise. She hadn't meant to embarrass him, and definitely hadn't meant that it looked bad – quite the opposite actually. She playfully pushed his shoulder.

"No, Paul, I didn't mean it looked bad. It's just not your usual - I was teasing. Don't worry about it, okay?" Paul relaxed, though his stomach buzzed at her touch. Clearing his throat nervously, he looked around and noticed for the first time that everyone had left the meeting room.

"I think, we're late for lunch," Paul noted, "Should we catch up with the others?" Jane looked down for a moment, then up at him, a hopeful gleam in her eyes.

"To be honest," she said, "I have a general aversion to the steamy food here. The smell's awful!"

"I heartily agree," Paul said with a chuckle, "I wish there was a place we could get proper food, but McDonald's is too far away from here."

"McDonald's is *not* proper food Paul," Jane eyed him with a smirk, "Have you tried the sandwiches at My Coffee Corner?"

"Do they sell sandwiches here?" he asked with surprise. Her expression turned secretive as she whispered,

"I have an arrangement with them to give me a good sandwich and salad every day."

"Well in that case," Paul said as he stood up, "Let's check it out." As he strode towards the door, Jane followed, calling after him,

"Wait for me - and please don't take my special sandwich."

A few minutes later, Jane caved. "Okay, Paul, you can have half of it on the condition that you pay for the lattes."

And that was the start of their daily routine of sharing Jane's 'secret sandwich' with lattes for lunch. Every day, both of them counted the minutes until 12:30 pm, when they could have their special time, just the two of them.

The more time Jane and Paul spent together, the more they bonded and felt the growth of this special connection. Yet neither of them made a move, and after a week Jane told Paul she'd be heading back to South Korea soon.

"What?" Paul tried to hide the panic in his tone, "But we don't have any of the bears up and running yet. Jane, how can you leave us like this?"

"Well," she said simply with a little smile, "I guess you'll have to come over to drop them off, Paul. I haven't got a clue how to get them working once they come in the mail."

"Don't worry," Paul said, visibly relaxing, "We'll send Thomas, and maybe I'll tag along too."

* * *

Francis sat in a conference room together with approximately fifty other colleagues from competing European mobile network operators. They were all working in their own network operating centres, or NOCs as they called them. The European parliament had decided that all centres needed to collaborate with one another in case of severe network outages.

Francis didn't mind - he was getting paid either way, and the hotel in Brussels was really swank. A very elegant woman walked onto the stage and introduced herself as Nikole Solon. She thanked everyone for their presence on behalf of the European commission and explained how important this operator collaboration was for Europe.

"Society relies on the wireless connectivity you offer. Your companies have indicated that you, as senior operations managers, are the ones responsible for keeping your networks up and running. First of all I would like to thank you for doing this." After a small round of applause from the audience Nikole raised her smartphone in the air.

"My friends, without this device my life would look completely different. To be honest, I don't think I could live without it anymore." Francis took this moment to look at his own smartphone. She continued, "This is why it's essential that, in case of a severe network outage, other networks act as back-ups. Citizens should always be able to call each other and have mobile internet access." Nikole took a drink of water and went on,

"Since multiple-day outages can still happen, the European parliament has decided additional precautions are required – and it's up to me to work this out. So, I'm here today to make sure this inter-operator backup mechanism is supported by each and every operator. As you are all senior operations managers, you must help prevent citizens from having to get alternative SIM-cards from phone stores when outages occur." Most of the audience nodded, then she finished up.

"I'm both exceedingly happy and proud that everyone present today will take responsibility and support this initiative by preparing network backup tests." More applause sounded as Nikole handed the microphone over to a test expert, who then outlined a basic test plan.

Though they discussed alternative approaches over the next few hours, everyone ended up agreeing on the 'Pull-the-Plug-Test'. Normally they'd do it on their own special test systems. The problem was that inter-operator connections between the test systems didn't exist, so they simply had to check it on their production systems. Nikole looked around happily as everyone talked and signed agreements – it was a great success so far.

* * *

"We apologize for this early time Mr. van Dijk, but we wanted to involve the entire team. Thanks for being available." Paul stared at his laptop's camera, sleepy and definitely surprised to see an entire group of UN members on the other end. He saw Jane sitting at the table, giving him a quick wave and smile. She was about to deliver a presentation on the bear project, and Paul was the remote expert, on standby to answer any questions.

The multidisciplinary UN-team consisted of the project leader, a doctor, a teacher, an anthropologist, an epidemiological expert and two nurses who'd worked in western Africa. The objective of the meeting was to get a feel for the SmartBear's educational potential in that area of Africa.

After introductions and jokes about bringing bears to Africa, Jane took off. Before she could finish her speech, the nurse with field experience said. "Jane, do I understand correctly that the bears can ask children simple 'yes-or-no' questions and are able to send the results back to my phone?"

"That's right," Jane nodded, "The bears will be connected to a central IoT-platform, so you'd be able to send out messages simply by accessing this platform with your laptop or smartphone. You could even contact a specific bear." Everyone looked impressed.

"So," the epidemiologist said, "Does that mean we can occasionally ask the kids if everybody in their family is still healthy?"

"Yeah, that's possible," Jane nodded excitedly, "Though we've designed the bears for teaching, we can simply add a questionnaire function, right Paul?" All eyes were on him as he answered,

"Yeah, we can do all of that, definitely." The epidemiologist frowned, not seeming to be convinced yet.

"Can we see the bears geographically? I mean, can we see if they're travelling or something?"

"Yes," Paul answered, leaning towards his webcam, "We can

extract location information from the mobile networks and GPS. More or less the same way your phone works." The epidemiologist now looked seriously impressed.

"That would mean we'd be able to time-monitor families and detect if they leave the area when they're afraid of virus outbreaks – this is amazing."

"So," the second nurse said, "We can even use the bear to verify if the children have taken their medication with spoken reminders?" She didn't wait for a response, but went on excitedly, "And if the kids trust these bears, we can even ask the children to remind their parents to visit us, since most of them forget about their preventative health check-ups."

"You're right," the project leader now came into the conversation, "If this really works like you say, it would be life changing."

"Its true guys," Paul smiled at the camera as he spoke, "The possibilities are unlimited - the only limitation is our imagination. We can add functions remotely as long the bear's hardware supports it." Everybody continued to brainstorm possibilities and after a few minutes, Jane looked over at the teacher, who'd been relatively quiet, and asked how he felt about the bear idea.

"First," the teacher replied, "I'm worried that these bears could take over my teaching function. And secondly, I wonder if the people will really accept being monitored 24/7. What about their privacy? With this system, we have direct access to all kids with these bears – will that be safe and secure?"

"Sorry," the UN meeting leader frowned, "I'm not so sure I'm convinced either. Though it's an amazing idea, right now I only see a regular teddy bear here on the table, with none of the functions you just explained. We're an organisation with limited resources and can't afford expensive or time-consuming pilot projects. You've got to understand that we can't afford the risk of being the first ones to test it out." He looked at Jane sympathetically and finished,

"To be honest, lots of places don't have electric facilities - they just roll out solar panels. I think your product isn't ready for such a third-world environment just yet. I suggest that you contact us again when your bears have already been in use for a while, okay?"

"I understand what you're saying," Jane said, biting her lip in frustration, "We're actually planning a controlled pilot project in South Korea, but I thought it was good to involve you in an early stage of development. Your comments will enable us to prepare the bears for the functions you suggested. We wouldn't have thought about the necessity of tracking, tracing and health surveys. This meeting and your feedback was very helpful, indeed – thank you."

* * *

"Sorry Paul," Rafael said through his blue-tooth as they skyped two days later, "We need you on the application side of this project. Jason and I have discussed it and want you to please do us a favour and step back from the bears themselves – give the FLQ guys some room and focus on the content part, alright?"

"Of course," Jason spoke up before Paul could respond, "You have a big role in this project - it was your idea and we're proud of you Paul. But, please hand the bear part over to your friend Bruce and the FLQ guys, okay? We need you to help us get the applications running and help Jane with starting her pilot in South Korea. You need to enable the development of content, and content is king you know?" Paul pushed down his initial instinct to protest this switch, and thought about how nice it would be to see and work with Jane.

"Okay, fine." Paul relented, "I'm not one-hundred percent happy about this, but I'll go and help Jane." He sounded disgruntled for Jason and Rafael's sake, but inside he felt a jolt of excitement at the prospect of seeing her again.

* * *

"Are you sure you understand the complete set-up? Do you have the software-libraries under control? Please don't forget to migrate from my home server to a decent hosting provider, okay?" Paul nervously told Bruce a few days later, once his friend had officially gotten full control of the FLQ team for the project.

"Don't worry Paul," Bruce said with a laugh, "I've got it completely under control. The bears will be fine. And I think it's great you're going to help the teacher develop content, you guys make a great team." He said this last part with a suggestive tone.

"Don't be stupid Bruce," Paul shot back, feeling his cheeks heat, "But I guess they're right - we need to speed up the content part. There's still so much to be done."

For the entire next day, Paul and Bruce sat together from morning 'til night and reviewed the development tools. Bruce reassured Paul at the end. "Don't worry, I'll treat it like my own baby." With that out of the way, Paul could now really look forward to seeing Jane. He texted her,

<I'll be flying there this Saturday and stay in a youth hostel in Namsan - ten minutes from your school!>

<<That's awesome Paul! Glad you can come help☺ Oh, and you should definitely come to this party I'm going to Saturday night after you get in – c ya soon!>>

CONNECTIONS

MARIA PLACED THE UN Letter of Intent that Rafael had made into his hands. "Rafael Silva," Her bottom lip trembled in anger, "Can you explain this to me?" He was surprised but kept his emotions under control.

"Oh that," Rafael responded coolly, "Yeah. It was a discussion with the UN funding manager. They contacted me, because of a Toys-for-Africa project. I told them we don't focus on the African market."

"What do you mean exactly, Rafael?" Maria's frown morphed into a scowl.

"Well," he replied, keeping his tone casual, "I was contacted by our TV partners who have a popular, highly-ranked show that always has tons of charities involved. This show's connected with the UN who's considering a campaign for educating African children, and they thought we might be interested. Don't worry, I've waved it away and…"

"Sorry," Maria cut in, "The *UN*? You just waved them away?"

"Exactly," Rafael said with a shrug, "It doesn't fit into our strategy, right? I've indicated that we're involved in similar Asian and European projects."

"Rafael," she said, relaxing a little, "Come on. This is the UN! You can't simply shove them away. Why didn't you discuss this with us or the marketing team?"

"Maria," he touched her arm reassuringly, "Don't worry so much. The UN is only considering this project, and I promised to look at it and come back in a month or two." He gave her a convincing smile then changed the subject. "How are the figures - are we on track?" She took a few steps back, and looked out her office window.

"Don't make me look stupid Silva, okay?" she said finally, ignoring his last question, "Keep me in the loop from now on, please. The UN and TV-shows might offer us opportunities - ones we'd all like to know about. Remember, if we do something good for children, it's also good for Idrel."

"Of course Maria," Rafael answered with a grin, "I'll be sure to let you know." Without her even realizing, Maria was now a little more on his side.

* * *

At 2:30 pm local time Paul landed in Seoul, a suitcase in either hand. One had dirty clothes because of the lack of time to go to the laundromat, and the other had bear samples. Not soft furry bears yet, only the potential electronical insides of them. As he walked through the Incheon International Airport, Paul felt a wave of disappointment – he'd sent Jane his flight details, but she was nowhere to be seen. She hadn't responded to any of his recent text messages either.

Trying to shrug it off, Paul grabbed a bus and checked into the youth hostel by a little after 4 pm. He would be sharing his room with two Australian students he'd come across in the lobby. All three of them had decided to drop their bags and grab some snacks at the hostel's little bar. After eating a bite of rice noodles, Paul's phone buzzed with a text. His heart leapt when he saw it was Jane.

<P! Welcome to .kr. We'll pick you up at your y-hostel for the party at around 10p, ok? J>

<<Yes! I'll bring some .au friends with me, is that ok?>>

<sure!>

Just as Paul and his new Aussie friends were finishing up some takeout dinner in the hostel lobby a bit later, Paul looked up to see Jane walk into the room with two guys. She walked right up to him with a huge smile, one that lit up her bright green eyes. "Hey Paul, good to see you!" Paul returned her smile, but inwardly wondered if one of those guys was her boyfriend.

After they hugged hello, and Paul introduced his new Aussie acquaintances. Jane introduced the guys as her two friends from New Zealand. She turned to her Kiwi friends and said, "Paul and I are preparing my next robot project."

Thirty minutes later, inside what had appeared to be an abandoned warehouse, Jane pulled an awkward-feeling Paul onto the dance floor. He was glad he'd worn contacts for the club since it was packed. Fast-paced music boomed in his ears and made the air around them vibrate along with the floor. Purple, green, white and pink laser lights flashed every which way, lighting up the fog that puffed out of several machines – it was crazy.

And just like that, in the daze of the lights, Jane dropped his hand and disappeared. There was no sign of her, so he sighed and joined his Aussie friends at the bar. He chose water over a beer, wanting to be alert and on the lookout for Jane – where the hell was she anyway? With those Kiwi guy friends? Releasing another frustrated sigh, Paul decided to just enjoy the insane atmosphere in this South Korean club. He grabbed a plastic beer cup from the Aussies and vanished into the fog.

* * *

The fog machines went on again and the combination of the booming beat, multi-coloured lights, stroboscopes and beer began to lift Paul's spirits. Just then he felt a touch on his shoulder and turned around to lock eyes with Jane. A smiling, glowing Jane. And just like that, he knew he couldn't waste any more time, he closed the distance between them and touched his lips to hers.

Jane closed her eyes, kissed back and literally saw stars. As Paul closed his eyes he saw millions of suns – galaxies even. When they both opened their eyes again, Paul grinned from ear to ear as Jane mirrored his smile right back. They couldn't really say anything to each other since it was way too loud in there, but he placed one hand on her cheek, the other in her hair and kissed her again. They didn't need words.

As the two continued their heated kiss, Jane wrapped her hands around the back of his neck and Paul's hands moved to hold her waist. The Aussies and Kiwis came around at that time and teased them with whistles and taking smartphone pictures, but the two lovebirds hardly noticed. They were in their own little galaxy.

Forty-five minutes later the club was closed and the Kiwi friends dropped both Jane and Paul off at her flat. The moment the door closed behind them, Paul drew close. "Hi," she whispered, smiling against his lips, "Now we can finally talk."

"Hi," he breathed back, "It wasn't talking I had in mind right now." He kissed her again and she fell into him, the sparks running between them, tingly and warm. He pulled back a fraction of an inch. As they gazed into each other's eyes, Paul felt a rush of nervous anticipation pulse through his veins.

"Jane, I've been wanting to meet you since that first chat on skype." Her cheeks turned pink and she looked down a little shyly, then led him into the living room, grabbing a bottle of wine and two glasses on the way.

"Want some?" she held them up. Paul nodded and Jane opened the bottle, poured two glasses of Shiraz, and handed one to him as they both sat on the sofa. "It's delicious," she said after taking a little sip.

Though his stomach was a flurry of uncertain nerves, Paul knew this was the moment. "It's not the only thing," he said quietly, leaning in, eyes glued to hers. He gently took the glass from her hands and set both glasses on the side table.

"You're exquisite," he said softly, face only a few inches from hers. Taking her hands in his, Paul held her gaze. Jane's breath hitched as his mouth came down on hers, lips soft and curious. Feeling instantly weak in the knees, Jane felt his kiss from her head all the way down to her toes. She usually had a strict 'don't mix work with pleasure' policy, but couldn't ignore her response to his kisses. She couldn't deny such deep, true feelings.

Jane trailed her fingers up the sides of his chest to wrap her arms around his broad shoulders as she started to kiss him back. Paul responded by tangling his hands into her hair, and deepened the kiss. They delved into a fiery interlock for a minute, maybe more. Neither of them had any sense of time – they were elevated above that.

When Jane pulled away it was only to catch her breath. She smiled at him. "That was nice," Paul said between breaths, chest heaving for air as well. His hands were still in her hair, and he brushed his fingertips across her scalp.

"Yeah," she breathed back, "It feels *really* nice." This time, Jane initiated, pulling him closer and kissing him fervently. Pleasantly surprised, Paul angled his body against hers and, together they shifted to lay side by side on the sofa. Pulling back for air again, Jane softly placed her hand on his ribcage just below his chest, feeling the firm muscles pulsing against his ribs, breathing in and out. "I can feel your heart beating," she smiled at him, eyes dancing, "It's going crazy fast."

Her head was spinning, more from being alone with Paul at last than the alcohol. "I can feel yours, too," Paul said as he ran his fingers down to the dip in her vee-neck shirt, just above her breasts.

"That's not where my heart is." Jane's green eyes had a golden fire behind them as she brought his hand to her left breast. He cupped it softly and she closed her eyes letting out a little gasp, savouring the sensation.

Your shirt is really soft," he whispered while he hooked a finger around the top seam of her shirt and pulled it to the side, exposing the left side of her lacy black bra. "And this is really soft too." He gave a mischievous smile and ran a finger across the top line of her bra. Goose bumps rose on her skin as he touched her. She raised a little to slide off her shirt, and lay back down.

Paul's eyes roamed up and down her curvy figure, from head to toe – every line and dip was breathtakingly beautiful. Half mesmerized, half like a hungry tiger, he trailed kisses across her chest while his hands moved to her back, unhooking her bra. Once she'd helped shrug it off and tossed it in a heap on the floor, Paul's eyes widened, staring at her bare breasts, cheeks colouring. She really was unbelievably exquisite.

Not able to wait anymore, Paul shifted their bodies so he was on top of her, his full, solid weight pressing down, hands roving and exploring her body while her hands moved from his head to his back. He kissed her from her mouth down to her stomach and back, causing Jane to release a small moan. Instincts started taking over, and within a minute, Jane guided off his shirt, then pulled off his shoes and socks.

Chest heaving she slid out from under him and led him into her bedroom. They left a trail of clothes along the way. By the time they'd reached the edge of her bed, they were both completely naked. Jane gave him the once-over, surprised that such a computer geek guy was so lean and muscular. "You work out," she looked at him, eyebrows raised in appreciation. He shrugged.

"I live next to a gym - it helps free my mind to work out."
After giving her fully exposed body a lingering once-over as well,
he pounced on her, pushing her back into the soft bed.

Their kisses were instantly deep, hands exploring everywhere,
legs completely entwined. After a few minutes, Paul lifted himself
a little, arms braced on either side, chest heaving. His eyes delved
into hers, and he saw the reflection of his love for her. Finally,
their bodies merged and they moved together in a slow, beautiful
rhythm. This was not just sex, this was true making love - a bond
between souls - connected on a deeper level.

His body moved faster and faster, hers matching the pace,
building up until it felt like tidal waves washing through.
Afterwards, Paul lay his head on her chest, both of them breathless.
Then, he rolled to the side and kissed her shoulder, a small intimate
touch. Basking in an ecstatic stupor, exhausted and utterly in love,
Paul and Jane fell into a deep, content sleep in each other's arms.

GETTING AHEAD

FRANCIS HAD TO wait and browsed one of the supplier's user forums to pass time. He couldn't help but laugh when he read that two Asian operators had problems with the signalling on their networks. "These guys always want to be the first ones to test new software," he thought. Francis was right, they were using a newer version than his own network. The forum thread showed that they first wanted to stabilize network traffic and then roll back to an older version of their system. The usual approach.

Suddenly, just after 3 am, a small European mobile network went into a planned outage. At 3:20 am, Francis reported to the group-chat that a few test subscribers had successfully found their way to the roaming server for foreign guest users on his mobile network. It had worked.

As he drank his coffee-machine cappuccino, Francis saw similar reports from other network operators. At 3:40 am the lead tester announced the end of the joint test and asked them all to store and share their log-files with him so the team could verify that the emergency roaming had gone as planned. Everyone had used backup networks, and the results looked promising.

Nikole felt a flood of excitement when she saw the results – her idea had become reality. She sat in a Belgian operator's control room near Brussels. "*This is a major step. We've discovered a robust safety net for network outages,*" she thought with a smile, "*And the amazing thing is, it didn't cost the citizens a thing.*" She texted her boss, Theobald, though everyone called him Theo, and took a taxi home.

At the same time, Francis was about to sleep when he noticed a twitter message from #NikoleEU:

<Congrats to the team! #Wireless #emRoaming in Europe was successfully carried out! #EUinnovations>

* * *

Paul woke up in Jane's flat as she whispered into his ear, "Let's have lunch, Paul van Dijk." He smiled with an impish glint in his eye.

"I only have one type of appetite at the moment." He grinned even wider as Jane playfully hit him in the arm and shook her head.

"You're incorrigible," she laughed teasingly. As Paul lay on his side and gazed at her, he thought about how lucky he was to have found this amazing young woman. It felt like Jane was the missing piece of a puzzle, one that he hadn't even realized was lacking in his life. He'd really cared about Katheryn, and had been hurt by the break-up, but he'd never had anything close to the powerful connection he felt with Jane.

"Well," Jane said, "While we do need to eat eventually, I suppose we could find something to do in the meantime." And then, she climbed on top and leaned down to kiss him, hair cascading softly over one shoulder.

* * *

Jane tore off a piece of her chocolate croissant. "I really want to stay with you all day Paul, but I have to go back to work."

"Forget work," Paul said, looking her straight in the eye, "And work with me on the code." She shook her head.

"As long as we're next to each other we won't touch any code, and you know it," she laughed. He leaned across the small café table and kissed her neck in answer. She pushed him away, trying to frown, but she broke into a blushing smile and whispered, "Paul, stop, we're in public." She stood up, gave him a quick kiss and went off to teach her class.

Left to work on his own, Paul reviewed the revised code Bruce had sent - if Paul gave his 'okay', this version would be used in a sample teddy bear at Idrel. Then he turned his attention to a message from Jason and frowned. According to him, Jane's school was waiting to start a pilot project. "She never mentioned that," he muttered to himself, "Jason's probably one step ahead as usual."

He shrugged it off and continued browsing through the updated code. But, it was way too long for just a 'quick review' and he simply wasn't able to verify all the detailed parts. "*Rafael did tell me to leave it in Bruce's hands*," he reminded himself.

* * *

Paul was taking the metro back to Jane's flat when Jason called. "I've just received approval from Bruce for the first production run. We're about to produce fifty prototypes and sew the electronics into the real bears. They'll be handmade." Jason rushed out in excitement. He continued on about the details for a while. Though it was hard to hear while on the metro, Paul understood that Jason would be shipping the bears to him for validation. After Paul's approval, Jane could start using them. His brow creased. "But, I'm not finished with the teaching applications yet." Bruce, who was also on the call, laughed.

"Well, you're going to have to speed it up - you're not fooling around with the teacher are you?" Paul ignored that comment and kept quiet.

"So," Jason chimed in, "The bears have white tee-shirts with 'UN-Volunteer' printed on them. I couldn't change that part in time, so if you guys could just take the shirts off before handing them out, that'd be great."

"Oh," Bruce added, "I've also sent some bears to Rafael and my own kids to get their opinion." And so it began.

* * *

The next few days resembled a whirlwind. Paul moved his stuff into Jane's flat and busily worked on the promised applications. In the meantime, Jane argued with her Korean colleagues who didn't want her to use the bears during lessons. She tried to persuade them and showed a copy of the Idrel 'Letter of Intent' to the UN, but it was no use.

"Jane, we're neither an iPad school nor a robot school," one of her fellow teachers said at lunch break, "Your robot project last year was a one-time-only thing, just to get national attention for KMO-Telecom. Personal attention to children is what this school preaches and practises." Face heating with frustration, Jane left the lunch room, finished her afternoon lessons and slumped back to her flat, pissed off and dejected.

And what she saw inside only made her feel more upset. The hall, living room and bedroom were completely filled with cardboard boxes, the words, 'Yes - we're Idrel Toys!' printed on each one. Paul just sat there in a gray t-shirt, using two of the boxes as a desk, and wearing a big grin. He had his laptop USB-wired to a teddy bear.

"Hey, look what came today," Paul announced. Jane's bottom lip quivered for a moment, then she burst into tears. He was immediately by her side, arms encircling her waist, and asked, "What happened honey? What's wrong?" He was more than a little confused by her reaction - he thought she'd be excited about the bears. Maybe she didn't like the mess?

"I can clean all this up quickly, I promise," he reassured. For a moment, Jane just cried against his chest as he held her tight, rubbing her back with one hand. Then, she spoke in between sniffles,

"It's not the mess. I just…" But she paused here, feeling so warm and safe in Paul's arms – like her worries were somehow melting away just by being with him. Her tears slowed down and she took a deep, calming breath.

"I just had a really hard day at work. And, seeing you here at my place," she pulled away and looked up at him with a half-smile, "It makes me feel like, no matter what happens, I have you - your support." Paul relaxed into a gentle smile and pulled her into his chest again. He kissed the top of her head and they stood in the hallway for several minutes in peaceful silence.

Jane finally pulled away and looked at him. "I can't believe you're actually here. We're really living together."

"Me neither – isn't it great? And I wanted to surprise you with the bear," Paul said as he gestured towards his makeshift desk with the teddy bear. Jane looked around the room, taking in all of the boxes. To Paul's relief, she didn't start crying again, but began to laugh.

"So, these are the much awaited bears?" she asked.

"These are them," he beamed, "They've been born at long last and delivered, like new-born babes."

"You know," she arched an eyebrow, "You turned my flat into a warehouse. We're gonna have to do something about this."

* * *

The girl felt a rush of excitement run down her spine. She was *in*. The code was finally cracked. It had been cleverly designed but messily implemented. Now that she'd solved the puzzle, the girl felt silly for not having seen it in the first place. The latest updates with test-routines had given her the essential clue.

There were fifteen individually remote-controlled cars

driving around for about twenty minutes. She'd discovered the data streams by tracing the internet IP-addresses. The data-format was simple and straight forward, so she could see their positions in real-time and read their engine settings. It was clear that the cars were driving around on some kind of racing circuit.

When she'd logged in during the weekend, she'd actually been able to see them moving on her screen. And though it was possible for her to interfere and take over the steering, she decided not to touch anything - only watch. The data stream contained some web-links referring to a forum for RC-racer development.

So, she created an account and before she knew it, she was part of the RC racing community. All doors were open to the newbie racer '2Fast4U', and she was ready to race the world.

RELEASED

"YOU SEE," JANE finally told Paul what had been bothering her the day before, "Nobody supported using the teddy bears at school – no one!" Her cheeks paled as she stared at her flat's window as they ate some takeout chicken for dinner. "I have absolutely no idea how to convince them, Paul," she continued, turning her gaze on him.

"The thing is," she added, "I told Rafael we'd already started a pilot. I just wanted to speed up the process you know?" Paul simply put his arms around her.

"What about the students?" he asked.

"What do you mean?" She frowned.

"Did you ask the kids if they'd like to work with teddy bears in class?" he clarified. She sat up more alert.

"No, of course I didn't. Paul. Kids would never say 'no'. But we don't need their approval, just the go-ahead from their parents." Paul nodded, looking thoughtful for a moment before saying,

"Okay, then did you ask the parents what they thought about their kids trying out the bears?" Jane's eyes started to shine, the idea dawning on her.

"Paul van Dijk, you're a genus," and she kissed him before saying, "Let's move the rest of the bears to your hostel storage room, okay?" They'd been moving bears and cleaning up the boxes since yesterday evening and were almost done.

Around midnight, Jane's flat was officially bear-free. Everything seemed brighter and fresher after she'd taken a shower and came out to her nice clean living room wearing a comfy tee-shirt and shorts. Phones were muted, laptops closed, and a bottle of Bordeaux was poured. Time to truly celebrate all their hard work.

***

"Just one will be fine, and I'll keep it on the balcony," Paul reassured himself as he drove from the hostel's storage room back to Jane's flat with one of the bears. Rafael and Jason both wanted to know how the pilot was going and whether the bears had his stamp of approval yet.

As Paul sped toward the flat he looked over at the passenger seat of the Toyota they'd borrowed from Jane's Kiwi friend. He'd propped the bear up in the seat and even buckled the little guy in with the seatbelt. It made Paul chuckle. Just before he pulled into the flat's parking space, the bear said,

"Hello there! Good to see you. What's your name? Please say your name."

"King Paul," he answered, suppressing a laugh. It took a few seconds but the bear responded.

"Oh that's a really nice name King Paul. Very nice. You know I've been sleeping for a while and forgot my own name. Could you please help me King Paul and tell me what my name is?"

"Eddy," Paul told him. After about seven seconds it replied,

"Oh yeah, you're right. I remember now. My name's Eddy - Eddy the teddy bear!" Eddy now started to follow a programme designed by Jane, giving encouragement and praise.

After Paul took him into the flat, Eddy indicated that he wanted to get some sleep.

"Please put me on my charging pillow King Paul and wake me up by stroking my back. Good night."

"Yeah," Paul found himself answering, "I will Eddy - sleep well." And the bear started snoring softly for a few minutes then faded into silence. Eddy was such a nice bear, and King Paul felt like a proud new daddy.

***

"So," Jane told Paul as they strolled around a small pond in the park near her flat the next day, "I spoke to some of the parents who were interested in that robot project I did last year, and told them I have a private project with educational teddy bears. And guess what?" Paul looked from the sun's glowing reflection in the water over to Jane, about to respond, yet she proceeded to answer her own question. "Every single one of them is interested in having their children try the bears out!"

Paul squeezed her hand with an excited grin, then asked, "So, you mean you've by-passed your colleagues?"

"Not really." Jane said, shaking her head, "But, most of the students also attend pre and after school care where a good friend of mine works. And, you know, I can't imagine that there'd be any-thing wrong with giving away free educational teddy bears during those programmes."

"I can't imagine they'd have a problem with that at all," Paul agreed with a sly grin. He was impressed with how well Jane had recovered from her school's push-back attitude. Just then, a flock of birds crossed over the pond and disappeared into the now almost twilight sky. After they walked hand-in-hand in peaceful silence for five minutes, Jane broke the silence.

"So, the plan is that Thursday afternoon I'll pass out the bears during after school care, right before the long weekend starts. Isn't that perfect?" Paul hesitated as they rounded the bend in the path that curved back towards her flat.

"It's a good plan. The only thing is, we haven't actually tested the bears out yet. And these are alpha pre-production versions."

"What do you mean?" she asked, brow creasing, "They were packed in boxes, ready to hand out, right?"

"Well," Paul said carefully, "The software is still in alpha-version which means we need to test them thoroughly before handing them out."

"Alpha? Pre-production?" Jane shook her head, "Come on Paul, these are the first, fully produced teddy bears. You're not backing out now are you? We only have four days to validate them, right?"

"Okay," Paul agreed after a moment of silence, "Let's say that if we both think Eddy is doing okay, you can hand them out Wednesday. Otherwise, we take another test week. Agreed?"

"Who's Eddy?"

***

Scry was a huge South Korean pop-star, constantly chased by fans, giving interviews and trying to avoid the paparazzi. In short, he was completely worn out. An extremely emotional and artistic guy, he always dressed up in fancy, sometimes eccentric clothes, earning him at least three pictures in the newspaper each week to show his outfit de jour along with his usual smile and show of the peace-sign with his fingers.

The press had spread a rumour that Scry was on drugs, which was not the case at all, but he was tired of explaining how he was, in fact, drug-free. His manager had insisted that Scry escape this weekend. "Please take some time for yourself and disappear for a few days, will you?" His manager had noticed how, lately, Scry always had heavy bags under his eyes as well as overly anxious behaviour.

In stressful situations, Scry had this somewhat embarrassing habit of crying - not big obvious sobs, just a single, silent tear down his cheek. But, it was enough to register on cameras. Headlines often read, "Another 'Cry of Scry'" when he answered difficult questions from the press. The stress wasn't good for his image, or his health for that matter.

So, when his manager suggested taking the weekend off, he immediately cancelled all six appearances that had been scheduled for the long weekend, muted his phone and ignored all calls, emails and social media feeds. Thankfully, his older sister had invited him to stay with her for a few days. No TV, no interviews just relaxing in the suburbs and playing with his nephew who didn't know about Scry being a pop star. It was perfect.

***

By Sunday morning, both Jane and Paul were utterly fed-up with Eddy. Partially as a joke and partially a serious trial, they'd intentionally carried him around everywhere they went - to the supermarket, going out with Jane's Kiwi co-workers, sitting on Paul's desk as he checked email and so on. Paul finally voiced his complaints to Jane.

"Okay," he said after a weary sigh, "This bear will drive kids completely crazy like this. He's too nice and asks too many questions - he needs an 'off' or 'mute' button!"

"He seriously does," Jane nodded in agreement, "Or at least some behaviour alterations." So, they got to work fine tuning Eddy's behaviour, changing some of the settings. Just as Paul was about to finish, Jane held up a hand, "Wait, is there any way we can push back the applications and give the kids some time to get used to the bear? Then, we can activate the learning modules afterwards?"

"You know," Paul eyed her, "That's the model Rafael suggested - getting the children addicted and once the bears are part of the daily routine, simply start premium upselling. I thought you didn't want that, right?"

"No, Paul," she said and let out an annoyed huff, "I didn't mean that addictive upselling crap. I simply want the kids to get used to the bears and like them before the gradual awakening of the learning modules."

"Okay, whatever you call it, the two plans are basically the same thing. But fine," he quickly added, before she could defend herself more, "We'll just time-schedule the premium lessons – one week after start-up. Sound good?"

***

When Monday afternoon rolled around, Paul had learned to count to twenty in Spanish, and was praised for being a good student. Tuesday evening Jane and Paul both agreed that Eddy had passed his little test and was friendly enough, yet not too friendly or annoying like before. Copying Eddy's settings, Paul remotely loaded them into the other teddy bears, which were either living in the hostel's storage or on their way to Rafael and Jason at this point.

Wednesday evening Jane learned to use the Bear IoT Management platform, enabling her to control and monitor the bears remotely. She'd kept one bear for herself, and named it Ada.

"Ada?" Paul asked her, "Named after your mom or something?"

"Are you serious?" she said, cutting him a look, "No – she's named after Ada Lovelace, the first person in the world who wrote a computer programme. As a programmer yourself, I can't believe you don't know that! Ada Lovelace inspired Alan Turing, ever hear of him?"

"Yeah," Paul nodded, "Of course." Jane continued to work on Ada as she added,

"You know it's not only the men who make a difference in this world Paul van Dijk." She'd definitely won on this point, and Paul conceded.

"I'm sorry, that's very true. Actually, Ada's the perfect default name for all the teddy bears. You know, in case the speech recognition doesn't work."

***

When Paul and Jane woke up Thursday morning, Ada and Eddy were still asleep. So, the two bears were left behind as their 'parents' used the Toyota to transport all the prototype bears in numbered boxes to the school. They'd written a quick-start letter for the parents, and the numbers on each box enabled them to track which bears were used by which student.

Before the long weekend began, forty-two bears were picked up by their new owners. That night Paul and Jane closely monitored the Bear IoT Management platform, but only two bears reported their presence – Eddy and Ada. After he'd made them both a rum and coke with fresh lime, Paul handed Jane hers and tried to cheer her up.

"Just wait and see," he grinned, "I bet by Sunday they'll be a lot more in use." Jane nodded, and they sat on the sofa, unwinding with their drinks paired with sliced baguette and Gruyere cheese. Jane turned to look at Paul after eating a slice of cheese.

"You know what we should do?" she said, face suddenly animated, "When this is all over, let's take a trip to Nepal together. I never got to go with my friend." Paul's dark blue eyes sparked with excitement. The thought that they were close enough in their relationship to go on a holiday together made him glow from the inside out.

***

Scry woke up early Sunday morning on his sister's sofa, where he felt the most comfortable sleeping, his heart pounding so fast he found it hard to catch a breath. It was probably part of the de-stressing process – a little hiccup of panic.

He tried to calm down but couldn't keep still, so he took out his phone and browsed through hundreds of false social media messages about him. People had reported seeing him at a clinic or even about possible suicidal plans.

Unable to stop it, the backs of his eyes began to prickle as they became watery. "What a hell I'm in - what kind of life is this?" he muttered in a croaky voice. Then the tears started to roll down and pour out silently, tasting salty on his lips. He made a quick cup of chamomile tea, and sat back down to try and get a hold of himself.

It was 5:30 in the morning and the family was still asleep. *"Let's see, what can I do?"* He racked his brains. There was no newspaper to read, but there was a box in the hall with, "Yes - We're Idrel Toys!" printed on the outside. Although it was for his nephew, Scry decided to open the box. "Let's see what we have here," he mumbled.

He pulled out a cute little teddy bear that wore a UN volunteer tee-shirt. He smiled, took the bear back to the living room, and threw the bear playfully into the air. Pulling out his phone, Scry put it in selfie-record mode. The teddy now sat on his lap facing the phone's camera. "See my friends, shouldn't we all put our energy into good things and behave like nice little teddy bears?" Scry started to say.

With a grin, Scry pointed towards his still recording phone and went on, "What's your plan to improve the world?" But before he could continue his little speech, the bear spoke.

"Hello, let me be your teddy bear!" Scry's eyebrows shot up and he laughed. "That's the spirit! And everybody should be a nice teddy bear to everyone else!" Like always, he raised his hand to make the famous, 'V' shaped peace symbol. But, this time he changed it so one hand made more of a 'U', and the other an upside-down 'V' to look like a capital 'N'. He repeated, "Please, let me be your teddy bear."

With that, a single tear-drop trickled down his cheek and onto the bear's furry head. Filled with uncontrollable emotions, and against the agreement of his manager, he did it. Scry posted the video on his social media feed accompanied with the text,

"Let's make a better world! Whose teddy bear are you?" Then, he threw the phone to the other side of the sofa.

At that point his sister came into the room, frowning. "Scry," she whispered loudly, "Can you please keep it down out here? You're like a little kid with all that noise. We're all still asleep you know." Then she looked more carefully at his face and her eyes softened. "Are you crying?"

PART 2 – THE DISRUPTION

VIRAL

"MARIA, I PROMISE I don't know anything about it. We don't have any official contact with the UN or a Korean pop star," Rafael said in earnest. Maria sounded so incredibly angry on the other end of the line that he could practically feel it through his phone. Idrel's marketing team and sales representatives were overwhelmed with calls from South Korea and Idrel needed to give a statement - *now*.

Everyone was asking for this new teddy bear product, one that didn't exist yet, not in its final form anyway. "Hold on, Maria," Rafael said as he pulled to the side of the highway, "I'll take a look now and call you back." His phone loaded the video and played. Maria was right. Rafael's eyebrows rose as he watched some strangely dressed Korean guy holding one of their teddy bears, wearing a UN shirt and sitting next to a box that was clearly from Idrel.

This guy had posted a selfie video of him and the bear, and he was crying. "Where the hell did he…" Rafael muttered to himself, wondering how this pop-star had gotten a hold of an Idrel bear. And why hadn't the UN shirt been taken off as he'd asked Paul and Jane to do? Without looking at the time difference, Rafael called Jason. But the line was busy, so he called Maria back - also busy. They were probably all trying to call one another. Shit, this was a mess.

After forwarding the video to his kids to ask if they knew who this odd-looking guy was, Rafael looked at the number of views - 850,000 since being posted yesterday. "This guy must be really famous," he mumbled. A knot formed in his stomach – he needed answers.

Paul was asleep with Jane as his phone buzzed. "Hello?" he answered, still half-asleep. The next moment, after a very anxious sounding Rafael told him about some video, Paul sat up straighter in bed and replied, "We did start the trial project and there are two teddy bears in use right now, out of the forty-two we handed out. But we only gave them to the students, not to some artsy-looking young man."

Paul quickly watched the video and recognized the guy. "Oh, that's Scry. I've seen him on the news. He's this mega, South Korean pop singer. How'd he get a bear?" He muttered this last part more to himself.

"Look," Rafael let out an impatient breath, "You need to contact the parents of the kids who have those trial bears. We need to know how this Scry person got a hold of one."

"Well," Paul stifled a yawn as he answered, "That's more in Jane's department. They're her students and she can contact them. But right now we're sleeping and…"

"Wait," Rafael interrupted him, "*We're* sleeping? Paul, are you hooking up with Jane?"

"Yeah," Paul said, swallowing hard, "We are - actually we're dating and I've moved into her flat." Rafael stayed silent for a moment.

"Okay," he told Paul, "If your relationship with Jane doesn't interfere with your work, it doesn't matter to me." Paul sat up straighter.

"Look Rafael," he sputtered into the phone, "I don't need your permission to date someone. I'm free to see anyone I choose. And for your information, we've been working day and night for you guys!"

"Gee," Rafael chortled after letting out a short laugh, "I wonder exactly what kind of 'work' you two are doing at night."

"Listen Rafael," Paul went on, ignoring this comment, "I'm going back to sleep. I'll tell Jane about the video. Just send me a message with what time you want to do a conference call."

* * *

"I'm really sorry guys," Jane said on the conference call with Paul, Maria, Rafael, Jason and Wendy, who was from Idrel's marketing department, several hours later. Jane went on, "We should've taken off the UN t-shirts ourselves. I'd asked the parents to do that in a little letter we enclosed with each bear, and I guess this particular parent didn't follow through. My apologies, seriously." After another minute of apologies, everyone calmed down considerably.

"Well, let's look on the bright side," Jason said, "At least we have a ton of attention for the product – the marketing has a solid start. Anyone got any ideas what we should do with this attention?"

"You know," Wendy from marketing responded with a concerned frown, "Idrel's site went down last night because it couldn't handle the number of visitors. So I asked one of our partners to prepare a pre-order website."

"Okay, that helps," Rafael said, "One thing I think we can all agree with is that, once something goes viral on social media, there's no stopping it. That's why we gotta try to turn it into a positive thing."

"So, what are we going to do exactly?" Jason asked.

"We've drafted a UN charity auction," Wendy said, looking around at everyone, "But weren't able to contact anyone from the UN, since their office was closed today."

"Okay then," Jason shrugged, "How can we get in touch with them? Does anyone here have a direct contact with the UN?" Jane had just been checking her phone and noticed that the UN project leader had tried to contact her multiple times that day.

"I have a contact," she spoke up, "And I'll put them in touch with you Wendy, okay?"

"That would be great, thanks Jane," Wendy smiled.

"What about this Scry guy?" Rafael asked, "We need to know what he's doing with them. I guess he's some kind of UN ambassador. Lots of pop stars are spokespeople for charities and NGOs, aren't they?"

"We've been searching online. Scry is a famous pop-star, but has nothing to do with charities or NGOs," Wendy replied, "We left a message on his booking manager's voicemail and also sent an email, which got an automated response that indicates we'll hear back within four business days."

"We can just let the bear ask its owner to contact us," Paul said, "And also set up a phone call to the bear itself, like a hands-free device. That's the easiest way."

"But, Paul," Jane turned to him, her lips pursed, "It's also the stupidest way. We have to respect people's privacy. We can't simply dial-in or listen-in - that's illegal, isn't it?"

"Do we have a statement on privacy and data protection yet?" Jason asked, "I mean, we have all this information about the users, even direct access to them."

"Let me be clear on this," Paul said, "In technology we can do it all; use the bear as a webcam, take pictures, listen-in and much more. But, of course we won't actually do that."

"We have to be responsible in this regard," Maria interrupted worriedly, "Since customers could get upset about their privacy. We have to address it in advance so parents and their children can fully trust our toys."

"At this stage," Paul said after thinking for a moment, "We can't promise anything. It's a pilot and we haven't implemented or validated privacy or data protection guidelines yet. We need help in making a proper plan since there are worldwide regulations we have to follow."

"That's right," Maria agreed, "Apart from obeying those rules we also have to create our own privacy policies based on company values, which will certainly exceed any governmental standards. I'll ask the consultants to have a look."

"Sorry to interrupt," Jason said, "But we have to set priorities right now. Let's first get this 'viral Scry' situation under control. Then we can move on to the other aspects, such as privacy." Everyone was in full agreement and decided to meet back for another conference call in three hours.

* * *

"Yes, we were surprised as well," Jane told the UN representative over the phone, "Of course it wasn't our intention." She paused to listen for a minute then replied, "Not happy, I understand. It was one of the test bears and those t-shirts weren't from us…No, I'm not sure where they came from." She raised her eyebrows at Paul as she listened some more.

"Yeah," she answered, "They're all doing fine. Um, no results yet since the trial is still running…Yes, the kids are absolutely happy with them. Uh huh. Yup, learning Spanish, counting and bedtime stories are all functions." She paused to listen yet again and Paul watched curiously as a smile grew across Jane's face.

"That would be great," she said into the phone, "Okay, I'll put him in contact with Idrel as soon as possible. Right, we're chasing Scry as well. Okay, talk to you later, bye." She turned to Paul and said, "The UN project leader is in close contact with their Unicef campaigning team and they insisted that they look at the bears again. People have been calling to ask which charity programme the bears are associated with, so they'd like to discuss fundraising possibilities."

Jane's face beamed as she went on, "I promised to get him in touch with Idrel." Her excitement and smiles did nothing to ease Paul's exasperation. He threw his hands in the air and almost yelled,

"But Jane, we haven't even started a real pilot yet. Most bears are still in their boxes, so how can you agree to this? We're not ready." Now it was Jane's turn to get pissed.

"Are you serious, Paul? I can't put the possibility of working with the UN on hold just because the engineers are telling us that we're not ready - engineers never think anything's ready - ever!" Jane threw her hands up for emphasis and continued, "Eddy and Ada are doing just fine and there's no reason to believe that the other bears are any different."

Paul ran his hands through his hair, ready to pull it out. "This is big shit, Jane. We need time to get results first. Eddy and Ada might look like they're doing fine, but with IoT the devil is in the detail you know? The volume on this Idrel project is huge, which means the impact's insanely high. We simply need more time." Jane tilted her chin up in defiance and turned away from him as she texted the mom of Bear #23 to 'please contact' her as soon as possible.

Moments later, the owner of Bear #23 called. "Jane, I'm so sorry about the video. And, sorry to ask, but can you please keep it top secret that Scry is my brother? That's how he found the bear and did that selfie video - he was staying at our place for a break this weekend. My son was so upset because it was his bear."

"I understand," Jane replied after a silent sigh, "We'll absolutely keep that secret. Does your son have the bear now - does he like it?"

"Yeah, he's got it and is now carrying Ada with him everywhere he goes – all day long." Before Jane could respond, she heard a high-pitched male voice come on the line.

"Hello - Scry here, how can I help you?"

"This is your nephew's teacher Jane. Your selfie video has gone viral and now everybody wants a bear, but the Idrel toys website's down…it's kind of a big mess."

"Sorry love," Scry said with an apologetic tone, "I had no idea it became so popular. I haven't touched my phone since that morning. I didn't mean to get you in trouble, I was just inspired by the bear. But, don't worry, I'll get you in touch with my manager – he'll know exactly how to handle this."

* * *

At the end of the day, a black limousine drove through a suburb of Seoul with Scry sitting in the back. It went directly to a studio where his song text writer was waiting. He'd adapted a song they hadn't used for his last album, and changed the title to 'Let Me Be Your Teddy'. It would be Scry's special Christmas charity song for the Unicef Child development programme he'd, very recently, adopted.

In the meantime a special website was launched, allowing people to pre-order the teddy bear. Seventy-five percent of sales would be donated to this special UN programme. And, as extra incentive, if a customer shared their pre-order on social media, they'd be listed in an online 'wall-of-fame'.

Two days later, Scry's new song was released during prime-time TV on a South Korean national programme. With a teddy wearing a UN shirt on his lap, Scry explained how he wanted to help children in need. During his live appearance, the new website was frequently shown, while Scry hugged the teddy with a tear rolling down his cheek.

At the end of the show, when footage of children in need was shown, 250,000 bears had been pre-ordered on the special site. And, because of social media spin offs, the count shot up to 470,000 and rising. Now, the pre-ordered consumers had all paid and were waiting for their purchased bears to arrive.

PROSPECTS

"AND THE NEW curtains really need to keep all the light out when closed during the day," Valentina told Paul's brother, Chris. Her husband agreed whole-heartedly as she now continued to drag herself from one room to another, her large, expectant belly leading the way. Valentina gave instructions on the things she wanted to add or improve in their new house as they went along. Chris had read about pregnant woman's hormones and really didn't want to argue, but he was getting extremely tired of the never-ending wish-list.

Their new house sat back from the main road on a smaller street that was lined with old oak trees and wound over a hill and down to their new country home. It was right next to a small river and, as a slightly hippy woman, it was Valentina's dream house. She was excited to have this new home to share with Chris, and soon, with their new baby too.

For Chris, the house was, well - it was okay. The only problem was he didn't have a landline phone, internet or cable TV just yet, and sometimes no mobile network. He'd tried all of the three operators that serviced the area, but none of them had good reception inside the house. Sometimes he even had to drive up the hill to sync his email or make a phone call. But, he tried to keep in good humour, laughing about how remote the place was. His closest neighbour, a single man, lived three-hundred meters away and only had a land-line, so he was extremely unhelpful with the mobile network problem.

Chris now double checked with Valentina, "Are you sure you want the baby room painted pink? Shouldn't I buy some blue or green paint just in case? I mean, in theory it could also be a boy."

"Chris," Valentina answered with her nose tilted up, "Believe me, it's going to be a girl. I just know it. I can *feel* it with my 'mother's instinct'." She was eager and nervous at the same time. Valentina's mom, who lived in Milan, was beyond thrilled and sent gifts for the baby every other week.

"What about Claudia?" Valentina now said with a dreamy look in her light brown eyes, "That's my grandmother's name."

"Claudia sounds great, sweetie," Chris smiled in earnest then added, "Uh, I'll be right back, okay?" And he walked down to the garage to inspect his car. Due to the rural environment, Chris wondered if he should change his sports car for a four-door, four-wheel drive, cross country model like his neighbour had. But, a baby and a new house was already so much change for him that giving up his sports car on top of it all was simply too much.

Valentina, on the other hand, didn't care about things like sports cars and fully embraced living in the country. This was the place their baby would enter into the world and their lives for the very first time. But they still had a while to adjust to country living and the idea of being parents since their baby wasn't due until the first week of January.

* * *

The complete board of directors from Idrel sat in a meeting along with two IoT consultants. Maria was in the back of the FLQ-electronics conference room, where they'd all decided to convene, with an older man and some other guys from Idrel's Atlanta office. An FLQ sales representative, whom Rafael had never seen, welcomed everyone and handed the floor to Maria. She spoke loud and clear.

"Our objective is obvious. We have three months to produce 1.5 million teddy bears. Since the UN is continuing this same programme in other countries and Christmas is nearly upon us in just eight weeks, we're expected to triple production within four months." Maria paused. Jason, who sat next to her, leaned over to whisper,

"That's impossible, we've never produced anything in this kind of quantity."

"Well," Maria whispered back, "What if we just take the orders and do our best to deliver on time?"

"We can't ask customers to wait four months," Jason hissed back, "We should be realistic and manage expectations. We can't make promises if we already know it's not feasible." The two consultants, who had received the task to work on 'Idrel-IoT-Innovations' a few weeks ago, now came to the front and started to show their slides as Maria stepped down.

A screen-shot of the consultant's SWOT matrix, including the strengths, weaknesses, opportunities and threats of what they called 'Plan A' was projected onto the wall. "Thanks Maria and welcome everybody. I'll quickly introduce ourselves. I'm Timothy and this is Ben. We're strategy product innovation consultants and we're here to help Idrel explore incorporating IoT into its future."

Here Timothy smiled at the room then continued, "During the last few weeks we've been talking to you all and looking at other markets like transportation, healthcare and the automotive industry. The conclusion is that the 'Internet of Things' technology will inevitably play a key role in every single market out there, including the toy market. To connect or not to connect? That is the question."

He paused for impact as everyone listened attentively, a few chuckling at his Hamlet reference. Timothy continued, "We see it every day in our lives. Mobile network connectivity changes complete landscapes, but business models, retail and governmental systems don't have control over the flow and fall of information. People expect faster, better, cheaper services and use their phones to guide them through daily life. Our lives are changing dramatically with supply chains being shorter and stocks disappearing." He looked around as he took a breath.

Here the other consultant, Ben took over. "Offer and demand get instantly informed by one another and businesses are shifting from product-based sales to paid services, with customer convenience leading the way. IoT is a catalyst for the creation of new markets, making the existing ones disappear, soon to become obsolete. IoT is inescapable and below the line, IoT improves quality of services and quality of life."

Ben took a sip of his coffee and concluded, "At this state we're taking the disruptive IoT technology into consideration. The thing is, disruption is not necessarily a bad thing, but potentially good - just not for those being disrupted. As the market leader, we're in a powerful position, and aren't being chased yet. Our margins are being pushed, but that's because of cost."

At this point, Rafael interjected, "By costs do you mean the fact our competition is using cheap child labour in overseas factories?"

"We've got our company values, Rafael," Maria told him as she crossed her arms over her chest, "We can't push the cost price lower on labour. We won't stoop to child slavery." Rafael didn't respond to her remark and Ben continued,

"We've been working on the Idrel IoT strategy in general, and particularly on the UN project this last week. After speaking with everyone involved, we find that the project's too big to leave any unanswered questions. So we're convinced that we need to have a Plan B – which is why we've created one based on your input." The image of a big 'B' with a question mark appeared on the screen and Timothy took over again.

"First of all, between us, we don't have to hurry with adapting to new technologies since there's no threatening start-ups in our market yet." He flipped a switch which showed the 'Plan A SWOT' again.

IoT SWOT Plan A (IoT - Bears)

Strengths
· Mature Mobile network technology
· Mature Internet services
· Production partner FLQ has track record

Weaknesses
· No consumer demand for services
· Consumers possibly not ready
· No other competitors active in IoT
· Idrel not experienced in selling content
· Idrel and FLQ not used to operating products

Opportunities
· UN Orders waiting
· Content up-selling possibilities
· Enables strategic change from product to services (CAPEX>OPEX shift)

Threads
· Product has never been tested in market
· Severe financial impact if technology fails
· Severe impact on brand if technology fails
· Severe impact on market position if technology fails

"Sorry to say, but when we look at this Plan A, there are clearly more threats and weaknesses than opportunities and strengths," Timothy said and waited for several beats to see the room's reaction. He then pushed on, "I would like to emphasize that not every disruptive technology improves the quality of the service for our customers. If we start with IoT inside these teddy bears, the care-taking is just beginning for us since we still need to operate them when they're in customer's homes."

Timothy took a long breath then concluded, "This requires having management platforms and customer-care call centres in place before sending the bears out. And last but not least, despite our future goals, the technology-implementation in our products hasn't been proven yet. We see high risks involved in this plan, especially if we take the extremely tight time-line into account." He paused and looked at the sleeping bear in the middle of the table.

Rafael kept his face neutral, but thought, "*What idiots. These guys are simply waving the opportunity away. Don't they know there are always tons of reasons to not do something new and innovative than to take the risk and try it?*" The FLQ representative tilted his head down, obviously disappointed. Ben took over once more.

"Let's ask ourselves this question: What did people actually order and what does Idrel need to ship to them? If I understand correctly, consumers pre-ordered a teddy bear that can say 'Let me be your teddy bear', right? That's it, nothing more, nothing less." He stopped talking to see if anyone had a response. But no one said a word, so he continued,

"We need to be realistic, so I suggest we deliver exactly what they expect from us. And we should do it within the time-line and use the exact same colour and packaging seen on Scry's video. We've been shipping toys with pre-recorded messages for years now. Let's just use this cheap, low-risk technology." The group started to mumble and talk to each other, but Timothy had one more thing to say.

"To summarize, my friends, we actually don't need to produce and deliver costly, high-risk, IoT-based bears, but just keep it simple for the time being and go with Plan B - 'TeddyLight'. What do you think?"

***

Nikole felt a warm rush of pride as the indicator bulb lit up during the Digital-Agenda-EU meeting where she had a front row seat. She'd initiated a few network operators to informally test the new emRoaming and it'd been a success. The Commissioner of the Digital Economy and Society met Nikole's golden-brown eyes and chuckled. He liked her pragmatic approach.

"Distinguished guests and dear friends," the Commissioner began, "There are countless reasons mobile networks are of such high importance these days. It's been interwoven with our everyday lives. But first, I'd like to underpin that I'm a liberal and support free market mechanisms. However, when public mobile networks started more than twenty years ago, network usage became a niche." He paused for effect and then continued,

While the frequencies were free back then, today we've proudly created value out of thin air and frequency spectrum is considered an important natural resource." Here Nikole nodded and smiled in agreement with the Commissioner. He smiled back at her for a moment, then continued, "As with any natural resource, we should hold it in esteem and stimulate max efficiency. Let's have a quick look into the future of mobile networks. For the short term, operators will keep using traditional networks formed from towers, base stations and so forth. These operate on specific frequencies and decide who's allowed to use the radio spectrum."

He paused yet again to look around the audience and then went on, "But in the coming years, the role of the operator will change. Smart algorithms in mobile devices and networks enable the operator to select the bandwidth and speed set by individual quality-of-service based subscriptions." Mutters and whispers went through the audience, some sounding confused.

The Commissioner smiled and explained. "You see, the question is: Do we really have to rely on the industry or do we encourage license-free open-source radio standards for society's mobile networks? I don't think we're ready to answer this today since future technical possibilities are too blurry. One thing is for sure - mobile network connectivity is a must have for all societies. And today our dear colleague Nikole Solon has used a simple demonstration project to show that we can make a difference and assist our civilians by offering emRoaming. Nikole, please come up on the stage."

The audience cheered as Nikole came onstage and received flowers. Her emRoaming was officially rolling out.

LEGACY

"WHAT DO YOU think?" Jason shifted on his chair as he looked at Rafael. Maria was completely silent. Jane had been rendered temporarily speechless, not able to comprehend that anyone would consider cutting their project. She turned to look mutely at Paul, eyes wide as if begging him to say something.

But, he had no idea what to say, sitting there with dark circles under his eyes and face unshaven. The bears were such a part of him. He'd written their software and put so much of himself into them that he felt almost like he was Eddy, or at least his dad. Plan B had put him and Jane into utter shock. Paul had been the one to say they needed to slow down, and he now recognized his own words in the SWOT matrix. But, he'd never meant those words to be used to cancel the project.

The bears, and all their hard work, including Paul's Turchaea, had been reduced to a single letter 'A'. Their project was now just a long-term alternative in case some start-up happened to disrupt their market. How could Idrel do this and then have the nerve to ask his and Jane's opinion? Paul's gaze dropped to Eddy, who was lying on his jacket in sleep mode and wearing the UN shirt.

"Timothy – Ben," Rafael broke the heavy silence. "Good

work. It's great that you took a serious look at all possibilities, and you're right in that we're not threatened yet. I think you have an interesting idea to simply put postcard-electronics into our bears, lean back and get the revenue. All problems solved." Paul and Jane gaped at him, hoping he was being sarcastic. But Rafael looked very serious, and as the consultants sat down, he faced Maria.

"We can of course still consider the use of IoT in future projects in our company, but now we can take a slower start, with the grow-as-you-go experience which I prefer. And after a year or so we can make an analysis about the next step." Rafael paused for a moment to look around the room, making sure he had everybody's attention, then continued,

"The key question is, are we, as a company, ready to have IoT technology inside our products, or do we stick to last millennium, talking postcard technology? To me, the answer is yes, despite uncertainty. I say we look at the future and consider IoT as part of it – part of our toys. And I also say we go for the original Plan A IoT based smart toys." Paul and Jane exchanged a surprised yet hopeful look, and turned to hear what else Rafael had to say.

"Let's take on this challenge with our production partner FLQ-electronics and not risk preventing Idrel's push into the future. So I pose to all of you this question - what kind of future do you want for Idrel?" Before he could finish his passionate speech, Rafael felt a gentle hand on his arm. The old man who'd sat between Rafael and Maria this whole time had put a finger up to silence him.

Who the hell was this ancient guy? But, Rafael stopped talking as the man slowly stood-up and walked to the front of the table with a wooden cane. As the old man sat down, he faced the projector light and asked in a fragile voice, "Can someone switch off the projector please, and open the curtains?" Timothy pulled the plug and the FLQ representative opened the blinds. Sunlight filled the dead-silent room, causing everyone to blink as their eyes adjusted.

"Maria," the old man said, "Can you hand me the book

please?" Maria came to the front with a plastic supermarket bag and put a large book on the table. It was an old photo-album and the man turned to the first page. Everyone looked at each other questioningly. What was this old man up to? The man continued, "My apologies for disturbing you with your good work and thank you for letting me attend."

He looked at Ben and Timothy who sat near him. "I come from a family of craftsman in the United States. My great-grandfather was a shoe-maker, though I unfortunately don't have any pictures of him. My grandpa told me that the entire family was involved in the process of manufacturing and selling shoes. They had a small factory in a shed behind their little house. Everybody from the sur-rounding towns wore shoes made by my great-grandfather and then my grandpa." Though he had no idea how this was relevant, Rafael suppressed a sigh and listened patiently as the man continued.

"My grandpa didn't go to school because he and his brother had to assist their father in the workshop – cleaning and getting supplies. In their spare time they often carved little animals and people from left over wood that was used in the fireplace and wood stove. When the industrialisation came, people started to earn money and slowly started wearing luxury leather shoes from the city instead of my grandpa's shoes." He paused to drink some water and went on,

"They fell on hard times, and when my grandpa and his brother turned thirteen and fourteen, they began doing farm work." He took a long breath and held up the photobook. "Here you see a picture of them together in the old house with their mom and five other younger brothers and sisters. On Sundays my grandpa and his brother always carved small wooden toys for boys and girls in the town. Their mom began to sell these at the market, and within a few years they were selling their own toys and were able to quit working on the farm. And thus, the company was born."

The man pointed his finger to an old black-and-white photo.

"Here you see a picture of their first products." The photo was fuzzy, but showed a craftsman in a workshop with carved wood figurines, posing for the camera. He continued,

"When my grandpa and his brother were fifteen and sixteen they had a common vision that they really wanted to develop. They definitely wanted to become the country's best toy makers and have their own toy shops throughout the nation. It was almost impossible because their dream was so big. They didn't see any chance because they were living in a little town near Atlanta."

"When they finally broke away from working on farms they must have thought they had a bit of a chance, because all they ever wanted to do was make toys, and not only make toys, but also sell them. At that time, in Atlanta, they already had specialized toy shops and department stores here and there. So my grandpa would take the train to the city and chat with every shop owner for maybe 30 minutes and explained about their workshop."

The old man took a deep breath and continued, "He had two suitcases with about eighty different samples and would sometimes sleep in the public parks because he didn't want to go back home before selling all of his samples. That helped them for about almost two years to survive in the beginning. When I started to work for them, they asked me what I wanted to do, and I said to them 'Let's make toys for the future.' I knew about plastic and thought, why don't I use plastic which is the material of the future."

"At that time I didn't have any idea what to do but I knew I needed a mold. So with the help of a black smith I made a simple mold. Then I knew that molded plastic could become a child's toy of the future but we didn't realize how much impact it would have. My grandpa and his brother were open to innovations and we were the first company in the world to manufacture plastic toys. My name is Johnathan Ian Drel, but everyone calls me Drel."

Drel closed the photo album and looked around at his captive audience. "Ladies and gentlemen, Idrel has faced a wide range of challenges, and I know you face yet another challenge today - this time a technological one. I'd like to ask you to think about the following: My grandpa had no overhead projector and never went to school to learn about making a SWOT or anything. My own dad used to say that we should never take all the profit, but use some of it to invest in the future. So I suggest that you consider the new Plan B, but in the meantime, I strongly urge each and every one of you to pursue this innovative IoT Plan A. Don't sit around waiting for the future to surprise you, but dare to face the challenges. Let's make toys of the future."

With that, Mr. Drel sat back down as he said, "That's all I have to say, thanks for your time. Maria, can you please assist me with my book?" As Drel passed Timothy, the consultant looked both impressed and irritated at once. The entire room was quiet as they all took in everything that the apparent founder of Idrel had just said. "Right then, let's have a coffee break?" Timothy suggested. They all had a lot to think about.

***

"That's a brilliant idea," Paul told Bruce over skype, "That FLQ guy is a genius – to develop software at the same time as bears are being produced round the clock, what a way to speed up the process."

"Exactly," Bruce said with a nod, "Then as soon as the bears get unwrapped for the first time, the latest official released software can simply be loaded into them remotely, through the network. And Paul, your Turchaea baby has already been tested thoroughly by the open source community, I'm convinced we'll be able to handle the remote software upgrade. It's all set, both Idrel, FLQ and the UN is on board with this plan."

"So the software release date will be in November so we can distribute these teddies before Christmas?" Paul asked.

"Yup, but the consumer sales should only start after the software is released by us. It's gonna be great - completely going along with the 'giving' spirit of the holidays."

After they'd ended the call, Paul leaned back in the sofa at Jane's flat and his mind flew back to a conversation he'd had with Mr. Drel a few weeks ago after that meeting. "So, what do you think the future looks like young man?" Drel had asked him. Paul had told him more about the Internet of Things and the fact that all products, objects or things would soon be connected. Then, when Drel had asked what Idrel's biggest hurdle would be, Paul answered,

"I'm able to develop my algorithms when I'm able to free my mind about developing methods and correct software structures. When I reach that stage, my mind is free and I can do anything I want. In those moments when nobody tells me what to do, and there is no preconception of what to do, smart algorithms slip into my mind." Paul had paused, face flushed from the passion of his words. He'd hesitated then added,

"I think the biggest hurdle for companies are the limitations they put on themselves - like simply going along the old route of following market demands. What Idrel needs is leadership and a shared vision to make toys for the future. To be honest Mr. Drel, I think Idrel knows how to create toys, but should enable other companies to distribute their content. Idrel Toys should simply open its IoT-platform and connect with other companies." Drel had been in silent thought for several moments, then spoke directly.

"Listen my son. I think we need to talk about the future of our toys more, which will definitely be a challenge for Idrel. We've excellent sales people and our marketing is good, but we're not familiar with IoT or any of the things you've mentioned. Therefore, I'd like to suggest that we team up, Idrel and you." Drel had looked him straight in the eye, and Paul hadn't been sure how to respond, so he simply smiled and nodded. Their age difference was about fifty years, but it seemed like they had something in common.

Before he'd left that meeting, Mr. Drel gave Paul his business card after handwriting his home phone number on the back. "Call me when you get a chance," he'd told Paul.

"I'll definitely think about it," Paul had replied. And he was still thinking about it now, as he sat on Jane's sofa waiting for her to come home from work.

***

Thomas had finished his work at Idrel and gone back to Germany to 'recover from the Asian kitchen' as he'd told Paul and Bruce was still a consultant for FLQ's development team. Meanwhile Paul wondered if he'd done the right thing. Nobody in Idrel challenged him since they were all too busy with production and logistics for the bears. The only thing Maria had told Paul was to 'follow his intuition' and do whatever he felt was best.

She'd also agreed that, after their hard work, he and Jane should take a well-deserved break for a few weeks. After their return they would catch up working on the content again. Paul still sat in Jane's flat waiting for her to get home from work and pulled out the business card Drel had given him.

"I bet once the bears are actually out there, then they'll start paying attention to the content part," Paul told himself, "I guess it's always the same with IoT services. In the beginning the focus stays on the physical product, like the app and dashboards. They always seem to underestimate the importance of interconnectivity and algorithms." Letting out a sigh, he dialled Drel's number. It rang three times then Drel answered.

"Thanks for calling me, Paul. I'm glad you decided to chat," Drel began, "So, what are you thinking of doing – what are your immediate plans?"

"First and foremost," Paul told him, "Jane and I are exhausted and need a break before continuing any more work."

"Of course." Drel said in an understanding tone, "You should definitely take time for yourselves. If you want to think about the future, you first need to free your mind." Paul smiled, happy that the old man really seemed to get him.

"Exactly," Paul agreed, "So, Jane and I want to take a trek on this trail in Nepal." And after he explained more about their vacation plans, Drel said,

"How about you let Jane go ahead on the trip at first, and you come for a quick visit with me at my house here in Atlanta? Then, you can catch up with Jane in Kathmandu."

"That sounds perfect. I'll see you then, and thanks for understanding." With that Paul wrapped up the call, feeling relaxed and grateful that Drel was such a cool old guy.

***

"This is going to be so awesome," Jane told Paul with sparkling eyes, "After all that insane work, it'll be great to just take time to relax and, well, for me and you to spend more time together." It was a few hours after Paul talked with Drel and the two of them sat on the sofa eating takeout for dinner. They'd been busy planning their trip to Nepal, and even now browsed a travel site to find various treks and sites they wanted to try.

"Exactly, just you and me," Paul said, "No teddy bears, no laptops and no crazy pop-stars. We can finally get away from it all and unwind." And with that, Paul leaned over and gave Jane an excited kiss.

As they ate and planned, Paul silently considered heading up to check in on his Amsterdam flat before leaving. But he'd had a friend who was currently looking for a new flat himself staying there for the time being. So, all of Paul's stuff, including his home NAS-server, was in safe hands – there was no need to go up there. Bruce had told Paul about some challenges with the bear's software, but they knew how to handle them. To be honest, Paul didn't want to work at FLQ-electronics anymore, he just wanted to stay with Jane. So, he pushed all thoughts of FLQ, smart bears and his flat aside.

QUALITY

"AND YOU CAN rest assured," Francis proudly told the group as he gave a tour of their network operations centre, "That the backup and redundancy mechanisms will ensure the seamless operation of networks in case of a failure." One of the directors on the tour asked,

"So, what would happen if this operating centre collapsed?"

"Well," Francis answered swiftly, "That wouldn't be a problem because the back-up NOC would take over within 180 seconds." He beamed with confidence, then another visitor asked,

"And what's that red blinking dot on the screen over there?" Francis followed the man's gaze,

"Ah," he answered, "That my friends is a failing radio access unit. However due to the fact that our base stations have geographical coverage overlap, even if we needed to use the unit, it wouldn't cause a problem." Francis then moved over to his operator colleague, Jerry, and asked, "Will you please tell our guests about the load of all surrounding base stations?"

"Well," Jerry told the crowd, "All the surrounding base stations are actually below 12% which gives us an amazing amount of security for our service. And the service level agreement we have with our supplier requires a solution within 2.5 hours – no problem at all for us." Francis looked around at the visitors and smiled as he observed the impressed looks on everyone's face. But there were still a few questions about emRoaming.

"So, Francis," another visitor piped up, "In what way are you in contact with the competitors?"

"That's a great question," Francis replied, "For normal operations, we have our ticket systems which follows service level agreement procedures. Now, emRoaming is pragmatically implemented, and has no ticket system in place. So, when we performed the emRoaming test for the first time, all of us senior network operators simply created a group account on a social media platform to be in contact during and after the tests."

"But that's the same platform my daughter uses," the visitor declared, "She uses it to chat with her friends." Francis simply smiled and said,

"Sometimes the simplest things work the best."

* * *

It was the Thursday before 'Freeze Friday' for the FLQ-electronics team. The day before all the software would be handed over to the bear-operations team. Jung, the FLQ lead test engineer, felt his stomach twist up with nerves. And it was due to the fact that today of all days, the day before the release, a red blocking issue had been reported. He'd asked the two testers who'd reported it to come over to his office.

They entered silently and sat down at the table directly across from Jung. As soon as the door was closed, Jung leaned over the table and looked sternly at the two. "Are you absolutely sure this is a Prio-1? Isn't it something we can fix remotely after roll-out?" With bowed heads, one of the two testers spoke softly and quickly.

"It's actually a blocking issue related to the start-up sequence.

We thought it was important enough to give it a priority level one." Jung understood why they'd done that, but he didn't let the testers know. He narrowed his eyes menacingly.

"You have to understand that we are about to release our software. We can't possibly afford any delays whatsoever. You are to release our software at the end of this day, is that understood?" He looked from one to the other and continued without waiting for an answer.

"Our production colleagues will start using it tomorrow at 7 am after the hand-over. On the other hand..." And now Jung's posture relaxed a bit. He thought for a moment and continued, "Maybe it's good that you've found this issue. We have to ensure that we can solve problems together with our partner – Idrel Toys. You know what I mean?" The two engineers didn't dare raise their eyes and just nodded.

"So," Jung went on, "The company's success is now in your hands. Can you help me find the guy who's responsible for this bug?"

"Yes, sir," they both answered softly.

"Okay," Jung gave a brief nod, "Come back here in one hour, please. Feel free to involve any engineer you need in order to find an appropriate solution. Know that you have my full commitment." The two testing engineers nodded and silently left the room. Once Jung was alone in his office, his gaze lingered on the framed 'Quality' awards on his wall. Jung knew that he'd have to give his quality signature on this bear project, the company was relying on him.

Jung called the lead engineer, explained the situation and twenty minutes later a very tired looking Bruce came into his office. "Don't worry," Jung assured him, "I already have a team working on it." Bruce's forehead creased, but he knew Jung was quite capable and trusted that the software guys would resolve everything just fine. Five minutes later, the two testers came back in with a third guy – the one who'd written the code with a bug.

The guilty party didn't dare meet anybody's eyes, but Bruce could tell he'd been crying and still held some tissues in his hand. Before Bruce could say anything the poor guy took a deep breath and stated, "I'm sorry to have made this mistake, it was my fault. I feel ashamed and will work harder for you sir. I apologize for this again, I was wrong and I'll solve it. This year I won't take any holiday. Please allow me to solve this for you sir."

"We've looked at the issue again," one of the other testers added, "If you agree we want to double check the solution with you, Mr. Bruce." Bruce was extremely sleep-deprived, but he agreed just the same. Maybe he could get a few hours of rest in after this. The responsible engineer proceeded to explain how he'd made the mistake in the start-up sequence. Bruce was beyond irritated, but he responded as nicely as he could.

"Okay, you're right. This is incorrect. I'll explain it again. It's very simple - the internal memory index consists of four register banks. All you have to do is multiply them with the function number you want to use in a particular situation. Let's have a look at function number three, we always start counting from zero. This means it's the fourth function - four banks of four equals twelve, so that means it directs to that function. You understand?" Bruce pointed his finger to the printed software update routine with number twelve and looked at the engineer.

The engineer's eyes intently scanned the code, then highlighted the twelfth software function in the code with a yellow marker.

"Okay, yes sir, I understand, thank you. I'll go fix it right now."

"Great," Jung told him, "Thank you. But listen, can we do a hotfix procedure instead of a normal fix? This saves us having to test the entire software all over again." Bruce thought for a moment and said,

"I'm not familiar with your test procedures."

"Well," Jung explained, "A completely new test would mean

we'd have to run each and every test script all over again. We'd never get it done in time for the release at the end of today. Now, if we only go in and change this one part of the code, it's called a 'hotfix'. No big difference, really."

"I guess you know how to deal with this better than me," Bruce said with a shrug, "You're in charge of testing. Do what you think is best." And so the three software guys meekly left the room to work on the hotfix, while the test team went on with the remaining tests at the same time. Jung looked at Bruce.

"Listen my friend, you should go back to your hotel and get some sleep. We can't make it on time today anyway. We'll continue testing through the night and if you can just be back here tomorrow at 6 am and we can hand-over to the operation guys, okay?" Bruce smiled with relief. Sleep at last.

* * *

Jung looked wiped out, but smiled widely at Bruce when he came in the next day at 6 am on the dot. He gave two thumbs up and pointed to his PC to show green indicators all over the test plan. Success. "Finally," Jung said happily, "And now I can hand this over to the bear-operations team. I'm going to call them right now."

Bruce smiled with relief and watched Jung make the call. Within minutes a guy from production came to pick up the software and documents. After the production guy left, Jung turned to Bruce, tired eyes crinkling at the edges. "Mission accomplished. We passed an important quality milestone today, and now it's time for some heavenly sleep." Bruce laughed at this, completely understanding how Jung felt. And now the bears were finally ready to go.

* * *

Jane grinned from ear to ear when she saw Paul's smiling picture along with the incoming call. She answered, "Hello baby. How was your day? No, you first... oh what?" Paul, who was waiting for his transfer flight to the U.S., responded,

"Sorry babe, the reception is quite bad - you at home? I can't really hear you...I'm fine, it's okay. I just need some sleep. Yes, I'm packing tonight. It's been a busy week." Then Paul heard kids scream in the background and he put the phone close to his mouth.

"I love you angel." Suddenly the connection was lost, only going to voicemail when he tried again.

The next day Jane excitedly packed her bag. She'd be leaving in just a few hours to catch her flight to Nepal and she couldn't wait to see Paul again. When almost done with packing, she heard a knock at the door. It was the mailman delivering a red parcel with her name on it. Jane thanked him and shut the door, tilting her head at the package. She unwrapped it to find a teddy bear who immediately let out a burp.

Laughing, Jane read the enclosed note. "On behalf of the FLQ team we thank you for your trust in our company. We look forward to assisting you with bringing your product onto the market. With respect - Mr. Dong-Watsu, Vice President FLQ Company." Looking back at the bear, Jane smiled when she saw it was wearing a white T-shirt with 'I love you Jane' printed on the front.

A bunch of perfumed red plastic flowers also lay in the package. It was such a sweet gift. A personalized, limited edition bear for the team who'd worked on the product. "That's really nice of those FLQ guys," she said to herself as she placed down the bear and flowers and went to make some tea. As her favorite ginger tea brewed, Jane texted Paul about the bear.

She sat with her tea and a raspberry scone, then unfolded the courtesy card that had come with the package. When opened, Scry's song, *Let Me Be Your Teddy Bear* played in a variety of languages. Jane listened and felt a swell of pride, though she was also exhausted. They'd made it. All the work and stress from the last few months now dropped from her shoulders.

But she was overcome with an ache from missing Paul, and gave the bear a hug. The words, "Let me be your Teddy Bear, what is your name?" sounded and made Jane jump in surprise. She stared at her teddy as waves of emotion washed through. She answered the bear,

"My dear angel," and let out a giggle as a single tear trickled down her cheek.

The bear started his programme and Jane liked the fact that the teddy kept calling her, 'my dear angel' the whole time. She put him on his charging pillow, and he said, "Thank you my dear angel," then went promptly into sleep mode as Jane grinned and texted Paul,

<Your dear angel is on her way!>

It was time to head to the airport, so she grabbed her luggage and locked the flat door. Her holiday had finally begun.

Journey's start

PAUL SAT IN a hotel room in Atlanta, waiting to meet with Mr. Drel. Tomorrow he'd fly to Kathmandu and meet up with Jane. They'd been continuously texting little smileys and hearts, counting down the hours. She was now in India waiting for her transfer flight to Kathmandu. But at the moment, Paul was texting with his brother, Chris, who'd ordered twenty bears to sell on e-bay. Chris texted,

<*So they shipped out yet?*>

<<*They're ready and heading out – you'll get them soon- no worries! How's Valentina?*>>

<*Good, a little bossy, very cranky, but she's mostly happy and the baby's healthy. You off to Nepal with that girl?*>

<<*Yeah – Jane* ☺ *And I'm glad the baby's good – can't believe you're going to be a dad soon - crazy!*>>

After a few more minutes of texting Chris signed off to get Valentina some fish and chips she was craving. Paul shook his head with a smile. Since they were kids, his older brother had always been good at trading things, and as a teenager Chris used to buy and sell stuff all the time. Times hadn't changed a bit, not really.

* * *

"Welcome to my home Paul," Drel smiled at him later that day as they sat down with coffee and pieces of peach cobbler, "Thanks for coming."

"Thanks for inviting me," Paul answered politely, "I've never been to the States before, and…" Here Paul stopped in surprise as Maria walked into the room. What was she doing here? Before he could say anything, Drel said,

"You know, this house is built right on the spot that, a long time ago, my grandpa's workshop stood." As Paul looked around the beautiful old Victorian house's sitting room he noticed some wood-carved toys in a glass-enclosed bookshelf. Drel took a bite of cobbler, swallowed and went on,

"I understand you're about to travel around Nepal, that's very exciting. I'd love to do a trip like that, but my knees aren't what they used to be," he chuckled, "But before we start talking about Nepal, Maria and I would like to thank you for your help." Maria studied Paul's face intensely for a moment.

"Nice to see you again Paul," she said, "Your input for this project has been critical. We give you most of the credit for this project - you were key to our success."

"Thanks," Paul said with flushed cheeks, "But it really was a team effort. Rafael pushed it forward and…" But Drel interrupted,

"That's bull-shit. You, Paul are the one who made it possible. And finally, Idrel is making toys for the future. Maria could you…?" Maria stood up and handed a large envelope over to Paul, who eyed it questioningly. Drel said, "Please open and read it." The letter looked very official, printed on thick paper and with the company's gold-edged logo.

Paul opened it and started to scan the text which was signed by the complete Idrel board. '...*will grant you by doubling the license fee for each bear (or any other IoT- enabled Idrel-Toy) shipped by Idrel, or any of its production partners, for the next ten years.*' He didn't know what to say. Money wasn't what drove his work, but having it was a nice side effect. He stood there and stared at the letter in silence.

Drel understood Paul's reaction and put his hand softly on the young man's shoulder. "First take some time for yourself and your young lady friend on the trip. I'd really enjoy and appreciate if we could have some kind of common future together, after you come back of course." Paul remained quiet for a few more moments, then looked at Drel and nodded.

"Thank you," Paul told him simply.

"We'll talk again after your vacation," Drel said as he patted him on the shoulder again, "So, let's go grab some lunch now?"

* * *

She'd recognized the block-chain technology because she herself had built a bitcoin miner a few months ago, only to find out if it was feasible, of course. All these RC racers seemed to use the same server somewhere in The Netherlands to find their way to this sophisticated network.

These things popped up everywhere and weren't driving around at all. Not just a few, but hundreds. No, not hundreds - *thousands*. She couldn't see what was inside the encrypted data, but by looking at the origin of their internet data, she could see that they used mobile phone networks and tracked them all back to somewhere in South Korea.

She also saw one in the U.S. "Interesting," she muttered to

herself, tucking a strand of light red hair behind her ear. The other strange thing was that they were never turned off, but kept communicating frequently. It was like they were on standby, signalling each other and simply waiting for something to happen and then closing their internet connections again.

She'd never seen anything like this before. Their network behaviour looked restless, buzzing around like little insects. Once they were operating it seemed like they'd start to transfer data, then suddenly halt, only to begin all over again. The girl decided to log their activities and left her house to do some last minute Christmas shopping with her mom.

* * *

In the meantime, a few thousand kilometres away from the teenage girl, Francis' wife Helen was totally pissed off. How could he do this? He was the senior guy in the team for heaven's sake! But, every year it was the same story - somebody had to sit in the network operating centre right around Christmas and, believe it or not, it was Francis. How could her husband have accepted this yet again?

Francis had tried to convince her, "But listen honey, the last time for me was two years ago. It's only for Christmas Eve and I'll get double the pay. And on Christmas Day itself, I'll be home at 7 am." Helen let out a heavy sigh.

"Yeah, but then you'll sleep all day long just like last time. This is not the Christmas I had in mind this year Francis." He tried to embrace his wife, but she pushed him away. He tried to calm her down by saying,

"To be honest, I don't think it's necessary, it's just company policy. The network's quite robust, so it's basically not necessary to have anyone sit in the network operating centre. But during Christmas, they don't want to take any risks. Don't worry sweetie, I'll be able to get some sleep there and we'll have a nice Christmas Day. You hadn't planned to go to church on Christmas Eve had you?'

"Francis, don't you ever listen?" Helen's tone was scornful, "You agreed to go to church with me and my sister this year. We've been working as volunteers in their garden and were invited to the special charity dinner. Don't you remember?" Francis vaguely recalled that she'd said something about a church club she worked with.

"Right, of course I remember, honey," he said, "I'll ask my boss if somebody else can take over my shift, okay?"

CHURNED UP

"BRUCE, WE'VE GOT a serious situation. They're burping instead of saying hello," the operations guy said as he burst into Bruce's office. Bruce drew back in surprise.

"What do you mean burp?" he asked.

"I mean that they're not starting up properly," the guy answered. Bruce felt a pit grow in the bottom of his stomach. This was not good – not good at all.

"Are you sure?" he demanded.

"Yes, absolutely. Here, try this one." He dropped a wrapped package on the desk and Bruce unwrapped the bear. At first it was silent, then, after two seconds, a loud burp filled the room. Bruce's stomach felt even heavier.

"This isn't what we promised to deliver," Bruce said, "Customers expect a cute bear that says 'let me be your teddy bear!' What kind of shit is this?"

"Exactly," the operations man said, "This isn't what we want at all." The guy sat down and held his head between his hands, close to tears. "We've shipped thousands of them now and people will report burps instead of a warm friendly hello message after unwrapping them."

Suddenly the bear on the table woke up and said, "Hello let me be your teddy bear. What's your name?"

The bear did say the right message, but it wasn't until after the initial burping sound. They had to solve this, and quickly. Production was running non-stop and every hour hundreds of bears were made and then shipped twice a day to distribution centres.

Bruce stood and stalked towards his office door to go figure something out, but before he left the operations guy said, "Sorry Bruce, this is your part. If it's not solved in an hour I have to report it to the quality team. In the meantime, we'll let the production continue." Bruce looked out the window, thought for a moment then grabbed his phone. He called two of the most dedicated, trustworthy senior software engineers and explained the issue.

"Try this one Bruce," one of the two senior software engineers dropped a wrapped up bear on Bruce's desk forty-five nerve-wracking minutes later. Trying not to get too excited until he was sure, Bruce carefully unfolded the plastic. A few seconds later, the bear said,

"Let me be your teddy bear!" Bruce felt the pit in his stomach dissolve. He slammed his palm onto the table with joy.

"Yes, well done, my friends!" He looked at each of them, "That's exactly what we want. Well done indeed! How did you do this?"

"Simple actually," one of the engineers said, "We just changed the default setting in the bear cloud, where they get their initial start-up sequence, by directing it to a different mp3 file within the bear. The only thing is that the bears burp when they're not able to connect to the central bear platform, but that's no problem I guess."

A moment later, Bruce called the operations guy. "It's all good. Everything's solved, so keep those bears coming."

* * *

Francis smirked to himself at the festive gathering Helen had put together after the church's Christmas Eve service. He felt quite clever about having his student operations worker, Kevin, do the shift at the centre for him. Francis was off the hook, and his wife had been appeased. Now he could enjoy himself, eating salmon with crackers and white wine.

While Francis chatted with some guys at the party, a message from Kevin popped up on his phone, showing a thumbs up "*Wonderful,*" Francis thought, "*Everything's going well.*" He was in excellent spirits, and slightly tipsy from the wine, as he listened to Helen's little speech about the hard work of the gardening volunteers, thanking all the guests for coming and so forth.

* * *

Paul gently kissed Jane's head as she slept against his shoulder. They'd been reunited at last and sat together on a cheap bus in Nepal, somewhere between Kathmandu and Pokhara. The bus swayed and shook as it went over the mountain roads. Sometimes the road curved so much that Paul couldn't see the pavement anymore, and the window looked down over a 500m vertical drop. He'd planned on getting sleep in Kathmandu first, but Jane had already arranged the connecting bus tickets, ready when he'd arrived. "You can sleep on the bus," she'd said with a smile. It was incredible to see Jane again after an entire week apart and they'd kissed for almost two minutes when they saw each other at the airport. Seeing her smiling eyes had felt somehow like coming home to Paul – they truly belonged together on such a deep level.

"Are we there yet?" Jane suddenly asked in a sleepy voice. Paul shook his head.

"Not yet, angel," he said softly, "Hey, can you hand me that chocolate bar? We can have a Christmas Eve feast of chocolate and water from my bottle." He grinned, holding up the Himalayan spring water bottle he'd bought in the airport. Jane laughed and handed him the chocolate.

"Merry Christmas Eve, Paul." She beamed and kissed him. As they munched on their holiday feast, the conversation rolled around to the teddy bear project. "What an insanely busy time that was," Jane said, shaking her head softly in thought.

"It was crazy," Paul agreed. Then he took her hand in his, interweaving their fingers. He noticed how electricity surged through his body at her touch. The charged attraction between them hadn't dissipated at all from being apart, it had only grown more intense.

A moment later, Paul began leafing through their Lonely Planet book, stopping to read a particular section aloud, "Listen to this Jane, 'If you're lucky, in Nepal you'll face the Himalayan Brown Bear - ursus-arctos-isa-something, also known as the Himalayan Red Bear. The bear is thought to be the source of the Yeti legend.'" He paused to look at her, eyebrows raised teasingly. "So, what are we going to do if we come face-to-face with a Yeti?" Paul playfully squeezed her fingers and suddenly leaned over to kiss her. When he pulled back, Jane laughed.

"I guess we simply say, 'would you be my teddy bear?' That will scare them off, won't it?" Paul burst out laughing along with Jane, then said,

"I've seen enough bears for the rest of my life, thank you very much. Besides, I'd rather concentrate on my own cuddly teddy bear, sitting right next to me." Paul's voice spoke more deeply and his eyes were a darker blue as he smiled over at her. Before she could respond, he kissed her again, longer and more passionately, using his free hand to tuck a stray piece of hair behind her ear. She leaned into the heated kiss, sighing happily against the softness of his lips – they were as comforting as coming home after a long trip. She pulled back and whispered, "We belong together, you know."

"I think we've been together our whole lives," Paul pulled back to say, "In soul, if not in body." They stared into each other's eyes, complexly in love, until they drifted to sleep, Jane's head back on his shoulder and his head leaning on top of hers. As the bus followed the twisting road towards Pokhara, Jane and Paul continued having what was the most special Christmas Eve either of them had ever had.

* * *

"Francis, there's a burglar outside," Helen whispered frantically into his ear as they lay in bed, "He's walking around the house." Francis blinked in confusion.

"Huh, what? Did you just say a burglar?" he asked.

"Yes, be quiet," she whispered back, "Listen." Francis woke up more fully now, sitting straight up in their bed, listening carefully. After a minute he heard a bustling sound outside. There was definitely someone out there.

"Okay, honey, don't panic," Francis whispered back, "Just keep the lights off and don't move." Helen's eyes got wider.

"I'll call the police, don't go and try to fight him Francis!" He shook his head.

"No, don't call the police. I'm not going to fight, I'm just going to have a little look first." With that, before Helen could protest, he got out of bed and slowly walked out of their bedroom and towards the stairs. Looking down from the second floor, he saw a small torch light coming through a first-floor window, casting its beam into the hall. There was somebody standing in front of his house, right at the front door.

"Call the police," he urgently whispered back through the bedroom door. Then, Francis tip-toed down the stairs to the hall and noticed the torch light had disappeared. But he still clearly saw the shadow of a man at his front door. Quieting his breath, Francis could hear his own heart racing a mile a minute.

It was 3 am, technically Christmas morning, and a burglar was standing at his house, about to break in. Suddenly a noise erupted in the dead quiet of the night, exploding in Francis' ear. It was the doorbell ringing. Why would a burglar ring the doorbell? "Who's there?" Francis asked loudly, facing the front door. A voice from the other side of the door answered, sounding muffled.

"Francis? It's me. Kevin!" Just then Helen called from the bedroom,

"Who is it?" she asked with a panicked voice. Francis let out a sigh of relief.

"It's just somebody from work," he called back up, "Don't call the police after all." When he opened the door, Kevin's hair was covered in snow and he held his smartphone in his hand using it as a torch. His eyebrows drew together, both anxious and apologetic.

"Sorry to wake you up at this hour boss, but I'm really relieved to see you." Francis felt a horrible sickening twist in his stomach. This couldn't be good.

"Come in Kevin, and please tell me what the hell is going on."

* * *

"Ow, that one really hurt," Valentina gripped her fingers around Chris' arm so hard that her fingernails dug into his skin. It was another contraction. Luckily, it faded quickly.

"Is this normal?" Chris asked with a concerned frown. Valentina smiled knowledgably at him.

"Yeah, it's totally natural, don't worry honey. The frequency will soon pick up. I think we'll be parents within twelve hours." Now Chris was really getting nervous. He looked at his phone and saw it had been fifteen minutes since her last contraction. His gaze moved to look outside the window, taking in the heavy snowfall. The local nurse had told them both to call anytime they needed, and Chris decided that he really needed to now.

The nurse answered with a crying baby in the background. He

told her the situation. "That sounds really good Chris. Thanks for letting me know. This means that early labour has started...and no, don't worry that it's a week early. Remember what we talked about?"

"Yeah, I remember," Chris answered.

"Okay," the nurse said, "This will go on for quite some time, then the contractions will slowly speed up. When they're about four minutes apart and regular, let me know, okay?"

"Yeah, okay," Chris replied nervously.

"In the meantime," the nurse finished up, "Try to get some sleep and make sure Valentina drinks plenty of water." Even though she spoke in a calm, reassuring tone, his heart hammered in his chest after hanging up. Chris could clearly see that Valentina was having a hard time. He'd insisted that she give birth in a hospital, but she'd decided that giving birth at home was much more natural, and insisted on it. Both the doctor and nurses were fine with her decision as well.

So here he was, sitting next to her bed and holding Valentina's hand, waiting for the four-minute-apart frequency. "Ow, damn!" She cried out louder this time, her nails digging even harder into the flesh of his arm. Then she called out a small string of curses in Italian, her eyes tightening up in pain. This whole situation was, quite frankly, terrifying.

The woman at the desk of their hostel had arranged for a driver to bring them to the start of the Annapurna trail, and the car was already waiting just outside.

"Crap, let's buy these and go!" After buying everything, including some extra plasters in case of blisters, they stuffed it all into their mostly full hiking backpacks. "Here we go," Paul grinned at Jane as they sat in the back of the taxi a few moments later, both out of breath from rushing.

Before they knew it, the driver had dropped them off at the edge of Nepal, the starting point for the trail that would take two weeks to hike. Bye-bye civilization - hello wilderness.

* * *

"And suddenly all kinds of warning messages popped up left and right, asking for confirmation," Kevin finished explaining.

"So why didn't you call me?" Francis asked, crossing his arms.

"Because it just went straight to your voicemail every time I tried," Kevin answered.

"Nonsense," Francis said, "I didn't turn off my phone. Let me go get it, I'll be right back." As Helen came into the kitchen where they'd been sitting, Francis went upstairs.

"Do you want some tea?" Helen asked Kevin. Before the young man could reply, they both heard a string of curses coming from upstairs. In under a minute, Francis came bounding down the stairs and into the kitchen, dressed in jeans and a t-shirt, face pale. "We need to go to the office, *now*." He marched towards the door, car keys in hand.

"But," Helen argued, "Can't we have some tea first at least, its Christmas Day after all." Francis simply shook his head, looking apologetic for a moment before gesturing for Kevin to follow him. After fifteen minutes of careful driving, Francis and Kevin went through the sliding doors of the operation centre where the

STORM

"SO, SHOULD WE start getting ready for our mountain trek?" Jane asked with an excited smile. They'd arrived at the Karma guesthouse finally - early Christmas Day. Paul pocketed his phone and grinned. "Absolutely, let's check if we can leave some of our unnecessary stuff here."

The lady at the lobby desk told him in slightly awkward English, "Yes - that you can." She pointed them to a store next door that sold common mountain trekking supplies. As they walked into the store, Paul told Jane,

"Thank goodness we can leave any extra things at the hostel, so we only have to carry around the necessary stuff." He paused and picked up a green emergency raincoat.

"Um, Paul," she said, tilting her head, "Do we really need those?" While speaking Jane placed several packs of instant noodles and dried fruit into her shopping basket.

"Why not, let's take two," Paul answered with a shrug. Jane walked up to a shelf with spare shoestrings and put a few in her basket.

"These could come in handy, too...oh and some chocolate!" She moved to the next shelf over and put several bars in her basket.

fluorescent lights automatically turned on. There was a phone on one of the desks that continuously rang, but Francis focused on the big screen.

In three seconds, he understood what was going on. Red indicators blinked everywhere, warning that two core network servers were down. Glancing at his phone, Francis saw 'Searching for Network'. He frowned, always feeling isolated and a bit panicked when disconnected.

But it wasn't just him and his phone, the network was down across the nation. Though probably most people weren't trying to use it so early that Christmas morning, it was still completely down. What if someone had an emergency and couldn't call an ambulance? Francis saw that the automatic recovery procedures running as usual, and the backup system was already booting.

While Francis studied the screens, Kevin answered the ringing phone on the desk. It was the customer helpdesk and the employee who was working the current nightshift said, "Thanks for answering. What's going on? People are calling and reporting network unavailability on social media. I can't use my own phone either."

"Yes, we also noticed," Kevin replied, swallowing hard,

"There's something wrong with a server, but my colleague Francis here is working on it as we speak. I'll take a note and he'll call you back."

Francis' eyes scanned the screens while he opened and closed several system menus. "What the hell is going on here?" he muttered to himself. He focused on the main screen where a status bar indicated, 'Signalling Channels Overload', then browsed through the log file which said 'Signalling Level Warnings'.

"Did you get any warning messages yesterday evening?" Francis asked his student. Kevin looked sheepish.

"I *did* see a notification in bright orange scroll across, but then a beep sounded and it showed, 'Back-up Successfully in Place', and everything turned green again. So this repeated after an hour and later on every thirty minutes until an hour ago. I tried to call you, but I couldn't reach you because the network was out. Sorry." Francis sighed and patted the young man on his shoulder.

"No worries, Kevin, I understand, you did what you could. I don't have the old fashioned land-line phone at home anymore, so there wasn't any way to reach me except in person." Francis felt dizzy as his mind swirled around, trying to figure out the next step. He should probably call his own superior next. Taking the desk phone, he looked up the number the old-fashioned way - in his phone book - and dialled it.

It went straight to voicemail. Of course, he'd forgotten. None of his colleagues or superiors had land-lines anymore. So, he dropped his boss an email saying, "Severe issue, network down. Keep you posted. You can reach me in the office."

Then Francis remembered the internet forum messages from the two Asian operators who had also reported signalling issues. Yet, before he could read their forum, a beep sounded and the green light indicated, 'Back-up System in Operation'. The system was recovering! Francis quickly checked the status and saw that thousands of mobile phones were automatically trying to contact the network to re-register. He eagerly switched his phone off and on as Kevin did the same.

The screen said, 'Searching for Network'. Francis kept his eyes focused on his phone and waited while Kevin stared at his own phone. The room was dead silent. After several long-seeming moments, his phone found the network. Francis pumped a fist in triumph and said, "Yes! Kevin, did yours find the network too?"

Kevin nodded and grinned. His hands shaking with eagerness, Francis dialled the desk phone at the other side of the room. It rang. Both guys let out a whoop of victory. Feeling relief wash through his body, Francis sat down on a chair and pulled a hand over his face, smiling. He looked back at the screens to see thousands of messages reading, 'Successful Registration'.

It appeared that the back-up system had taken over now, and seemed to be running well. The main system was still down, which Francis would need to look at, but he decided to wait until after the back-up system had fully taken over without any slip-ups.

On another screen Francis saw that user traffic increased - people were calling each other. Within ten minutes all screens were flashing green and, though it was using the back-up, all systems were operating again. They were back!

Exchanging a relieved look with Kevin, Francis let out a breath and his gaze fell down to his feet. He was wearing Helen's flip-flops. "*Sometimes you've got to prioritise*," he thought with a chuckle. So, what had happened with the systems - what was the root cause? Something must've been wrong, but he couldn't tell what. It was all very strange.

Kevin sat down in a chair near Francis, rubbing his eyes in exhaustion. The young man glanced at his boss, feeling a wave of guilt, even though he hadn't caused any of this. He still had a bad feeling, like something else might go wrong. Francis regarded him and said, "You know, why don't you head home and get some rest – enjoy your Christmas. I'll stay here."

"No," Kevin shook his head, "That's okay. I'd rather stay to make sure everything's okay. I'm curious to find out what caused all this." Francis opened his mouth to respond, but a rapid beeping noise began, causing both of them to lurch and stare at the main status screen. A red blinking text read, "Signalling Overload on Back-up System. Switching to Primary System."

Francis went pale. "Shit, it's going down - there we go again! Kevin: Fasten your seatbelt. This could be a bumpy ride."

* * *

Nikole slowly woke up at her parents' house in the quaint yet gorgeous town of Parga in western Greece. The house sat on a cobbled street just two blocks from the sea, and was the home and town where Nikole, or known in this town as Nikoleta, grew up.

As she rubbed the sleep out of her eyes, she heard her grown-up children's voices downstairs, talking with her own parents. Sniffing the air, Nikole smiled at the mouth-watering smell of fried fish. The traditional family Christmas breakfast was definitely underway.

She stared up at the ceiling for a moment – it hadn't changed a bit since she was a kid. Nikole's children had spent the night, along with her daughter's new boyfriend and her son's college friend, all in her sister's room with cots and sleeping bags. They were eighteen and twenty-one now - officially grown-up and living their own lives, both also living in other countries.

As Nikole smelled the scent of coffee mixing with the lemony fried fish downstairs, she turned to snuggle under the warmth of her quilt. Just a few more moments of rest, then she'd go down for the scrumptious breakfast. It felt good to be back with her parents and in her old room.

Since Nikole had moved to Brussels a lot of things had happened. She'd gotten a divorce a few years ago, which upset her parents a great deal. It hadn't been a messy situation, but she felt a bit guilty since this wasn't what her parents had expected from her.

"Nikoleta, breakfast is ready," her mom called up.

"Coming," Nikole called back down. Before heading down, she did what most people in the world now did the moment they got up – she checked her phone. No messages. As she came into the kitchen a moment later, her dad gave her forehead a kiss and said,

"Good morning my love." Her mom was just taking fresh bread from the oven - it smelled heavenly.

"Morning honey," her mom called over from the oven, "Happy

Christmas." Nikole helped her put the bread on the wooden cutting board.

"Happy Christmas, mom," she smiled. Both Alysia and Alexander, Nikole's daughter and son, helped their grandma by putting everything on the table. Alysia's boyfriend Stavos and Alexander's college friend from Cambridge, Keith, were still upstairs getting ready. Alysia smiled and came over to Nikole.

"Morning mom, happy Christmas," she said with a quick kiss on her mom's cheek. Alexander came over too.

"Yeah, happy Christmas mom," he said kissing Nikole's other cheek.

"Thanks kids, happy Christmas," Nikole put an arm around each of her children's shoulders for a quick family hug.

Moments later, as they sat around the kitchen table, Nikole noticed the extra happy expressions on her parent's faces – they really loved having the house full of family, especially the young ones. Stavos and Keith had come down and joined them at the table by this point.

Nikole smiled contentedly too as the family cat snuck around everyone's legs, carefully observing and sniffing at everybody. Per tradition, after they'd eaten for a while, everyone exchanged Christmas gifts.

When all but one present had been opened, everyone watched as Alysia tore into a big box from Stavos, who looked both eager and nervous. She opened the card before the present, and read aloud:

Dear Alysia,
A teddy bear is a faithful friend.
That you can trust until the end.
His fur is the color of breakfast toast,

And he's always there
When you need him most.
Alysia, to let you know I really care
Please let me be your Teddy Bear!

Alysia's cheeks turned pink and a huge grin spread across her face as she gave Stavos a quick kiss and thank you. Everyone at the table applauded. Nikole's tearful eyes met her mom's across the table, and they smiled at each other, both loving how happy her daughter looked. "*Ah, young love*," Nikole thought a little wistfully as Alysia unwrapped the actual present. It was that cute teddy bear from the TV show.

"Aw, he's adorable, thank you Stavos," Alysia said, hugging the bear, "I think he's cuddlier than you," she teased. As Stavos opened his mouth to respond, a big burp filled the room, coming from the bear.

"He must've had a rough night," Nikole's dad joked. The whole table erupted into laughter. Nikole laughed so hard she had more tears in her eyes.

After more eating, talking and joking, Nikole turned to her dad. "You know, you guys should come with us to Brussels for that holiday you talked about taking soon. You'd love it!" Dad smiled but shook his head.

"Thanks, but I think that's too crowded for us, sweetie. We prefer a nice, simple trip to Athens or Crete, staying in a little bed and breakfast." He exchanged a knowing glance with Nikole's mom.

Alysia, who now held Stavos' hand casually resting at the table's edge, chimed in, "Speaking of trips, we're planning one to New York City in the summer and…"

But she was cut short by her new teddy bear who now said, "Hello, Let me be your Teddy Bear. What's your name?"

* * *

Everything was going wrong, horribly wrong for Francis, who now sat hunched in concentration, studying the back-up system screen. The primary system still hadn't recovered and the load on the CPUs was 100%. The network use was huge, far too much to handle. Francis had never seen this amount of signalling information on his network.

"What is signalling exactly?" Kevin asked.

"Well," Francis kept looking at the screen as he explained. "Apart from transferring data, network and mobile devices also exchange management information with each other. This is called signalling information. For example, it's used to indicate that a phone call has started then ended, or when a mobile connection with the internet is in place. It also ensures that a user maintains their connection when he or she travels and passes various mobile network base station towers."

Kevin nodded and wanted to ask more, but he noticed the increasingly anxious look on Francis' face and decided to stay quiet. As Francis observed the screen, he saw hundreds of thousands of devices continuously connecting to the network, then promptly disconnecting. Their network simply couldn't handle the volume. It was like a storm - a network signalling storm.

In two minutes, the network went completely down and Francis saw his phone screen show, 'Searching for Network'. He looked at Kevin, eyes full of dread. "We're in deep, deep trouble Kevin. I think I need to switch everything off and restart it all manually. I need to find the root cause then isolate it. And, I'm going to need my colleagues to help." Kevin looked at his watch - it was 5 am on Christmas morning.

"How are we going to reach them?" Kevin asked. Francis raced through the options out loud,

"Sending out emails? No, nobody would read a business email

on Christmas. Hey, can you drive a car?" Kevin nodded, but looked wary.

"Yeah," he said, "But I don't have a driver's license yet. And it's snowing." Francis decided to ignore these facts and held out his car keys.

"Here, take my car and pick up my colleagues as quickly and safely as you can. Bring them back here, okay?" Kevin hesitantly took the keys while Francis found his colleague's home addresses on the administrative assistant's spreadsheet.

After Kevin left, Francis decided he really couldn't rely on the auto recovery procedure - like he was the pilot of a plane who needed to switch off autopilot and fly manually. Francis wondered if he even knew how to navigate through these procedures. They'd never practised this before, and he had no idea what would happen after lift-off.

Meanwhile, Kevin drove carefully through the night, happy that it had at least stopped snowing for the moment. Before leaving, he'd put the addresses into his phone's navigational app, but unfortunately the app wasn't working because the network was down again. His phone only displayed, 'Searching for Network'. "Shit," he muttered to himself. This didn't look good, and he was utterly exhausted which didn't help matters.

And then the snow started to fall again. "Double shit," he cursed, peering up at the heavy clouds. Driving in the snow could be challenging, and the fact that Kevin had never driven on a main road in his life made it twice as dangerous. Thankfully, there was no other traffic on the road and he slowly came to a stop in the middle of the main street to figure out how to turn on the windshield wipers.

He finally got the wipers to work, but then he looked ahead and frowned. Without his navigational app working, he had no idea which way to go. He looked in the rear-view mirror to see a car pulling up behind him. As Kevin began to steer to the side so they could pass, lights flashed from the top of the other car and he heard a voice calling out through a megaphone, "Police, stay where you are."

***

"Let's be careful, dad, okay?" Nikole helped her dad into his light jacket after they'd finished their post-breakfast coffee. Although it took close to ten minutes for everyone to get walking shoes and light sweaters or coats on, the whole group was now ready for a short walk along the coast. This was another family tradition, taking a walk along the beach on Christmas Day.

Alysia, Alexander, Stavos and Keith had all gone ahead and were probably already enjoying the steady sea breeze and sparkling blue water, when Nikole came out with her mom and dad. "You know dad," Nikole said as they slowly ambled down the cobbled street towards the sea, "It's really nice to be back here and away from Brussels and the busy streets."

"Well," her dad replied, "To be honest Nikoleta, the streets here are also much busier than they used to be – tourists coming for their holidays and everything." Nikole just nodded while secretly smiling to herself - she knew her parents didn't have any idea what her life in Brussels looked like. Her days were packed with meetings, lunches and work-related dinners. Nikole often looked for ways to escape from the hectic business life to get a chance to relax and think about things.

When there was time, she'd slip away to jog along 'Boise de la Cambre', not far from her flat. During holidays and weekends that she wasn't busy, Nikole was able to get some perspective on all her work and life. Sure, she liked her job, yet during these moments, when she was further away from the daily chaos and stress of work, Nikole truly wondered what affect her efforts really had in everyone's life.

As they now walked through her parent's front garden, she asked, "Dad, do you *really* see any results from my work out here in Greece – in our little village?"

"Nikoleta - honey," he said with a smile, "Your mom and I are very proud of you. We know you're doing important work over there."

"That's right," her mom added, "Your dad's always watching the news on TV to see if you appear. When you're on, the whole village knows about it."

"Yes," her dad laughed, "It's true. But I don't look at all those idiot TV shows, you know."

"Being on TV is just like anything else in life," Nikole said, "It can be fun but depends on the situation." At this point, they were about to cross the street when a large black car with tinted windows suddenly stopped in front of them.

"What on earth is that driver doing?" her dad asked with a frown as her mom grabbed his arm in surprise. Two men wearing sunglasses swiftly came out of the car.

"Sorry to disturb you madam, but are you Nikoleta Solon?"

"Yes," she answered, blinking in surprise, "That's me. Why do you want to know?" Her expression was guarded.

"Ministry of Foreign Affairs," the man said as he took off his sunglasses, "We've been asked to assist you with your transfer to Brussels."

"I'm sorry," Nikole said, furrowing her brow in confusion, "I haven't heard anything about a transfer, and…" But the other man interrupted her as he handed over a satellite telephone. Exchanging a worried glance with her mom and dad, Nikole took the phone and placed the bulky device against her ear.

"Hello, Nikole Solon speaking. Who's this?'" She listened carefully while her parents looked anxiously on. It must be something pretty big if they came to interrupt their daughter's Christmas holiday. Nikole now said, "Listen Theo, isn't this a bit exaggerated? It's Christmas and I'm here with my parents. I'll be back in two days to catch up, is that okay with you?"

A long silence followed as Nikole listened to Theo's response. She then took out her own smartphone and looked at the display.

It showed, 'Searching for Network'. She softly said, "Right, I understand. I will." And with that Nikole handed the phone back to the man. "Sorry mom – sorry dad - I need to go back to the office."

"Was that the Commissioner on the other line?" Her mom asked with a frown.

"Yeah," Nikole said glumly, "I really need to go. We have a serious situation with our mobile phone networks." She paused to look at the two men and added, "Before I go, I want to walk along the coast a bit so I can say goodbye to my children, is that okay?"

"Sorry," the driver shook his head, looking apologetic, "But our orders are to bring you straight to the military airport where a helicopter awaits to take you to a plane to Brussels. We need to leave now."

"Please," Nikole pleaded, tears welling up behind her eyes, "You must understand - all I want is a quick walk with my parents and to be able to say goodbye to my son and daughter. All I'm asking is that you wait three blocks down along the beach for me, and I'll only be ten minutes." The men looked at each other and shrugged.

"Okay," one of them answered, "But then we leave immediately. We'll pick up your bag and passport here at your parents on the way to the airport."

"Thank you," she told them sincerely, then turned to her parents, "Sorry to wreck our Christmas together. I really have to go after the stroll." Her dad put a gentle hand on her shoulder.

"Your life is just like a James Bond movie. Does this happen often?" He held a slightly joking tone. Nikole dabbed at her wet eyes with a handkerchief and laughed.

"Not really, this is quite out of the ordinary actually."

"Then I assure you," her dad said with a grin, "We'll be watching the TV tonight and record everything on the news."

FLIP-FLOPS

IT WAS FOUR o'clock in the morning when Valentina screamed at the top of her lungs, eyes closed tight, hands on her pregnant belly. "Chris, call the nurse *now*! Call her…it's happening…it's time!" Heart racing, Chris looked down at his phone. It had been seven minutes since the last contraction. Valentina, spouting off a slew of Italian curse words, reached to dig her nails into his arm again.

Chris gave her a towel to grip so he could call the nurse. But, when he tried dialling the number, his screen said, 'Searching for Network'. "Damn," he muttered, "It must be the snow. It's affecting the coverage of the mobile network." He took out his other two phones, having been extra prepared with a total of three smartphones. Yet they all said the same thing - 'Searching for Network'.

A chill of dread crept up his spine. "*Now what*," Chris thought, starting to panic. Although he wasn't, of course, about to give birth himself, he was utterly exhausted from not having a proper night's sleep in days. "Be right back, sweetie," he told Valentina, as he started to run up the stairs to the attic, before she could answer. Perhaps he'd have better reception up there.

Standing near the small, hexagonal attic window, Chris looked at each of his three phones. All still said, 'Searching for Network'. "Shit…*shit*," he said to himself as he switched the phones off then on again. It seemed they took forever to restart as he nervously drummed his fingers against the wall and tapped his left foot. There was no time for this.

Finally on again, Chris entered the default pin codes with shaking fingers and waited. The displays said, 'Searching for Network,' and he put them all up on the ledge of the little window, hoping it would help. After a minute or so, one of the screens now showed, 'No network available'. "Damn it…come on - one of you has to work," he muttered, waiting for the other two. Within seconds both of their screens also said, 'No network available'.

Chris dropped his head into the palms of his hands, trying to not completely freak out, though it was a little late for that. He was just about in full-blown panic mode. He heard Valentina's muffled cries even up there, and heard his name bellowed out among the screams. Having no idea what he was going to do, Chris grabbed the phones and ran back down to his wife.

"I need to drive up the hill to call the nurse, there's no connection at all because of the snow," Chris told Valentina, eyes apologetic and anxious at once. Her dark brown eyes now opened wide, full of panic. Grabbing his hand, she pleaded,

"No! Chris, don't leave me here alone! Are you kidding me? You can't leave me…I…ahhh!" Her own cry of pain interrupted followed by more cursing. Chris squeezed her hand once, but then pulled away – he had to hurry.

"I'm so sorry, Valentina, I'm not really leaving at all. I just need to drive up the hill and I'll be right back in mere moments, okay? I love you!" He called out, already out the door before he could hear her response.

"No, it's *not* okay! Agh!" He heard her yelling out, but he was already at the front door and headed out. He hated leaving her in this state, but he simply had to reach the nurse. Moments later, after sliding just a little in the snow in his sports car, Chris parked at the top of the hill where the reception always seemed the strongest.

Looking down at all three phone displays, he grunted with frustration. They all still said, 'Searching for Network'. With a heavy sigh, he turned them off and restarted them once again, which took several, nerve-wracking minutes. Finally, he entered his pin codes and waited as they showed, 'Searching for Network'. A minute later, again, they all changed to 'No Network Available'.

Now, true panic washed over Chris and his pulse pounded in his head, which started to feel dizzy. His head thumped down hard on the steering wheel, causing a small beep to sound from the car's horn. "Fuck!" he cried out. What the hell could he do now? Then, he suddenly remembered his neighbor who happened to have an old-fashioned landline phone. That's right, he could go there to make the call.

Before going to the neighbour's house, Chris decided to drive home, check on Valentina and let her know where he was going. Turning the car around, he accelerated gently causing it's wheels to spin a little. The road was definitely slippery, but his car kept strong and steady down the hill.

As Chris approached the bend in the road, he took his foot slowly off the gas and gently pushed the brakes. He felt the ABS-system intervening and an alarm began to sound. He couldn't slow down. Trying to think and act clearly, Chris turned the steering wheel towards the right to follow the curve in the road, but he was going too fast. His heart leapt into his throat as he felt the car moving away from the road, straight towards an oak tree.

As soon as Chris saw the tree in the beam of his headlights, his foot slammed down on the brake and he turned the steering wheel hard to the left. But it was useless. As though it was all happening in slow motion, the car crashed straight into the old oak, just as Chris instinctively put his hands over his face as a shield. The last thing he remembered was a loud screeching metallic sound piercing his ears. Then everything was dark.

* * *

"Don't worry, sugarplum, you're doing very well," Jonathon Drel told Maria, "You've got it all under control." And he looked from his toy display to the teddy bear on the charging pillow. He continued talking, eyes remaining on the bear, "Sometimes you grow a little, sometimes you go backwards and sometimes you experience crazy speed-growth. That's just life, and it's perfectly normal."

Maria's gaze also fell on the bear. "I'm not sure dad, the last few weeks have been really tough. I mean, working with a TV studio is okay, but having the UN, popstars and thousands of fans asking for products that we didn't even have. That was a bit much. You can't imagine the social media pressure we have for deliveries. We have *three* customer care teams on it 24/7. Even now during Christmas." She released a heavy sigh.

"Yeah," Drel said, "The world's changed a lot." Then he mumbled, "I wonder if the bears are also active on social media?"

"What do you mean?" Maria quirked an eyebrow at him, smile playing at her lips.

"Are the bear's themselves posting messages, pictures or asking the kids to take care of them?" Her dad asked.

"No," Maria said, "We don't have that yet. In fact I hadn't even thought of that, it's an interesting idea dad. But, we've been one-hundred percent focused on getting the bears shipped on time. In a few weeks, when Paul and Jane come back from their vacation, we'll evaluate the functions and plan to make more content available. We need consumers to get used to them before offering new things."

"You know," her dad said softly, "I still can't get used to the fact that your mom's not here anymore. Thanks for being here this evening, honey." Maria smiled and gave her dad a hug.

"Of course, no problem at all dad."

* * *

"On top of the world," Paul said with a grin, "What amazing wilderness." Although Jane's feet were starting to hurt, she matched his grin and agreed. The view was dazzling. They'd followed the Annapurna trail for a day now, and it felt like being on a completely different planet.

"Can you imagine," Jane said, "The people who live here are utterly isolated – separate from the rest of the world. They don't even have internet access, so they don't have to worry about their on-line status all the time. Can you picture living off-line like that?"

"Not at all," Paul shook his head, "I don't think I could handle living off-line, not now. I'd have to sit around re-inventing board games and reading a lot. I wonder if such an off-line life leads to cognitive laziness." Jane gave a short laugh, stepping slowly over a large rock – her feet were really aching now.

"Come on, Paul. Do you think the ancient Greeks were cognitively lazy? Or what about Einstein? None of them were online and it's safe to say they had quite active, searching minds!" Paul tilted his head in thought, leaping over several rocks on the trail, definitely less tired than Jane. She added, "It's also good to have some time to get your thoughts aligned. That's probably why they have so many meditation centres in this area. You know, I was just thinking, if we see any, I'd like to do a meditation workshop."

Paul laughed, not looking back. "You're joking, right?"

"I'm dead serious," Jane responded indignantly, "No joke at all. And I think it would be nice for you to try it as well." Now Paul stopped and turned to look at her.

"Right - *me* meditating?" He asked, half amused.

"That's right," she replied, holding his gaze in all seriousness,

"You - meditating. Why not? How do you know you won't like it unless you try?" she coaxed.

"Okay, fine," Paul relented with a dubious smile, "I'll think about it." He looked back ahead once Jane had caught up to him and added, "So, I think we need to walk for about three more hours until we get to the next village. We can ask them, over there at that monastery, or whatever it is." He gestured to their right where a large stone building sat.

Paul took out his phone to search for what the building was, but there was no reception. He let out a long sigh, "Never-mind, there's no network coverage here in the mountains. Let's just continue on our way."

Five minutes later the light darkened as heavy gray clouds filled the sky. And then, it began to snow. "Oh look," Jane cried as several powdery flakes landed on her nose and cheeks, "It's beautiful. Snow for Christmas!"

"This is incredible," Paul agreed, "And aren't you glad I got those raincoats now? They can help protect us from the snow." Moments later they both wore the raincoats and trekked through the quickly accumulating snow, being careful not to slip. Paul looked behind them and saw their footprints side by side just behind.

"It's amazing – walking in the snow, tracing steps with you." And he kissed her under the cascading flakes.

* * *

Francis woke up when he heard footsteps across the operating centre floor. He slowly raised his head off of the desk, drawing his hands over his face to help wake up. "*How the hell long have I been asleep?*" he wondered to himself. He now attempted to smile as two of his colleagues, a police officer and Kevin, holding Francis' work ID badge, walked over to the desk. Luckily, the police officer understood the situation and left with a quick, "Good luck," to them all.

"I'm so sorry for the delay," Kevin rushed out, "The snow was tricky to drive on."

"No need to apologize," Francis put a hand on his student's

shoulder, "I'm glad you're safe." His eyes glanced from Kevin to a clock on the wall which read 5:15 am.

"So," Kevin frowned, "How's the situation?" Heaving a sigh, Francis glanced from Kevin to his two colleagues,

"It's still the same. Morning guys, guess I better explain." He quickly caught them up to speed, both quiet and pale when he finished.

"Um," Kevin chimed in, "I think I need to get some sleep really soon - I can hardly keep my eyes open." Francis nodded, then they all turned to look at the backup system screen. It was down and they all took out their phones to see, 'Searching for Network'.

"Okay, we really are in some deep trouble," Francis said grimly, "Everybody's going to be up in a few hours and go to their jobs."

"Did you contact the supplier?'" His colleague, Jerry, asked.

"Yeah," Francis answered, "But they're insanely busy so I've been trying to resolve it myself. Though these damn auto-recovery procedures aren't working. It keeps crashing due to huge amounts of signalling."

"You mean," the other colleague, Nasier, spoke up, "We have a signalling storm in our network? I had no idea that was actually possible."

Francis let out a joyless laugh. "Neither did I, but it looks like it's indeed very possible. And the bad news is we're not the only ones with a storm." He pointed to the web forum screen.

"Wow," Nasier's eyes widened, "Okay, first let's write up a proper description of the problem and put in a ticket to the supplier. Then at least we've stuck to SLA procedure."

"Okay," Kevin commented, "Though that won't change the situation or fix the actual problem."

"That's true," Nasier said, "But it will show the superiors that we've officially done something about it." With that, they all helped write up a detailed report of the incident and put in the ticket with the supplier. An automated reply told them it could take up to four business days before receiving a response.

While Jerry and Nasier started to look more closely at the situation, Francis and Kevin decided to sleep in the lobby for a few hours, before all the other colleagues arrived. Kevin was asleep on a small sofa within seconds and Francis took out his phone, setting the alarm for 7:30 am. At least his smartphone's alarm clock still worked.

* * *

"I'm not sure what's going on Mr Lee, I'm so sorry," Maria said into her phone as she sat in her dad's garden in Atlanta. Her phone hadn't been working, but seemed to have temporarily found a signal. Here it was, Christmas Day, and the Vice President of their mobile connectivity partner, KMO-Telecom, was demanding answers. Unfortunately, Maria didn't have any answers yet.

"Okay," she said, "Let me try and talk to Rafael, though he hasn't been picking up, and…" She tried to explain, but the connection was suddenly cut and Maria tried to call back but couldn't reach Mr. Lee anymore. After numerous attempts Maria was at least able to get in touch with Rafael. She heard his panicked voice through the line.

"Maria, something's not right with the bears, and Bruce is no help at all. Where's Paul – what's going on? I have hundreds of reports that, after opening their bears for Christmas, none of them are working properly. There's some talk of mobile outages and…" But even as he spoke, the connection dropped.

"Shit," Maria muttered to herself as she tried to find the network, but even after turning it off and on again, it gave her the message, 'Searching for Network'. An anxious lump formed in her throat that made it hard to swallow. "This can't be good," she told herself, "This can't be good at all."

Meanwhile, Mr. Lee kept trying to call Maria back but got no answer, and then his phone lost the signal completely. He couldn't believe she'd ended the call to get out of this situation – he was so furious he prepared to file a claim. Mr. Lee meant business.

* * *

Tawfeek, head of finance at a European mobile operator, hit his brakes - it looked like an accident had just happened. All the cars around him stopped in the still-dark December morning. After a few minutes of sitting completely still in the traffic jam, he took out his phone, but it said, 'Searching for Network'.

Even after turning it off and on again, it didn't have service. "Damn," he muttered. Then his eyes landed on a petrol station up ahead. He didn't need any fuel, but really wanted a cup of coffee and a pomegranate muffin on top of needing to use their restroom. Moments later, after using the bathroom, he went up to the register at the petrol station store. The lady behind the counter rang up the coffee and muffin then said, "That's EUR 7.00 please." Tawfeek handed over his bank debit card. She pointed to a paper taped to the wall next to the register that read, 'Payment terminals out of order. Only cash accepted'. "Sorry, sir, do you have any cash?" she asked.

"Uh," Tawfeek sighed as he looked through his wallet, "Sorry I don't have enough cash. I only have a EUR 5.00 banknote."

"I'm sorry sir," she shrugged, "But I can't sell you these for less."

"Fine," he said, reluctantly putting the muffin back, "I'll just get the coffee then." On the way back to his car, Tawfeek smiled and thought, *"I guess not having enough cash is a good way to watch the weight."*

As Tawfeek pulled out of the petrol station, he laughed aloud and told himself, "Can you imagine? I work in finance and my wife works as well - we have a double income and I can't pay for a stupid muffin!" His navigation app still didn't show how long the traffic jam would take, but the cars had at least started to inch forward.

In about thirty minutes, he finally entered his office garage. It was 7:30 am, surely he was one of the only persons there. *"This will be a nice, relaxing day,"* Tawfeek thought as he entered the building. However, he stopped short upon seeing a man with flip-flops asleep on a sofa in the lobby. Probably some homeless guy who'd managed to sneak in.

"*What should I do,*" Tawfeek pondered, "*The receptionist will arrive in half an hour, so she can deal with him I guess.*" He walked back to the elevator and pushed the up button. In thirty seconds, the doors opened and a man came out. It was one of Steve's men - an operations guy who now looked stressed beyond belief.

"Good morning Mr. Tawfeek," the man said.

"Morning to you as well. Sorry to see that you had to work." Tawfeek replied.

"Well," the man gave a weary sigh, "There's actually a very serious situation here. Do you know how we can get in touch with Steve?" Tawfeek let the elevator doors close behind him, staying in the lobby to talk to this guy.

"Okay," he said with a furrowing brow, "I do know where he is, but I'm not sure it's going to be much help. Steve is in South Africa right now. What's the issue?"

Before the poor guy could explain, the homeless man in flip-flops walked towards them, ignored Tawfeek and started to talk to the operations guy, "How's it going?" he asked.

"Not good," the operations guy replied, "We can't keep them under control manually either. The network keeps going down – still that same horrible signalling storm."

Tawfeek stood there, blinking in surprise, then finally recognized the 'homeless guy' as one of the operation managers. Tawfeek now turned to the guy in flip-flops.

"Okay," he demanded, "Tell me *everything*." As the three of them walked to the control room, the atmosphere grew more and more tense.

"So," the operations guy, Nasier, elaborated, "Mobile devices are continuously connecting and disconnecting from the network. I believe it's a signalling storm and we just can't handle it. It's too massive."

"You know," the flip-flopped colleague, Francis, added, "I think we need to delete or disable them somehow. Do you think it's a popular app or something causing it?"

"We really don't know yet," Nasier answered, "It looks like huge amounts of failing data transfer sessions. We're looking at the systems as we speak."

"How are the other networks doing?" Francis asked, as Tawfeek listened attentively.

"Good question," Nasier replied, "Let's have a look." As Nasier looked through the forum messages on the desk computer, Tawfeek turned to Francis.

"Does this mean that our complete network is down?" he asked.

"Unfortunately, that's right," Francis answered, "We've been down for a few hours now and it's affecting customers nationwide."

Tawfeek put his laptop bag on the ground. "Wow, this sounds beyond serious. Can't we call the experts?" They all remained quiet for a few moments. Nasier kept looking at the screen as he said,

"Honestly, Mr. Tawfeek, we're the ones who you call when it gets complicated. I'm sorry to say, but we *are* the experts." While Tawfeek dropped his head into his hands, Nasier continued, "It seems that we're not the only ones, though. I see dozens of networks worldwide reporting similar situations."

"We run this network," Francis mumbled, "We're in deep, deep trouble. The sky is basically falling down and all we can do is watch."

EERIE SILENCE

CHRIS HEARD THE sound of an alarm ringing and slowly opened his eyes. He blinked in confusion, looking around in what appeared to be airbag dust in his car. When his brain woke up more, he felt the icy cold and a tremendous pain in his left arm.

It all came flooding back – the slippery snow and his brakes failing...the oak tree. Though the pain was almost unbearable, Chris was able to crawl over to the passenger seat and open the door. Cradling his left arm with his right, he managed to get out of the car, wincing as he stood up, surrounded by the dark night. Thankfully, the snow had stopped.

Looking down in a daze, he saw the front of his car bending around the huge old oak. Breathing in short gasps that made little puffs of cloud in the cold air, Chris locked his eyes determinedly on his house, just a few hundred meters away. He struggled to push down the acute pain in his arm and the oncoming sense of panic and stumbled through the snow to the house and through the front door.

Everything was eerily silent as Chris went up to their bedroom. Valentina looked over at him from the bed when he walked in, her face was pale and wet from sweating. In a soft voice she asked,

"Where's the nurse?" Then her eyes fell to the blood on his hand and her eyes grew wide.

"Wh…what happened to you…where have you been?" she stuttered.

"I couldn't make the call because of the snow," Chris answered, "Then it was too slippery and my car crashed, but I'm fine just a minor injury." He added this last part quickly as her expression grew even more concerned, pushing down any show of pain. "I'll walk to our neighbour Michael's house to use his landline phone. Are you okay?"

"Sort of," she managed to say with a weak nod, "I think it's shorter between contractions and…ah!" She cried mid-sentence as her face scrunched up in a grimace. Tears in her eyes, Valentina whispered, "I hope the baby's okay." Chris came and gave her hand a reassuring squeeze with his uninjured right hand.

"Don't worry, sweetie. She's completely fine, and she'll be born beautiful and healthy, you'll see. I promise to be back quickly this time." He kissed her sweaty forehead and went down to the front door. Just before he went outside, Chris saw the pile of gifts from Valentina's mom in the hall. Taking a baby monitor package, he left and trudged his way through the snow as speedily as possible towards their neighbour's house.

Heart racing and his left shoulder pulsing in agony, Chris knocked on the door. As soon as Michael opened it, his eyes rounded with shock. There stood his new next-door neighbour with dried blood on his hand and what looked to be a dislocated shoulder. "I need help, can I come in and use your landline phone?" Michael nodded as he let him in and led him to the phone, Chris quickly explaining as they walked.

When Michael dialled the emergency number, an operator answered on the first ring. Chris felt a deep wash of relief and his posture slumped a bit. Everything was going to be okay now. Michael looked at him and repeated the operator's question, "Are there any complications with your wife or the baby?"

"No," Chris shook his head, "I think they're fine. But she's in labour as we speak, she could actually be giving birth any moment. Somebody needs to come now."

Michael repeated what Chris had said to the operator and listened carefully. While watching and waiting, Chris scowled and gently touched his left shoulder as it throbbed more and more. "Hold on one second, please," Michael told the operator. He looked at Chris and said, "They can't reach any of the nurses due to a problem with the mobile networks. We need to help Valentina give birth ourselves and the operator will assist us by phone." Chris felt his face blanch, mouth dropping open.

"No fucking way," he yelled in desperation, panic seizing his body. "Somebody needs to come over, I'm injured and bleeding and I know nothing about giving birth or babies!" And before Michael could stop him, Chris grabbed the phone out of his hand and shouted. "Are you insane? You'd better send someone over, we need medical assistance right now!"

"Sorry sir," the operator answered, "I understand this is a highly difficult situation. Please try to relax. You need to calm down and listen…and stop yelling." Chris closed his eyes tightly and took several deep breaths, calming down as best he could, then handed the phone back to Michael. He then proceeded to open the baby monitor package, plugged the parent receiver part into an outlet in the wall and saw the little red light come on.

"Listen to me Mike," Chris turned to his neighbor, "Please keep your phone line open with the operator and listen to this baby monitor. I'm going to set up the other part at my house – to talk to me, you just push this button." He pointed to a button on the side of the receiver, then continued, "Just give me a minute."

Mike opened his mouth to respond, but Chris was already out the door. Taking a deep relaxing breath himself, Mike explained the situation to the operator and watched out his window. He could see a dark, bent figure slowly walking through the snow towards the neighboring house in the early morning light. Holding the monitor in one hand and the landline phone in the other, Mike waited two nerve-wracking minutes, then heard a loud crackle from the receiver. A voice came through loud and clear.

"Can you hear me, Mike?" Chris called through the monitor. Mike pushed the talk button.

"Chris," he spoke into the receiver, "do you hear me? Over."

"Loud and clear," Chris replied, "Please ask the operator what I should do. Valentina's okay but really tired. Over." The next few minutes were astonishingly complex. The emergency operator had set up a conference call with a doctor. Mike held the landline phone close to the baby monitor.

He had to listen carefully to ensure he pushed the talk button at the right moment in order to facilitate the conversation.

Over in the other house, Chris used his one good arm to prepare hot water and towels. Valentina seemed to be on another planet as the contraction intervals shortened. She was definitely ready, it wouldn't be much longer now.

***

"Okay, now it's been going on for twenty-four hours, making the impact on everyone much more severe," Theo continued while Nikole listened patiently, trying to keep her anxiety down. "Apart from people losing mobile phone and mobile internet connectivity, not even the emergency numbers are working. The multi-million dollar systems we have in place to broadcast emergency text SMS messages to our citizens is now utterly worthless."

He paused for a breath as Nikole pursed her lips in concern. Then Theo continued, "The police are reporting an increase of car theft because alarm systems aren't able to send out the necessary signals. It's a nightmare out there!" He slammed his palm down on the table, more upset than Nikole had ever seen him before. It was all she could do to take silent, long deep breaths to at least attempt to keep herself calm. Face getting redder by the second, Theo went on,

"The commission has advised that all countries increase their police patrol numbers in the cities. The French are even considering the help of military police on the street. Nikole, this has to be solved! What's your plan?" She glanced nervously at her hands, which now gripped together in an anxious clasp. He was right of course, the impact was unbelievably severe. *"Basically, it's the world turned upside down,"* Nikole thought grimly.

And now, mobile phone users were getting truly angry and aggressive to the point where staff at smartphone retail stores felt unsafe. They'd actually closed their stores to prevent damage or danger – there'd already been stone-throwing incidents at the glass windows.

***

"They acted like tiny insects. Each of them tried to find the optimum communication settings to distribute new software to the bears. In the beginning it was random, but after they'd found each other in their Turchaea cloud they compared performances, exchanged parameters and individually kept fine tuning. Continuously and massively. But they didn't succeed and simply kept trying to transfer data.

Their only objectives were to keep the connection to their cloud open and keep the communication costs low. They didn't care about the mobile phone networks or any of its users. Their algorithm caused these IoT-Bears to continuously set-up and close mobile internet connections.

Not regularly, but very frequently and much faster than humans could physically do with their own phones. The mobile networks never faced so many users with this behaviour before. It was too much to handle. They went down."

Francis could hardly keep his eyes open but immediately understood the message on the internet forum. The South Korean guys had found it - the signalling storms were caused by the popular teddy bears. And after they'd kicked the bears off their networks, the servers no longer crashed.

Finally, Francis knew what to do. After running a backup, he took the log files and scanned through the traffic information. He couldn't recognize which ones were the bears and which weren't, so he simply selected the IoT-based devices that generated the most signalling traffic. So with a sequence of commands, he carried out the 'Korean solution' and re-started the network servers.

Looking at the management system, he noticed that thousands of mobile phones were automatically re-registered. He turned his own phone off and on. After three seconds, his phone had found the network. With shaking fingers and a cautious smile, Francis selected Helen's mobile number and pushed the green dial button. It was ringing.

"Francis, are you okay?" she answered on the second ring. He fought back tears of joy.

"Yeah, I'm fine honey." His voice shook with emotion.

"What happened and where are you? I couldn't reach you at all," she told him.

"I'm at the office," he answered, "I'll call you back later and explain everything. But I have to run now, okay?"

"Okay," Helen said, "But please be careful honey."

After getting off the phone, a very happy Francis looked over at Kevin and said happily, "I think we have solved it!"

For the next twenty minutes, they went through to verify that all systems worked properly. They did. And then, the backup system also received the 'Korean treatment'. It had been about forty-five minutes when the head of finance tapped Francis' shoulder.

"Not bad for a man in flip-flops," Tawfeek grinned at Francis. They all erupted into laughter, then everyone called home, suddenly feeling very good, though also very tired.

CONTROL

"YEAH, HER PULSE is really fast, but I think she's still fine. Over." Chris listened to the doctor through the baby monitor as the sound of an ambulance wailed louder and louder. Help was on its way. Just moments later, two nurses and a police officer entered their bedroom.

The officer spoke into his walkie-talkie. "202 here, we've entered the house of the injured man and birth-giving woman." A voice came through the walkie-talkie's speaker,

"Roger 202, please inform when we need to go to prio two."

"202 - Roger," the officer answered, "Keep three for now. Standby." As the two officers communicated, one of the nurses checked up on Valentina and the other one, a young male nurse, sat down next to Chris. He met his gaze and said,

"Well done Chris. We'll take it from here." Chris gave a weak smile in response - he was utterly exhausted.

"Come on, let's take care of those injuries," the nurse next to Chris said, standing up. So, leaving the other nurse and the officer with Valentina, he followed the guy nurse down to the living room.

He quickly cleaned up Chris' wounds, put a bandage around his shoulder, and gave him some water.

"You're fine Chris. Your shoulder's dislocated, but you don't need any operations. We'll fix it properly in the hospital later on."

Moments later, on the nurses' orders, Chris was stretched out to rest on the sofa as the guy sat in an armchair nearby. Just before drifting to sleep, he mumbled, "Please wake me when my new baby girl is here and…" but Chris was fast asleep before he could finish. He had no idea how long he was out, but a low voice and gentle nudge to his uninjured arm woke him.

"Chris, it's time, come with me," the male nurse said, helping him get up. With a smile, he led Chris to the bedroom. Heart racing with anticipation as he rubbed the sleep out of his eyes, Chris came into the room to see a radiant Valentina holding their baby in her arms. They both looked healthy. Eyes filled with love and amazement, Chris walked up to the two, kissed Valentina and whispered,

"You look lovely, and she looks healthy - so beautiful." He gazed adoringly down at the baby, carefully stroking her hand. Valentina looked at him. "It's a *he* Chris. It's a boy," she whispered with a smile. He gaped at her.

"You're joking! Really?" he asked.

Valentia laughed and beamed up at him. "You want to choose his name?" Chris was speechless. They never considered boy names because of Valentina's intuition. The nurse who'd helped Valentina deliver told him,

"Please, take your time Chris. But I *do* need to fill it in the forms here and the first question is the name of the baby." He felt an overwhelming rush of emotions and looked around the room. Chris thought about his dad, grandma and his deceased grandfather, and gazed thoughtfully out the window. In the distance he saw his car covered with a layer of snow, front still bent around the oak. Just then, the sound of Mike's voice came through the baby monitor and interrupted his thoughts.

"Congratulations Chris! Can I be the godfather? Over."

"Thanks Mike," Chris smiled, "Thanks for everything – I'll check with Valentina! You can get proper sleep now. I'll catch up with you later after my hospital check. Over."

"No problem," Mike said, "You and Valentina take care, and enjoy your new little one. I'm switching off the monitor now. Feel free to come over when you get a chance. But please at a decent hour this time. Over."

"I'll try my best," Chris joked, "Thanks again. Over and out." Chris turned off the monitor. For several moments, he stared down at the monitor in his hand, reading the brand name, 'Marconi Baby Monitor' etched in golden italics.

Suddenly Chris looked up at Valentina and their new baby boy. "Marconi. His name's going to be Marconi, but everyone can call him Marco."

* * *

Nikole stepped from the seventh floor, where she'd just come from Theo's office, into the elevator with a young guy in his mid-twenties and a silver-haired man in an impeccably tailored suit. "Good afternoon," the older man smiled at her as she stepped into the elevator and the doors closed. The younger man just gave a brief nod as a greeting. These two were probably coming from the big law firm with offices on the 8th floor in the eight-story building.

"Afternoon to you too," Nikole forced a smile back. She was still riled by Theo's panicked lecture and demands that she fix the network outage situation right away. As she turned to watch the glowing numbers light up as they descended, a sudden jolt and flashing of lights startled Nikole out of her thoughts.

"Shit, what in the…?" the younger man's voice rang out in the enclosed space. The elevator had lurched to a stop and though the main lights had gone out, a low emergency light went on above them, casting an eerie, greenish glow around the three of them. Nikole's heart had jumped into her throat and stayed there – she was momentarily speechless.

The older man looked between her and the young man, then he spoke in a calm, reassuring voice. "It's alright Jean. No need to panic." He glanced back at Nikole and said, "I'm Mathieu, and this is my law intern Jean. You're Nikole Solon, right?" Her eyebrows shot up, though most people in the building did know who she was. Perhaps he'd seen her on TV as well.

"That's right, nice to meet you," she replied, her voice shaky. The silver-haired man went on, "You too, Ms. Solon. Now, I suppose we'd better push the emergency call button here. Don't worry, they'll have us out of here in no time." He assured them both as he stepped forward and pressed the red-rimmed button at the bottom of the numbers. Nothing happened.

"Let me try," Jean said impatiently as he pushed the button in rapid succession. Still no response. Nikole gave the young man an irritated frown and said,

"Well, you'll just break it even more that way – here." She walked over to give the button a slow yet firm push. Absolutely nothing – no alarm sound and no lighting up. "*Shit,*" Nikole thought as she looked from the broken button to Mathieu and Jean, a cold sweat forming on her forehead.

"Merde," Jean muttered in French, "I don't have time for this." He took his phone out and pressed a speed-dial button for emergency services. "Damn! It says 'Searching for Network'," Jean cursed. Nikole and Mathieu both silently took out their phones and tried as well – the same message showed on their screens.

Nikole tried to keep her panic from rising, but her stomach clenched with a sick kind of dread. "Well," she said, "I wonder if it's because we're in the elevator, or because of the global mobile network outage." While the emergency light was working, the air had stopped running and, in spite of the cold temperature outside, the small space was becoming hot and stuffy from the lack of circulating air.

Jean just stared at his phone, turning it off and on again, while Mathieu responded, "Even if the network's down, we should be capable of accessing emergency services." Nikole swallowed hard, feeling a weight of guilt – this is exactly what her emRoaming was supposed to prevent. And it had failed.

Mathieu continued, "I'm guessing it's the…" but his words trailed off and Nikole watched the older man fall to the floor as if in slow motion. He landed with a heavy *thud*. With a horrified gasp, Nikole immediately knelt down next to him and eased his body over to lay face-up, all while Jean stood and gaped in shock. She looked up at the young man, eyes wide with fear.

"Jean, quick – call…" but Nikole cut herself off, remembering with a sickening flip to her gut that they had no way of getting in touch with emergency services. Hell, they couldn't even get the building's security officer.

"I…is he…?" Jean started to ask, voice quivering. Nikole didn't see Mathieu's chest moving, but she placed two fingers on the side of his neck near the back part of his jaw to be sure. There was no pulse.

* * *

"The thing is, Bruce, that they're pushing our bears off-line." Bruce could hear Maria's words, but wasn't quite gasping what she was actually saying.

"Wait," he said, "But who - who's pushing them off-line?" Maria was in the Atlanta office with Rafael, and highly upset at the moment.

"The mobile operators," she explained in frustration, "They told us that we weren't using their mobile networks properly and that our bears caused tremendous problems. Some of them even said they're thinking about making claims against us. Even Mr. Lee, the director of KMO-Telecom, threatened a claim." Bruce was quiet for a moment as he sat on the other end of the skype chat. He knew a lot about software and networks, but did not specialize in mobile IoT connectivity.

Bruce did know that if the connectivity ever had issues, they just drew a white cloud in the architecture to transport the internet-data. The bears had simply used that cloud, which Paul knew more about than him. Bruce finally responded, "Let me have a chat with the FLQ operation guys here and I'll call you back in twenty minutes, all right?"

"Okay," Maria said, "But I insist that FLQ also gets involved. We're drafting a press statement and need your technical input."

Bruce didn't even wait for an elevator, but ran down the stairs. Once he'd told an operation woman the situation, she looked at the IoT Bear management platform. "It seems that most bears are not in range of a network," she told him, "They aren't connected or responding to us. Any commands we send are queued in our servers, and the bears will follow them as soon as they've re-established internet connection."

"It's impossible for bears to suddenly disappear," Bruce said in confusion, "Hold on, I'll be right back." Then he ran again, grabbed a demo bear from the lobby, one that used to work, and ran back to the operations woman.

"What's the status of this specific bear?" Bruce asked, handing her the bear. She looked at the printed number in the bear's ear and browsed the database.

"Okay, here it is," she answered, "This bear last reported one hour and thirty-five minutes ago. Let me send a status request message." She clicked some icons and waited. After a minute of silence, the operations woman was convinced. "This bear is off-line Bruce. I don't know why it's been happening – we have to investigate."

Yet again Bruce ran off, this time to their small warehouse which held all the new bears. Once he returned, Bruce opened the parcel and unwrapped the bear, who stayed quiet at this point. "I think we have an issue Paul," Bruce mumbled to himself. While the operations woman told him that this bear didn't show up in the platform either, a loud burp filled the room. The bear had woken up, but wasn't able to connect to the cloud.

The woman stated, "Let's investigate that one as well, okay?" Bruce just nodded and walked back to his work area, mind confused and buzzing.

"So, why did they disable the connectivity? What's happened?" Maria asked, now sitting with two other colleagues as well as Rafael again on Skype. "Can you tell us anything, Bruce? The sample bears in our Atlanta office, which used to work fine, also seem to be off-line." Bruce looked at his screen in dismay.

"You're right Maria," he said simply, "We have a serious issue. Most of the bears out there are off-line, we can't reach them anymore. Also new bears seem to have the same connectivity issue. We must investigate and contact KMO-Telecom who provides the connectivity. It's not us, but them that has a problem and needs to solve it."

"Bruce, listen," Maria responded with a ferocity that caused him to shiver, "This isn't just something about contracts. Not only does this service provider have a problem, but FLQ, Idrel and the UN as partners have problems. I insist we join forces and use all required resources in order to solve this and I hope I've made myself very clear."

With a pale face, Bruce swallowed hard and said, "Yes – crystal clear. However, I'm going to need some support. The connectivity part of the software is complicated – it was written by Paul."

"Then we need to fly Paul in – when is he coming back?" Maria asked.

"I don't know," Bruce replied, raking a hand through his hair, "We'll try to contact him. But please start right away on your side, okay?"

"We'll look and see if we can find out where Paul is as well," Rafael chimed in.

Bruce closed the skype connection feeling sick to his stomach. They'd completely lost control of the bears. It couldn't get any worse than this.

* * *

"Okay," Paul told Jane, "My mind feels all quiet and stuff, but then all I do is start falling asleep. So, how do you get to the next meditation level?"

"You need to be relaxed," Jane said as she smiled and shook her head, "Which it sounds like you're doing, but you also have to be totally *focused* on the silence, then wait. When you practice enough it'll happen."

"Hmm," Paul peered skeptically at her, "So what level are you on?"

"Paul," Jane giggled and gave his shoulder a playful shove, "This isn't a video game or a match. But, if you insist, I'm on the 3rd level and yes, I can lower my heartbeat quite a bit if I want."

"Well," Paul said, trying not to look jealous, "That's good for you." Then a sly smile crept on his face. "Hey, I bet I can think of a way to speed your heartbeat back up again." And he raised both eyebrows twice, suggestively. Jane laughed and pushed him in the shoulder again, harder this time as they walked through some beautiful, tall trees.

It had been almost two days of walking at this point. Jane turned to Paul. "I loved staying at the monastery for the last few days, but I can't imagine actually living there. Did you see that monk's face when I asked where the shower was? I can't believe there's no showers at all up here."

Paul chuckled and said, "Forget no showers, how about the fact that they have no newspaper, no internet and no mobile access? There's nothing up here."

"Well," Jane tilted her head in thought, "It does have *some* things. I mean, the environment is gorgeous - the air is so fresh and all. And everyone that lives here has everything they could want in life."

"Yeah," Paul replied, "I guess that's true. How can they miss something they've never had in the first place, right?" He paused and looked up at the sky through all the trees. "I wonder how long it'll keep snowing, I'm starting to get a bit wet in spite of this raincoat and it's so cold."

"I don't know," Jane shrugged, "But I think we'll reach the next village within the hour and can warm up in the hostel." Paul looked at his phone, but there was no mobile network coverage here, of course. It would be a waste of money for operators to invest in a communication infrastructure up here. The population was so low and those that lived here preferred to spend their money on necessities like food and clothes.

Paul mused aloud, "I wonder, if people here ever got internet and mobile connection, would they be addicted just like the rest of us?"

"You know," Jane said, "I haven't looked at my phone at all for the last few days, except for using the torch app." She looked very proud of herself.

"And the compass," Paul said with a wry smile.

To Paul's relief there was an internet café in the next village, along with some restaurants and small shops. And on top of that, the busy hostel had a private room for them – he could finally have some alone time with Jane.

Once warm and clean from showers, the two went back down to the lobby and read old National Geographic magazinés. A little later, the owner came over and showed them a printed email. "Is this about you guys?" he asked, handing over the paper. Paul read aloud:

TO ALL GUEST HOUSES AROUND THE ANNAPURNA TRAIL
*** $1000,- REWARD FINDING FEE ***

DEAR GUESTHOUSE OWNER,

WE'RE URGENTLY TRYING TO GET IN TOUCH WITH OUR DEAR FRIEND PAUL VAN DIJK WHO'S TRAVELLING IN NEPAL WITH HIS GIRLFRIEND JANE.

THE REASON WE'RE TRYING TO GET IN TOUCH WITH HIM IS THAT WE VERY MUCH NEED HIS HELP.

PLEASE KINDLY ASK HIM TO CONTACT US IMMEDIATELY.

HE KNOWS OUR CONTACT INFORMATION AND WILL PASS YOUR DETAILS TO US.

IF YOU'RE THE FIRST ONE, WHO GETS US IN TOUCH WITH HIM, WE'RE HAPPY TO GRANT THE $1000 FINDING FEE TO YOU.

THANKS FOR YOUR EFFORT!
KIND REGARDS,
RAFAEL SILVA

*** VALID UNTIL 1ST FEB ***

Paul looked over it again and checked the date. It'd been distributed to all guest hostels in the area today. He had a sickening feeling in his stomach – this was no joke. Jane spoke up, "No, that's not us, sorry. But when we see them, we'll direct them to you, okay?"

"Okay, sounds good," the owner said, taking the paper back,

"And if that happens, my friends, we'll have a good drink and share the $1000."

"Sounds good to us too," Paul said with a forced smile. Then the owner pinned the email back up on the notification board in the lobby.

Once back in their room, Paul said, "Rafael put money on my head!"

"You're right," Jane sighed, "This is ridiculous. He probably needs to have your presence at some kind of customer sales meeting with new opportunities. I know how he is! Sales guys always want to have the experts around."

"True," Paul agreed, "And there's no way they need me that desperately. Bruce has all the code now, so they can just ask him if they have questions. Besides, if they have an issue they can email me."

"Good," Jane smiled with relief, "So tomorrow we carry on with our trek, and we can forget about all that bear work!" Paul smiled back, but then dug out the golden Idrel letter from the bottom of his backpack, looked at it and wondered what to do.

"I guess it's too obvious if we ask for the Wi-Fi access code now isn't it? Why don't we check our messages in the internet cafe at the end of the street?" Paul suggested.

"No," Jane said adamantly, "Let's not. We're here on holiday, Paul. I'd like it if you tried to stay off-line for a while. You know, I've skipped coming to Nepal several times now, and I don't want anything else interfering with our trip, okay?"

Paul studied her serious, almost pouting expression, and put the letter back in his backpack. "In that case," he said, "I suggest we go for some pizza." He grinned, and that's exactly what they did. As they ate, Paul and Jane met other back packers who were walking the trail in the other direction. With cheap wine they exchanged where-to-stay information and little tips.

The next morning, though the two had headaches from the wine, they had great walking weather and dry clothes. Just before heading back onto the trail, Paul looked at their Lonely Planet book and said, "Okay, according to this, we have about an eight hour trek until the next village. And that one is completely isolated from the rest of the world." He looked up at Jane with a half-smile and added, "Hey, maybe I can reach the 3rd level of meditation like you there."

Jane laughed. "Maybe. But I'm still winning," she teased. And so they started their day's journey. Paul couldn't be further away from Idrel than he was right now.

***

"The last few days they had continuously tried to use their preferred mobile network, but their access was somehow blocked.

After three days, they were automatically granted access to other networks.

It was what they had to do according to the #emRoaming agreement successfully initiated by #NikoleEU.

They had been very patient and now crept in fast and stealthy. Thousands, tens of thousands - no hundreds of thousands of subscribers were starting to use his network. Their bandwidth thirst was unquenchable and they filled their cloud and took all available network resources.

Like anxious ants, they communicated intensely in their cloud, searching and asking each other for optimum connection settings and parameters."

Francis saw all of this happening, his heart sinking heavily into his stomach. Face draining of all blood, he watched the red indicators. They were everywhere. Within three minutes, down it went again. Massive network resources were requested and the backup system couldn't even start up properly.

Within ten minutes, all mobile phones in Europe indicated 'Searching for Network' on their screens.

PART 3 - THE LESSONS

LIFE AND DEATH

THE BACKUP SECURITY guard and two members of the Brussels' fire department met up with Nikole and the initial security guard on the fourth floor, since the elevator was stuck between the 4th and 5th floors. They'd overridden the auto-controls and it now dinged, about to open as they all stood in the hallway.

Nikole could hardly breathe as the shiny metal doors slid open, a mix of fearful trepidation and hope swirling in her mind. Her eyes flew down to where young Jean sat next to Mathieu, who was still motionless. One look at Jean's defeated, dazed expression told Nikole everything.

Her heart dropped into her stomach in a strange, cold feeling as her insides churned. Jean stood and Nikole numbly moved forward to hug the now sobbing young man. She was vaguely aware of the voices buzzing around, and watched with a dizziness that blurred both her vision and hearing as one of the firemen knelt, checked the silver-haired man and turned to slowly shake his head.

Nikole answered all of the questions and bid everyone thanks in a dark whirl, the pain in her gut increasing but not a single tear falling. As she drove home to her city flat, her mind was back in the hallway, on the ashen face of Mathieu who had…No, she couldn't think of it – not now.

She held it all in, still in shock, until she walked into her flat and shut the front door. Then it all came flooding over her – overwhelming and all-consuming. Nikole crumpled to the floor of the front hallway and wept with abandon into her hands. She sobbed for a good five minutes, then stiffly pulled her body to the kitchen to make some chamomile tea. Horrible didn't even begin to describe what had happened and the way she felt, but somehow, she had to pull it together and deal with another crisis – one that had, in Nikole's mind, allowed that man to die. The mobile network outage disaster.

* * *

Newbie racer '2Fast4U' was pissed off, just like all the other RC-Racer members. The operators had simply kicked them all off their networks without a warning. None of the cars would go - they were completely grounded. And why? Even though there'd been a mobile network outage for a few days, it hadn't affected the use of their racer cars before, so why weren't they working now?

Their internet forum had exploded with questions and outraged comments, and now all they could do was wait for someone to post a solution. So far, nobody had come up with anything, and there hadn't even been any post from Paul, that Dutch guy who usually distributed new versions. And there was absolute silence from the software distributors. "*Well*," the newbie racer thought, "*Since nobody's doing anything, I'll just have to figure it out myself.*"

'2Fast4U' thought it would take her two days to 'deep dive' into the system, and so she got to work by first downloading all the open source code and tools. The newbie girl prepared herself by grabbing bags of chips, a candy bar and a pack of Cokes, then told her mom, "I'm gonna be busy for the next few days – really busy, okay mom?"

The seventeen-year-old's mom was used to this kind of behaviour and simply replied, "Okay honey, just let me know if you want any real food or anything."

The girl opened a Coke and bag of vinegar chips and started her work. She'd seen the code before, but had never looked too deeply into its core. It took her a while before fully understanding the software structure, which had been set up by this Paul fellow and later on enhanced by a bunch of Chinese programmers.

Two snack-bags of chips and three sodas later, the newbie racer suddenly noticed something strange - an empty software 'hook-routine' named "ffu_direct_rf_paul". She understood that "direct_rf" referred to radio technology but as far as she knew, that kind of technology wasn't in use for the racers. "What on earth does 'ffu' mean?" she muttered to herself, peering closely at the screen, "Maybe 'failed finding network up' or 'fast find upgrade', or perhaps 'feel free to use'?"

The newbie girl looked at the empty software hook-routine more closely. It was located just before the car was supposed to start using the mobile network. Suddenly it dawned on her that all the RC-racers would first try using other, and in this case, short-range direct car-to-car connections. So she carefully examined the electronic circuit board in her own car and found a tiny antenna.

"Yes!" she exclaimed out loud. There was a radio chip on the board, but it wasn't in use yet, and now she knew – 'ffu' meant 'For Future Use'. As a programmer herself, the newbie would've done the same thing. She knew what to do now, took a deep breath and dove down all the way into the system.

***

A few days later, far from where the newbie girl sat examining the depths of the RC-racer software, Rafael Silva was highly disappointed. Idrel hadn't been able to get in touch with Paul and neither Bruce nor FLQ knew what to do. "This probably would've never happened if we'd taken more time," he mused to himself, "We simply needed to wait for the product and services to mature - maybe talk with test panels like we always do with our regular toys."

Yet, how could they have taken more time when the market situation had forced their hand to speed up? Rafael growled and hit his desk with the palm of his hand in frustration. He hated not being able to do anything - the feeling of being useless and just waiting around. If only he could actually *do* something.

But at this time, for Rafael, the project was dead with all the bears offline and nothing to be done about it. He had to forget the upsell and subscription model opportunities and was forced to relax back at home.

So, Saturday morning Rafael went with his son Jackson to the RC Club and saw everyone standing in the test zone while he grabbed a latte. Jackson had said something about software issues during the drive to the club this morning, but that was typical, besides the fact that their cars were also somehow affected by the global network outages.

Rafael began to chat with another RC-racer dad as they both watched their sons put the cars on the track and switched them on like always. But instead of the artificial motor erupting through the loudspeakers of the cars, Rafael was shocked to hear burps – just like the teddy bears. Once the noise died down, the green traffic light went on and the cars silently accelerated. Rafael's jaw dropped and he turned to the other dad. "What the hell was that?"

* * *

Nikole opened Theo's office door and saw him pacing in circles like a caged lion. It had been a few days since the elevator incident, and Nikole was able to put it more and more behind her, as traumatic as it had been. She'd told Theo about it, and he'd given his sympathy for such a harrowing experience.

Now, as she walked into his office, Nikole saw how pale and

nervous Theo's face looked. "Nikole," he said, "Thanks for coming. I thought the issue was resolved, but apparently it's not. I'm not going to ask for any action plan on this, we simply need results. *Fast*. Please do something about it."

"Give me twenty minutes, Theo," she reassured him, "I'll have the whole EU-crisis team here." And she began sending emails as well as making calls to office land-line phones until she'd contacted every member. Within a minute, the whole team began to trickle into Theo's office one by one. Everyone was surprised, thinking the issue had been resolved, but apparently it had come back like a boomerang.

"Do I understand correctly," one team member asked after Nikole had updated everyone on the situation, "That the reoccurring outages have been caused by our own new emergency roaming service?"

"Yes," Nikole gave a curt nod, "We think so at least. It's a very unlikely situation, yet, as we've found out, it *is* happening. The strange thing is, the outage is only happening within the EU zone now." Theo was quiet for several long moments, considering his options. He raised his pale-white face, looking right at Nikole.

"What are the possibilities Nikole?" he asked in a low voice.

"We simply need to pull the plug from the emRoaming system," she answered decidedly, "I've been in contact with three major operators and they're all awaiting our approval. Their experts know what to do, at least that's what they said." Theo laced his fingers together and propped up his chin, deep in thought.

"What are the alternatives?" he asked. Everyone watched Nikole with anticipation.

"To be honest Theo," she replied serenely, "There aren't really any. This is what they advise us to do. You know, we can always put it back in place later even if it doesn't work properly now." It was at this point that Theo truly realized they were seriously out of control, with absolutely no alternative options whatsoever. People's lives were being heavily disrupted and all he could do was watch.

Theo forcibly put his mind back together and said, "Is this 'pull-the-plug' scenario confirmed by the network suppliers?"

"Actually," Nikole responded after clearing her throat, "We haven't heard back from the network suppliers since they're still busy recovering the other worldwide networks."

"You know," another crisis team member chimed in, "The public is having tremendous problems from the outages these last few days. It really goes to show how much society relies on mobile network connectivity – we can't seem to survive without it."

"Very true," Nikole agreed, "Not only have people lost communication, but all Smart Cities' critical infrastructures, such as waste water management and electricity distribution, are negatively affected. Mobile machine-to-machine communication has become utterly interwoven with everyone's daily life."

Theo's head was spinning as everyone spoke and the severity of the situation continued to sink in. He interjected, "Shouldn't we be thinking about an improved backup plan after this situation's resolved? Can we really leave communication up to the market? To my understanding, the telecommunication infrastructure has the same priority for a society as electricity, main roads, rail roads and water companies."

Theo took a deep breath and added, "So I suggest we do what the experts propose." The entire crisis team agreed.

With a silent sigh, Nikole walked back to her office, took her Wi-Fi connected smartphone out and posted a message in a social media group she had with the senior network operating guys she'd met a few months ago.

Dear EU operator friends,

This is not a test. Within the EU-zone we're having severe network availability issues which are most probably caused by our emRoaming system. This is resulting in network outages in the EU-zone. Please temporarily disable our emRoaming system asap. It's causing prioritized roaming traffic from the IoT UN-bears which I presume you have disabled by now. Thanks for your swift follow-up and sharing your findings with all of us.

Thanks, Nikole.

She took a deep breath and said a little prayer, *"Please let this work out."* Then Nikole hit the send button and went back to the meeting room where everyone looked up as she entered. "Ladies and gentlemen, please be patient. They're working on it as we speak."

* * *

"I still have a bad feeling about this," Paul said while they descended the mountain path, "I mean, Rafael would never put this kind of effort to find me for a simple chat - $1,000 is a lot of money. He knows how much turn-over he needs to make to be able to spend it. That's how he's thinking you know?"

Jane carefully watched her steps, considering Paul's words. "No, I actually don't think he is - he probably wants to fly you in for a business talk with some huge potential business partner." Paul didn't respond, focusing on the path ahead of them.

After another hour or so, they reached a crossing and saw another backpacking couple stopped ahead, just to the side. It seemed the woman was having a problem with one of her backpack straps and the guy was trying to fix it. "Hey, you guys need some help?" Jane called out as she and Paul walked up.

"That would be great," the guy smiled, "The strap just broke a little on the bottom. I'm Adam by the way, and this is Miriam." Paul and Jane smiled.

"Good to meet you," Jane said, "I'm Jane and this is Paul. You guys been trekking for long?" As she talked, Paul had taken out a spare shoe string and was working with Adam to fix the bottom of the strap.

"We're from Israel," Miriam answered, "We've been traveling for almost six months now. Plan to continue another six months for a full year trip." At this point Miriam's strap was fixed and the two couples continued along together towards the mountain guesthouse where they all planned on spending the night.

"Did you guys also have connection problems with your phones?" Adam asked.

"There aren't any networks around here," Paul said. Adam shook his head.

"We used to be able to check email everywhere," he told them,

"But after the global outages our phones aren't working anymore." Paul exchanged a worried look with Jane.

"What global outages?" Paul asked. Adam proceeded to explain how most mobile phone networks throughout the world had been having serious problems for the last few days.

"Wow," Jane said, eyebrows raised, "We had no idea since we were in a monastery for a few days and didn't look at the news."

"Do they know the cause?" Paul wanted to know.

"I think it had something to do with those UN-bears, that's what the news is saying anyway," Adam answered. Jane stopped short and let out a gasp, eyes wide in horror, now understanding why Rafael wanted to get in touch with them so badly. Paul stood stock-still, face now drained of all colour.

"What the f…" Then he dropped his backpack on the ground and said, "We need to call him right now!" His voice was panicked. Miriam and Adam watched with confused frowns as Paul pulled out his phone and turned it on. It read, 'Searching for Network'.

"Okay," Adam finally said, "What's going on? I know it's an inconvenience, but that's a pretty strong reaction." But Paul was incapable of speech as he stared at his phone screen and Jane's eyes were welling up with tears as she checked her phone. Like Paul, she only saw, 'Searching for Network'.

"We need to call some people right away," she looked from Miriam and Adam to Paul, feeling queasy. "Those bears – the UN ones - there our bears. We helped make them. The outages are our fault!" Her voice was now high and wobbly. Paul still focussed on his phone screen which now said, 'No Network Available'.

"Damn, damn, damn it," Paul muttered, ready to throw her phone at the pebbled ground in frustration, "It's not working. Can we use your phone?" He looked desperately at Adam, who had started to hand over his phone, saying,

"Here - but I doubt it's going to work either. We haven't been able to use it for the last four days."

"David," Paul said, "Could you try switching it off and on again, please?"

"Yeah," Adam replied, "No problem, but the battery is getting low."

So there they were, standing in the middle of nowhere, Nepal, on top of the world and staring at their phone screens as they turned them off and on. They were totally and completely disconnected.

SHORTCUT

"WE NEED TO get to the mountain guesthouse, as soon as possible," Paul declared, trying to get his head in order after the shocking news, "We can call Rafael from there. I think there's about an hour and a half to go." He sped up.

"Not too fast," Jane called after him, "I have some serious blisters here, remember!"

As they walked, Paul and Jane explained the entire bear project to Adam and Miriam. Their new friends were impressed and understood the importance of Paul and Jane's role in the project. Paul frowned.

"Something must've gone *very* wrong," he mused, "I just can't believe it was our bears that caused it."

At 3:45 pm, the four of them trudged up to the mountain guesthouse, which was remotely located between two snowbound villages. Jane released an audible gasp of relief, as they stopped in front of an older woman who worked at the house. She'd seen them coming and had a steaming pot of tea ready to welcome her new guests.

All four travellers smiled and greeted the older woman, and before taking off his backpack, Paul asked,

"Can I make a phone call please?"

"Sorry," the woman answered, "We don't have any phones here, but you can leave a postcard with me and they'll go out with the weekly mail carrier. My name's Margaret, by the way." She gave a sweet smile.

After quick introductions, Miriam and Adam left to drop their backpacks in the communal dorm room. Then Paul tried again. "So, we kind of need to get in touch with some people back home. Do you have Wi-Fi available - do we need a code to use it?"

"I'm sorry dear," Margaret said with a laugh, "We don't have the internet either. But please come in, make yourselves at home, relax a little." The woman was used to backpackers who wanted to check their email and social media accounts, but these two looked extra desperate. "If you'd like to call or email you can do it tomorrow, in the village just to the west. But, for now you can just relax your feet and have some of my fresh mountain tea – all out in the rock garden."

Paul stood there in silence as everyone watched and waited for his response. After several beats, he looked at Jane. "Okay, we'll need to keep going and make it to the next village today." Jane opened her mouth to respond, but Margaret interjected,

"That's way too far, son. It's a good three hours' walk, and there's only two and a half hours until sunset. That trek is far too dangerous in the dark." Without a word, Paul pulled out the Lonely Planet and began to scan its pages. He saw that taking the route they'd just come, the one over the mountain, wasn't an option. It would take at least six hours.

"Here listen," Paul said suddenly, looking up, "It says there's a shortcut to the village that only takes an hour and a half – through the rock forest." Jane gave him a wary look and Margaret shook her head vigorously.

"There *is* a shortcut," the older woman said, "But it's extremely dangerous, which is why only locals use it. It's simply too steep for tourists, and you can easily get lost. I strongly advise that you take the regular route tomorrow." At this point Adam and Miriam walked back into the front room.

"Thank you ma'am," Jane told Margaret with a smile, "I think you're advice sounds like our best option." She gave Paul a pointed look.

"What's going on?" Adam asked.

The four moved a little bit away from Margaret where Paul briefed Adam and Miriam on his dilemma, and about the risky shortcut. Ignoring the incredulous look from Jane, Adam responded with, "If it's really that important for you, we can take this shortcut with you to make sure you're safe."

"Absolutely," Miriam agreed, "We had a similar situation in Argentina two months ago when somebody needed medicine. We'll walk with you if you want." Jane threw her hands up in resignation – at this point, her feet would be permanently injured. As they spoke, Margaret watched from behind the front desk. She'd heard their conversation and shook her head in dismay. Yet she knew it was useless - nothing she could say would change that young man's mind.

Jane sighed and looked at Paul. "Well, I don't like the idea of a steep, maze-like route over a mountain, but it's three against one – I guess I'll come too." Jane managed a little smile as she gave her feet a quick massage and changed into fresh socks. As the four of them shuffled back outside, Margaret followed them and handed a bag to Paul.

"Here, take some cookies and please be careful." Then the old woman pointed to their right. "See that rock there? That's the start of the shortcut path. Look for piled stones as the trail markers so you won't lose your way." Paul immediately took the lead toward the path, turning to wave to Margaret.

"Thanks for everything," he called back. And they were on their way. "We've just enough time to reach the village within thirty minutes of sunset. Let's move guys!" Paul told the others as he set a speedy pace.

Everything seemed great as they made their way along the shortcut path. The weather was good – cold but crisp and sunny. And the trail was easy to follow, with the piled stone markers at regular intervals.

They had a marvellous view of the mountain range, snowy peaks glowing almost magically as the golden light from the sun hit them. It was a bit steep, but that was hardly a challenge with their hiking boots. Zig-zagging down the mountain, they now had to descend at least 700 meters. This part of the trail was covered in gravel stones.

After twenty minutes, the four travellers finally saw the villages' rooftops peeking out from the valley below. It seemed this had been the best choice after all, despite Margaret's cautions and Jane's hesitation.

But, Paul couldn't really revel in that fact. His mind was too busy with continuous questions. *What the hell could've gone wrong with those bears - a hardware issue? No, otherwise Thomas would've fixed it. Was it properly tested? It must've been or Bruce wouldn't have released it.*

As soon as Paul reached the village, he'd call Bruce. No - Jonathan Drel, since he had the number in his wallet. "Not too fast for me Paul, please," Jane called from the back, "My blisters are killing me. I think they're bleeding now." He stopped and turned around to look at her. This last leg of the path, leading into the valley *was* rather steep.

"Sorry," he replied, "Go at your own pace, and hang in there just a little longer. I promise to get you a nice, medicinal glass of whiskey when we get there, okay?" With a playful wink, he turned back around.

Jane let out a laugh and said, "I think that will definitely do the trick." With the new motivation, she began to carefully make her way down the steep, gravelly path, step by step. She lagged way behind the others.

All of the sudden, as Jane placed her right foot down, she lost her footing. She immediately swung her arms around and backward, trying to catch her balance. However, her backpack threw her completely off-kilter, causing her to land hard on her right side and begin sliding. "Aaahh!" Jane screamed as she felt her body helplessly slip down the hill-path on the loose stones.

The three others stopped and turned to see what was happening. "Heeelp," Jane cried out as the path became even steeper, causing her body to race straight towards the canyon's edge. It was no use, she couldn't stop at this point. Paul, who'd been standing their frozen in shock, stared at Jane's speedy descent.

"No!" Paul yelled out in desperation, "Jane - plant your feet!" But he knew she wouldn't be able to do that, not at the rate she was moving. He watched in horror, fear and adrenaline gripping his insides as Jane plummeted towards the cliff edge with a cloud of dust trailing behind. Adam and Miriam watched, mouths agape, paralyzed with panic.

Not ten meters from the edge, Jane's body came to a sudden halt when she collided with a large rock. "Oof," was the last noise they heard from her before she lay there, limp and motionless.

MISTAKES

"HOLY SHIT," PAUL muttered as he started to run down towards Jane body where it lay unmoving against the large rock.

"Wait, stop," Adam called after him, "It's too dangerous, you could slide as well, and you might not be lucky enough to hit the rock." Adam, Miriam and Paul stared down at Jane's body as it began to twitch a little and move again. She screamed out in shock, then erupted into soft crying with a sob here and there.

"Jane," Paul shouted down, "Don't move a muscle. We'll get to you and get you back up." Then, he turned to Adam. "Call the emergency services for a chopper, will you?" Adam took out his phone and tried to call - no service.

"Damn, bloody fucking phone!" Paul dropped his head into his hands for a moment, tears welling up in his eyes, then looked down at Jane again.

"We'll come get you. You're going to be okay, I promise." He called to her. Amid his panic, Paul tried to collect his thoughts and discuss rescue options with the others. Adam looked directly at Paul, seriousness emanating from his expression.

"Listen to me Paul," he spoke calmly yet firmly, "It's too

dangerous to go all the way down to her. You can't let emotion cloud your judgment." Paul nodded, then Adam pointed down and to the left and said, "If we can get to that other large rock, then we'll have a safer approach. I can make a kind of rope from our backpacks if we use a knife to cut them into cloth and leather strips. Then, we'll use that to get Jane away from the edge."

"Listen," Miriam said, looking pale, "I can run back to Margaret at the guesthouse and get some rope from her if you want."

"Forget it," Adam said, "That'll take too long and then the temperature will take a rapid drop after sunset. And Jane's probably injured, we need to get her medical help as soon as possible." Miriam nodded, then she and Paul quickly emptied their backpacks. Using his military knife, Adam tore them apart and constructed an improvised rope.

After carefully getting down to the other large rock, closer to Jane, they prepared to throw the makeshift rope over. Jane had managed to take off her backpack, though she kept her legs and feet still, something was extremely painful. "Agh - my right foot hurts like hell. Guys I can't move it!" She called over, a fresh stream of tears coming down. The salty tears turned icy cold as they dried on her cheeks.

"It's okay, angel," Paul called over, "We'll get you to a doctor before you know it. Okay, leave your backpack there and put both your hand and wrist through the loop at the end of this strap, okay?" Adam and Paul braced themselves against the other large rock, nervously glancing at the terrifyingly close edge, and threw the makeshift rope towards Jane. After three attempts, it got close enough and Jane snatched it with both hands. Once she'd put her right hand through the loop, Adam called over,

"Do you have the strength to hold on?"

"Yeah," Jane nodded, "I think so." She moved her weight away from the rock, wincing as her foot and leg injuries shot pain through her limbs. As the three pulled on the rope, Jane's body inched upward and over a little, towards the second rock. She relied fully on the improvised rope. Now, if someone slipped or let go, Jane was sure to slide over the edge.

But Paul, Adam and Miriam simply focused on pulling, ignoring any sense of fear or panic. After three more steady pulls, Jane was safe and sound behind the second rock. She shared a quick, very tearful embrace with Paul, before they began crawling, inch by inch, back up to the path. Once back on the trail, tears flowed freely down Jane's face as she lay there.

"Honey, have some cookies and water," Paul said, eyes filling with tears as he gave her the food and drink, "I'm so sorry. It's all my fault. I never should've dragged you on this crazy shortcut." He gently hugged Jane again, careful not to touch her injuries. She sniffed, and let out a little laugh.

"Remind me never to listen to your crazy ideas ever again!" She looked at her foot which seemed to be injured and softly said, "I want to go home."

"Okay guys," Adam interjected, "We can discuss all this later. Right now we have to continue on to the village before the sun sets completely. We haven't much time." Leaving their backpacks behind, everyone kept essential items such as money and smartphones, in their pockets, and Miriam brought her sleeping bag to carry a little food and water.

As they trekked slowly down, Adam and Paul supported the poor, limping Jane. In half an hour it'd grown totally dark and the weary travelers could see lights from the village growing closer and closer below them. Guided by the torch app on Paul's phone, they finally reached solid, level ground and released sighs of relief.

"Here," Paul said as he walked up to the first house they came across, "We need to get you help quickly." He knocked on the door and a man with two little kids and a wife peering behind him, opened it and let them in. As the wife got them water and hot tea, Paul turned to the husband,

"We need a doctor," he gestured to Jane who sat on a chair in the living room, "Is there one around here?" The man nodded, grabbed his coat and led the four back out into the cold night to the doctor's house.

"Thank you," Miriam told the man as he left and the four shuffled into the doctor's house.

"You poor thing," the older, bearded doctor told Jane, "Come and lay on the sofa, let me cut your shoe off to check your foot."

"Thanks," Jane smiled. Tears welled up in her eyes as the doctor cut open her hiking boot with very strong, surgical looking scissors. The other three watched as he examined Jane's bruised and battered foot.

"You must've had a hard time, my dear. But, thankfully you've been lucky. No broken bones - possibly a mild sprain, but you'll be fine. You need to rest and recover though, so let's get you to the guesthouse around the corner." Everyone smiled in relief, especially Jane. No serious injuries and all would be well soon.

* * *

The next morning Jane blinked in the mid-morning sunshine streaming through the guesthouse window. All four of them had slept in a family room on cots and sofas. Jane looked down at the dark bloodspots on her jeans and to her ankle and foot that looked swollen and bruised. She then gazed all around - Paul and Adam were gone. "They went to find a store and replace everything we left in our backpacks." Miriam's voice from behind startled her.

"Oh, that's a good idea," Jane smiled as Miriam came around to sit on the edge of Jane's cot.

"How are you feeling?" Miriam asked. Jane touched her leg injuries and right foot gingerly.

"I think I'm okay," she answered, "But I want to go home as

soon as possible. I kind of never want to see a mountain again," Jane laughed.

"Well," Miriam said with a chuckle, "That's understandable. For now, just relax, maybe take a shower. There's a really nice one here."

Minutes later, after limping to the bathroom, Jane felt her body relax under the fresh, warm water. It was so soothing, washing away the mountain dust and dried blood. The clean smell of lathered shampoo entered her nostrils, making her smile as she rinsed her hair. It had been a little tricky getting off her pants, but she'd managed to slowly peel them off and handle the pain.

Just then, a gentle knock sounded from the bathroom door, and Miriam called in, "Jane, I borrowed some clean clothes from other travellers for both of us. Also my phone is working again, isn't that great?" Jane smiled and wondered if she'd remembered to bring her phone. But, she didn't really care - she was just happy to still be alive.

Both feeling fresh and relaxed after showers and crisp, clean clothes, Jane and Miriam sat in the living room happily eating breakfast. The guesthouse owner was working on his computer at the desk. Jane's gaze shifted from the owner up to Paul who'd just walked into the room, phone to his ear. "…a blue and a red one," she heard him say.

As soon as Paul's eyes met Jane's, he said, "I've got to hang up now. She's awake." He came over and kissed her good morning, eyes shining with love and concern. "How are you feeling today, angel?"

"Better," Jane replied with a half-smile, "Thanks honey. But, I'm dying to end this holiday now." Before Paul could respond, Adam joined them, and everyone ate a hearty breakfast, chattering about what had happened yesterday. Paul, who sat next to Jane on a two-seater sofa, smiled at her and gave her a kiss.

"You're lucky to be alive," he told her gently.

"It's true," Jane agreed, "That rock may have stopped my fall, but you guys rescued me from the rock, thank you." She shifted her gaze to Adam and Miriam then back on Paul.

"You know," he told her, "I was terrified you'd slip, but you made it. I'm really sorry for taking the shortcut, angel, I feel a bit responsible, but at least we ended up on the more interesting side of the mountain." He added with a weak attempt at humour. Jane gave a short laugh, but inside, part of her was still pissed as hell at Paul for insisting on the risky path – his calls could've waited until today.

Paul's phones kept buzzing, flooded with messages, but he kept his focus on Jane. "Adam and I got some supplies to replace the stuff left in our backpacks, but we still need some new, basic clothes." Jane looked at her injured foot, now elevated on a foot rest to reduce swelling.

"You guys go ahead," she told them, "I need to rest and recover more. It still hurts like crazy. Paul, can you get me some magazines, please? And listen," her expression grew more serious as she locked intently at Paul, "When you get back, we need to talk about our flight home."

Paul blinked in surprise for a moment, then said, "Uh, sure. I'll get you some magazines. But shouldn't we just recover a bit before we make up our minds about going home?"

"Babe," she said with a gentle hand on his forearm, "I seriously think I need to get out of this place and get home as soon as possible. We can come back in a few months to walk the rest of the trail," she offered.

"Hmm," Paul replied, scratching his two-day stubble, "Let's think about it, okay? I'll be back in a bit."

"Okay," Jane said with a weary sigh, "I'll be up in the rooftop hammock the owner mentioned – resting."

* * *

It was early evening when Jane woke up. Paul was just coming to check on her again. They'd come back earlier with new clothes, Miriam having picked some out for Jane, and supplies, but Jane had been asleep then.

"Hey sleepyhead," Paul said after giving Jane a gentle kiss, "I brought you that medicinal whiskey, chocolates and some crisps. But, the closest thing they had to magazines at the store I went to was a local newspaper, sorry." He gave her his most charming smile and set everything on the table next to the hammock.

"Thanks Paul," she said with a tired smile, "Um, I've been doing some more thinking. I'm really quite ready to go home now. Let's go back, *please*." Paul handed her the whiskey glass, filled with ice, and took a sip of his own. He studied his glass for a moment, sitting in a lounge chair right next to the hammock. Then he looked at her and said,

"Just give me a few days to help the guys back home with the bears, okay?"

"Paul van Dijk," Jane narrowed her eyes, arms crossed over her chest, "I don't think you're *really* listening to me. I need to go home." Her voice rose with frustration. Paul sighed heavily and, before responding, his eyes caught the newspaper's front page article – it was about the 'UN Teddy Bears'.

"Look," he responded, feeling his anxiety level rising by the second, "We'll discuss this later. I need to go check my messages and make some calls." Arching an eyebrow, Jane followed his gaze to the article. Her expression was a mixture of irritation and understanding,

"Fine," she said at last, "I guess you'd better do that. But, we need to talk again when you're done, okay?" She took another sip of whiskey and popped in one of the dark chocolate truffles he'd brought her. The alcohol and chocolate did seem to calm her nerves, her head already swirling a bit.

"I'll come right back when I'm done," Paul assured her, "I promise. Just keep drinking, eating and relaxing – you'll feel better in no time." He gave her another kiss, stood and went back inside.

Logging into Wi-Fi, Paul synced his phone, which was now loading email upon email. At first, it just loaded some regular emails, but then it showed a bunch of highly prioritized messages with all-caps in the subject lines. "Ah, hell, this is gonna be fun," he grumbled, taking a long drink of whiskey before calling Bruce.

* * *

"Paul, I feel terrible," Bruce sounded almost hysterical on the phone, "It feels like blood is on my hands. I'm the operations guy and I had this thing to call my own. And I know I'm completely responsible, not you. But, Paul, I just can't figure it out. Thank God we got in touch with you." Bruce was seriously rambling now, obviously quite upset. He continued before Paul even got a chance to respond,

"I never meant to take over so completely. I mean, you and I both know that this platform was built by *you*. You're the founder and know the most about it." Bruce took a deep breath and Paul was finally able to respond.

"Relax Bruce," he said, "Just tell me what happened and I'm sure we can figure it out." Paul tried to sound calm and confidant, but he felt a nervous twist in his stomach all the same.

"We still don't know exactly what they did," Bruce began, "But it seems that we've made a serious mistake somewhere, related to the software update mechanism. It might just be a minor flaw, but whatever it is had an enormous impact with these global outages. It's more horrible than my worst nightmares."

Paul could hear the despair in Bruce's voice as he went on, "The operators claim we've overloaded their networks with intensive signaling. The bears are apparently misbehaving – they repeatedly set up and then disconnect, and the mobile networks can't handle it

and so they all went down. They say it's our fault because we didn't stick to the GSMA network connectivity IoT guidelines. And Paul, I can't do anything now because I have no control over these bears anymore. All we can do is watch it happening. It's horrible!"

Paul listened quietly to Bruce, who now sounded near tears, trying to process everything. He didn't quite know what to say, so he offered, "What have the networks done about this?"

"Well," Bruce said with a sigh, "They simply kicked all the bears from their networks by disabling our subscriptions."

"Would I be able to login to the Bear IoT platform and have a look?" Paul asked after thinking for a moment.

"Yes," Bruce replied immediately, "Absolutely – and please do take a look soon. You know Paul, honestly and just between us, I'm so confused I can't see it anymore."

* * *

Paul squinted in bewilderment as he saw the pattern of each bear continuously connecting to their cloud, partly downloading firmware and disconnecting – then each bear immediately reconnected and repeated the cycle over and over. It was like somebody dialling a number, starting a conversation with "Hello", suddenly hanging up, then calling again and repeating the process again and again. These continuous loops occurred extremely fast.

Paul's mind spun from it all. Did the software deep inside each bear exchange information by simply setting up and closing connections? Had the Turchaea algorithm optimized itself and was he now facing the end result? Starting to feel dizzy as his heart hammered in his chest Paul realized that a 3.5-inch smartphone screen was not enough.

This required a larger screen like a laptop or a desktop. The guesthouse had only one old PC and it was located at the reception desk where the owner used it for administration and personal

internet access. But unfortunately, the man had said his computer wasn't available for guests to use. Paul decided to try again.

Walking up to the front desk, he held up the article about the bears in his newspaper. The man nodded and smiled. "Yes, bear. No bear here, only computer."

"Yes I know," Paul replied with a patient smile, "Can I borrow your computer tonight to look at a file?" And Paul pointed to the article and added, "These bears need my help. Can I use your computer so I can help them please?"

"Sorry," the man answered, keeping the same smile on his face, "No bear. No such file here in this house." Paul held back an exasperated sigh - it was impossible to communicate with this man. He only had a basic command of English in order to run his guesthouse.

Suddenly the man pointed at the picture in the newspaper and said, "Bears in mini market," and pointed toward the door in the direction of a small shop. Paul nodded and asked,

"Do they also sell laptops?"

"No laptop," the man shook his head, "Only food and phones. Are you hungry?" He held up a plate of spaghetti and meatballs with a grin.

"No thanks," Paul held up his hand and walked back upstairs to Jane. "I'm going to a shop nearby," Paul told Jane, "Could you try to figure out a way to ask the man down at the front desk if I can use his computer tonight? We're having, uh, communication issues and I want to login to the bear management platform to have a look."

"Sure," Jane shrugged, "I'll try my best. And please look for some magazines for me while you're out, will you? You don't know how boring it is sitting around, recovering."

"Don't worry," Paul smiled reassuringly, "I'll find you some magazines. And thanks."

It was just about an hour when Paul walked back into the

guesthouse, carrying two wrapped bears. He saw Jane turning from the front desk man and she walked over with a wide grin. "Guess what," Jane told him, "You can use Djired's PC this evening! He usually doesn't let anyone near it, but he took one look at my injured foot, and heard about my life-or-death experience, and bingo."

"Jane," Paul's face had lit up, "That's great! Nice job using your injuries to manipulate him – thanks. I'll chat with Bruce soon, so he can prepare remote access." Paul proceeded to unwrap one of the bears which immediately woke up with a burp. Then, the bear asked Paul to give him a name.

Paul grinned and said, "Eddy2" It seemed like such a long time ago, but he recognized the wake-up sequence. It was still the same way they'd designed it.

While Paul put Eddy2 on its charging pillow, Jane opened the other bear and named it "Ada2". She tossed her new bear to Paul. "Good," Paul said, "I'll put them both in the corner of the room where they can chat," Paul gave a playful smile.

As Eddy2 and Ada2 lay next to each other on their charging pillows, they softly chatted and 'paired' as friends who hadn't seen each other in years. After he called and asked Bruce to prepare remote access to the platform, all he had to do was wait until he could use Djired's computer. So, Paul went up and tried to get some rest next to Jane in the hammock, and thankfully his busy mind quieted down enough to drift into a light nap.

It was 5 pm when Jane woke him up. She'd been happily reading a magazine in the hammock next to him and now looked over, eyes glowing. "Paul, let's eat out at this cosy looking restaurant I saw in the local newspaper tonight - all four of us okay? We owe Adam and Miriam something nice, you know? And it would be fun to do something a little different."

At that point, Paul's mind had drifted to the Bear's cloud and whether Bruce had enabled him access yet. He'd only half-listened as he checked his phone for any emails, and gave the delayed response of, "Sure, no problem, honey." Jane put down her magazine and let out an annoyed breath.

"Listen Paul," she spoke louder now, "I'm fed up with this place. I've been talking with Djired and it's a five hour bus ride from the city to the airport and…" This time Paul did look up.

"Sorry," he said with a frown, "Can we talk about that later? I just woke up and I'm right in the middle of reading this email from Bruce. The world is on fire, and we caused it."

Jane's frustration escalated as she scowled over at him, sitting up in her hammock as best she could. "Look Paul, I almost died. We agreed to talk about the return trip and you keep putting it off or ignoring me!" But, it was too late. Paul was already focused back on the email from Bruce.

That was it. Jane swivelled her head to look him straight in the face. "Paul van Dijk – are you listening to me?"

"Yes," Paul answered as he stood up and released his own exasperated sigh, "I'm listening, and we'll talk about it. But first I need to use that dusty old PC to help Bruce. He's waiting for my feedback and needs support, okay?" Jane glared at him, mouth gaping as Paul simply stalked out the door and downstairs, without another word.

It was perfect timing for Paul - Djired had just left. Sitting down behind the reception desk, Paul looked at the ancient computer. Its internet connection was ridiculously slow, and was already trying his patience. However, Paul and Bruce had counted on this and he used an old fashioned command line interface to connect to the central bear management server. Bruce and Thomas were ready on standby in the smartphone chatroom.

After a few minutes, Jane came down to the reception area, still limping slightly. She spoke in a hard, cold tone. "I'm going to the restaurant now. Miriam and Adam are already on their way to meet me there. Are you coming or not?"

"Yeah," Paul answered, still not looking up, "Sure. I just need to start some downloads first. Then I'll be right there." Jane rolled her eyes in annoyance and huffed out of the guesthouse. Still Paul only barely glanced up before swiftly logging in and finding the server log files.

There were a ton, and it would probably take some time to download the system log files with all the history event information, so Paul started the download, put a paper on the monitor that read, 'Please Do Not Touch' and stood up to head for the door, intending to go to the restaurant. Before moving away from the desk, Paul quickly checked the monitor one more time, putting the 'Please Do Not Touch' paper aside, and saw: 'Download Failed'.

"Damn," Paul muttered to himself, "Probably a time-out from this insanely slow connection." He sat back down on the chair and logged into the Bear server again. He proceeded to cut the files into smaller pieces so they'd download more easily. Scrolling through the smaller log files, Paul didn't find anything strange. Bears frequently reported their presence and sometimes new ones reported their first wake up.

Paul scratched his head in confusion - this wasn't what he'd expected at all. There were no massive activities to be seen. He continued to investigate by looking at earlier log files when he heard his phone buzzing on the desk with a message from Jane. Shit, he'd forgotten.

<Hello, earth to Paul! We're starting to eat. Are you joining????>

<<Yes, just a sec. problems with the connection. Plz order food for me too and a beer ;-) >>

Paul put his phone back down and continued to search through the files, recognizing the various regions and countries by their IP-addresses. The bears popped-up all over the world. "Just a quick try," he said to himself while importing several log files to a spreadsheet and filtering random bears. Now he could see it more clearly.

Once the bears woke up, they'd loaded their settings, initiated a download and that was basically it. Then Paul noticed something peculiar, and leaned toward the screen for a better look. There was a notification from one of the bears that indicated he'd reported his findings to another back-up system. Paul frowned, racking his brains. Did the Chinese have a back-up system in place already?

For a moment, his thoughts went to Jane and the restaurant, but his attention was soon utterly taken up by the log files, blocking out everything else from his mind. Scrolling back a few days in the log, Paul found more notification messages to this unknown back-up system. His brow creased even more and he went to another directory and looked to see what that back-up server was and where it was located. It was mounted via the internet to the primary bear IoT server.

"Strange," he mumbled to himself, "Very strange indeed." It took a while to open the host file from the other system, and then the internet connection seemed to drop again. There was no response. Irritated, Paul verified his phone's internet connection in the guesthouse, and it was still okay. He looked back at the selected file and instead of 315Kbytes it was 3.15Mbytes – the file appeared.

"Okay, this looks more like what I'd imagined," he thought. Paul now saw a host file with thousands of torrent links. The Turchaeas had used these links to share their capacity and cooperate. Looking at the torrent list, he recognized the algorithm, and it was basically the way he'd designed it.

"So," Paul said to himself, "Guess someone needs to look inside one of the bears to find out what happened." But first he checked the bear platform again and found a few still on-line scattered across different regions. They were probably the bears which hadn't been noticed by the mobile network operators or the ones unwrapped during the outage. Paul quickly downloaded a system log from one of the bears via the central bear server and opened it.

He recognized it - like a punch to the gut - the host file, with the list of back-up servers showed a familiar internet IP-address. It was his own server back at home in Amsterdam! "What the fuck," Paul mumbled to himself. For some reason, the Bear IoT-management server was linked to his home server. Who had done this and why?

Truly baffled, Paul decided to take a break. He pulled his arms behind his back to stretch out his spine and fingers, then looked around the reception area. It was the only room with lights on at the moment and printed paper files encircled him, visible from the cast of the pale desk light. The vague realization hit Paul - Jane had said something about dinner plans. Then he remembered.

As quickly as possible, Paul walked to the cosy restaurant. As soon as he entered, he ran into Miriam, Jane and Adam as they stood to leave. Jane had a hardened look on her face, mouth at a downward bent. She didn't even look at him, when she said, "Enjoy your meal Paul. They've put it in the fridge and we've already paid for it. You're welcome." She spoke in a cold tone, devoid of all emotion except of the slightest trembling hurt underneath. Paul held up his hand apologetically.

"Sorry Jane, but I…" Yet his words trailed off as he took in the angry frowns on both Miriam and Adam's faces. Paul looked back at Jane - he'd never seen her this pissed off. She finally looked at him, with her most intimidating glare.

"Forget it, Paul. Your priorities are clear - very clear." The three of them then walked out and headed back to the guesthouse while Paul sat alone in the restaurant. As the waiter microwaved his dish he grabbed his beer and took out his phone to text.

<Bruce, can you send me a system log of a bear that's been disconnected? I'd like to see what's happened under the hood.>

<<U mean I open a bear and get the log from the Bear itself? I never thought to look inside!>>

<I just thought of it myself, no worries ☺ J Just send me the complete file okay?>

<<Gimme 30 min, will take a demo bear we have lying around.>>

Putting his phone down on the table, Paul finished his meal alone and he went back to check if Jane was okay. He found her sleeping in the hammock with her injured foot raised up, so he quietly walked back to the reception desk computer, not wanting to disturb her rest.

After a moment of looking at the bear's behaviour, Paul ruffled his hair with a confused frown. It didn't look unusual at all, and he couldn't understand why they'd used his home server to store the host files. "Those FLQ-idiots," he muttered, "They'd agreed to not use my home server since it was only supposed to be for the original demo, not be a production server."

* * *

A few thousands kilometres away Bruce plunged into one of the bears with a knife and put a USB cable deep into the furry little guy. With a single click on his laptop, he extracted the bear's log file history.

Back up in the Nepali Mountains, Paul looked down as his phone buzzed with,

<Check ur mail for the bear's inside log.>

Paul opened the file and his mouth fell open in shock. This bear had opened and closed its internet sessions without sending any data, and had done it thousands of times. Not to any server, but by using proxies to other bears. Paul had never seen that before - ever. Who would do...?

Sitting straighter in the old desk chair, Paul continued to search the database, looking for the bears that first began to show odd behaviour. It was like finding a needle in a haystack.

After two hours, he heaved a sigh and gave up. "Shit," he grouched to himself, "I have to find another way." At this point it was 4 am and he was sick of drinking caffeinated tea, so Paul took a small break and browsed his RC-Forum. It appeared everyone was pissed off that they couldn't drive their cars. *"Well of course they can't,"* Paul thought, shaking his head, *"The code in those cars is partly shared with the bears. Wow, they even referred to my name here in the forum."*

He read on, seeing that a newbie racer had referred to the ffu source part, causing Paul to tilt his head with interest. The newbie had asked for feedback on her findings, but nobody had replied. There weren't many who understood this part of the source code, so the lack of response didn't surprise Paul in the least. He was impressed that this newbie was on the right track, and curious to see her mention that she was continuing to search for a solution.

Scrolling down in the forum logs, Paul found the same newbie appearing over and over again. "Does this girl ever sleep?" Paul asked aloud with a smirk. The newbie asked a number of questions on the hardware interfacing and chip device drivers, and in the end, she referred to a YouTube video she'd posted. Paul clicked on the link and waited as the old bandwidth connection slowly loaded the video.

When it finally ran, the video showed an RC-racer car without any housing placed on a kitchen floor, the camera shot being on level with the car. Without showing a face, a teenage girl's voice with a French-sounding accent said, "I'll boot and drive it now," and a hand appeared on the screen, flipping a switch.

After several seconds a green light went on then a loud burp sounded as the car immediately took off, proceeding to smash against the wall. Paul stared silently for a few moments, then put his face down into his hands in thought. This girl had somehow bypassed the mobile network start-up sequence and had gotten the car to move – but how the hell had she done that?

Paul brought his head back up and continued watching in astonishment. "Amazing," the voice of the very clever newbie declared, "After the start-up, the software jumped to the firmware upgrade routine and used a local short-range radio connection."

It was 7 am when Djired came in to find Paul working on the front desk PC. The young man glanced up, looking weary and pale, and said, "Sorry, I'm still using it." Djired regarded Paul for a moment then said,

"Good morning sir. I need to work again."

"Um," Paul gave a pleading look, "Can I just have five more minutes to transfer some code to my friend – please?"

"Okay," Djired told him after thinking for a moment, "You have ten minutes but then you need go."

Needing to hurry, Paul wrote a short email to Bruce and added, 'PS. This newbie RC-Racer-forum girl figured out a clever trick that we should try out on the bears. Look at her kitchen RC-racer video and check the bypassing boot sequence she did.' Then Paul hit 'Send', logged out of his email account and stood to start cleaning up the mess he'd made.

"Thanks for letting me use your computer. That was very kind, not to mention helpful." Paul said with a smile.

"So," Djired said after a nod, "Did you save bears this night?"

"Almost," Paul replied, "We're very close." Then he gave a big yawn as Djired put his hand on Paul's shoulder.

"No problem my friend," the kind man said, "You can use it again tonight after I finish my work if you need."

Minutes later, the exhaustion and stress of working all night suddenly washed over Paul. He went to the bedroom and found Jane still asleep in the hammock, so he softly kissed her and quietly tiptoed away. He felt bad about being late – extremely late - for dinner at the restaurant. Of course, it wasn't the first time he'd done something like that.

Paul's mind flicked to his ex-girlfriend Kat's face as she'd hurled the key at him. Kat had broken up with him for the same thing he'd just done to Jane - making her wait and putting his computer and work at a higher priority than her. He simply couldn't repeat that with Jane – this beautiful woman that really and truly loved him. Paul was resolved. Tomorrow he'd beg for forgiveness, doing whatever it took until she accepted his apology.

FAREWELL

THE FIRST THING Paul noticed when he woke up were beams of light hitting his face. He reached for his phone to see the time – just after noon. "But, what is…?" he muttered to himself as he felt a piece of paper next to his phone on the night table. He sat up, rubbed his eyes and blinked down at the note. It looked like Jane's handwriting.

His sleepy eyes focused more sharply now as he put on his glasses and read.

Dear Paul, I've been trying to talk with you the last few days – to reconnect. But you seem to be completely in your own world. Not showing up at the restaurant was not only embarrassing, but it hurt – really hurt. I'd think if you really cared, you'd take some time for me. I think we'll both be better off if we go our separate ways. Please don't follow me. Good luck with the bears, I know you'll fix it. x Jane.

"No - shit," Paul mumbled to himself, pulling one hand over his face as if to clear his head. As he lowered the note, a wash of emptiness and anguish flooded his body. "Bloody hell," he cursed loudly, "This can't be happening again." His mind flashed back to Kat yet again, "Not with Jane, she's different – she's the one." It was true, Jane wasn't only his romantic partner, but his best friend – his soulmate.

And Paul knew for certain that he'd just made a serious mistake. He'd virtually abandoned her to recover in the hammock, just tossing a few magazines, whiskey and chocolates her way. Only now did Paul realize he should've given her more attention. While Jane had been miserably lying around all day, injured, he'd been focussed on programming and the bear fiasco. A wave of guilt rippled through him. It seemed he hadn't learned his lesson from the Kat situation.

Grabbing his phone, Paul found her name in his contacts. It rang...and rang...and rang some more. Then, a lady's mechanical voice sounded, "The number you've dialled cannot be reached, please try again." He threw the phone in his pocket. "Damn it to hell!" Paul cried out before running outside. His eyes cut over to Djired who stood just out front. "Have you seen my girlfriend, Jane?"

Djired nodded and smiled. "She continued her way this morning." Paul clenched his hands into anxious fists by his sides. "Where was she heading? Was she on foot?" Paul asked.

"She on foot," Djired told him, "I not know where to though, perhaps over there." He pointed over towards the mountains, then glanced at his watch. "She left maybe one hour ago and told you would stay longer. She would travel with bus."

"Shit," Paul muttered. He felt his pulse quicken, not knowing what to do. Even if he caught up with her, how could he convince her he was sorry, and truly wanted to be together? This whole thing had blown up - out of control.

Paul looked over at Djired. "Where's the Israeli couple?"

"Took day walking trip," Djired replied, waving his hand in a different direction, "They return this afternoon." Thanking Djired for his help, Paul released a long, frustrated sigh and walked back to the room. He looked around. Jane had taken her passport, bankcard, her clothes and even the bear she'd named Ada2. The image of her looking so cute, naming that bear flashed in his mind. It increased the ache he'd begun to feel in his gut.

Shaking his head, he tried to sort out what to do next. Where would Jane be heading – which bus would she take? Had she hitched a ride and already gotten on it? He tried to call her again, but her phone was switched off. After thinking a moment, Paul rushed to the lobby and studied the area's map. There weren't many roads and he didn't think she'd risk heading into the mountains. Jane still couldn't walk properly.

Most likely, she was headed into the city, 25 kilometres down in the valley. There she'd probably take a long distance bus. "That's it then, I'd better move." Paul told himself, veins beginning to hum with adrenaline. He would race to the city and look for Jane at the bus station, even if he got there ahead of her and had to wait. Djired had come back into the lobby. Paul went up to him and asked, "Can I borrow a car or could someone take me to the city?"

"Sorry," Djired answered, "No cars here today. Everybody to big market. You can take other bus this afternoon."

"That's no good," Paul said, shaking his head, "It'll be too late. Is there no other option?" he asked, desperation seeping in. Djired could tell it was very important to Paul, so he took out his phone. One quick call later and the man looked apologetic.

"Sorry," he told Paul, "There really are no cars here now."

"*Damn*," Paul cursed in his head. Djired was right, everybody had gone to the big monthly market – of course there weren't any cars. His eye was suddenly caught by a mountain bike leaning against the wall just outside the front window. What other choice did he have? Before he thought it through properly, Paul said. "Can I borrow that bike out there?"

"Yes," Djired nodded, "No problem. But be careful." Yet Paul was already racing into his room to grab his wallet, a jacket and Teddy2. On his way out, he grabbed some dusty plastic flowers from the reception desk - Djired smiled, understanding that this young man needed those flowers more than him.

"Wait, make sure you take this path," Djired called out to Paul, pointing to the map. Paul came back over, he'd been in such a rush, and so clouded by emotions, he hadn't thought about which way to go.

"Thanks," Paul said, "I'll take a picture just in case." Using his smartphone, he snapped a shot of the map. Just before Paul left the guesthouse, Djired tossed him a milk-chocolate bar he had at the desk as a snack.

"Good luck," Djired winked and focused back on his old computer. Paul grinned and waved his thanks after pocketing the chocolate. Anything he could get to help win Jane back– now he had old plastic flowers and chocolate.

After a quick pressure check on the tires, Paul grabbed the bike and took off. It was old, but had still been used now and then by Djired. Paul had put a plastic bag with his stuff on the luggage carrier of the bike and was now following the unpaved path down the hill. "*This isn't so bad - this is pretty easy actually*", he thought, smiling to himself.

Paul felt the fresh mountain air in his face as he sped up. It was invigorating and kind of fun – adventurous. The path was narrow with a steep wall of the mountain on his left and a deep drop on the right. It seemed crazy to go fast on this path, but if he rode too slowly, the loose rocks made it difficult to steer. When he pedalled faster, he could keep the steering in control. Paul now flew over the rocks and swiftly began his descent.

As the road ahead curved, he followed the bend of the steep mountain wall, making sure to be careful, using the hand brakes to help stay on track. Paul couldn't see the village yet, and after about ten minutes, he took a break to relieve himself against the mountain. It was then he felt his stomach knot up in hunger – he'd been so rushed he'd forgotten to eat anything. On top of that, his palms throbbed and pulsed from gripping the shaking handlebars. Paul looked around, taking in the spectacular view of the mountain. It made him think of Jane, she would've loved this. Though he didn't know whether or not she'd even look at it, Paul took a picture and sent it to Jane with a message. It read,

<Although the mountain is high and the valley is low, they belong together, despite their differences. I love and miss you. I'm sorry, please come back!>

He added some hearts and kissing face emoticons, then hit the send button. As Paul continued his bumpy journey, a car appeared in the distance. It was heading slowly towards him. Perhaps he could convince whoever was in the car to stop and taxi him back down. He'd pay well. As it got closer, the vehicle honked. Paul stopped to wave his hands, trying to flag the driver down. Only, when the car got close, the man driving it simply looked at Paul, waved with a smile, and continued on his way.

"That's just great," Paul grumbled to himself, "He thought I was just waving 'hello'." He mounted the bike again and kept going. After two more turns, he saw the city-bound bus in the distance crawling along the path toward the valley. And just like that, Paul *knew* Jane was on it. His pulse quickened - he might be able to catch her before she got to the city.

Surging with adrenaline that now tingled up and down his spine, Paul was suddenly sure he could catch up with the bus. He could picture Jane's face now, shocked and in awe of him as he overtook the bus and forced it to stop. Then, he could go to her, apologizing and explaining everything - after handing her the flowers and chocolate bar of course. As Paul pedalled faster and faster, a huge smile spread across his face. Yup - everything was going to be just fine.

At that moment, another climbing vehicle appeared in the distance. It was a pick-up truck. As the truck got closer, coming toward him, the driver honked, but Paul didn't want to lose any time – he kept biking. Right before passing, the man beeped again, yet he didn't leave much space on the path. Paul was forced to ride close to the edge. He didn't dare look down, but he could *feel* the emptiness next to him. It was way too close for comfort.

Squeezing the hand brakes, the bike suddenly slipped just as the truck passed. Thankfully, instead of slipping off the edge, Paul was able to steer towards the mountain wall – just barely. "Agh," he cried, hitting the ground hard. As soon as he collided with the ground, Paul felt a pain shoot through his right hand. The pick-up truck must not have seen him, or just didn't care, because he didn't stop. Trying to let the pain and shock pass for a few seconds, Paul then pushed himself to stand up.

"Ow," he said, wincing at the pain in his hand as he pushed off the ground. He looked down to see that his hand was scratched and a little bloodied, but not too bad. His gaze shifted to the bike, which now had a completely broken gear-shifting cage plate. "Shit - double shit," he muttered. He knew enough about bikes to see it would be nearly impossible to ride now.

But, Paul was beyond determined to catch that bus. He hopped back on the bike and checked to see if the wheels could still rotate. He smiled – they could. He might not be able to pedal, but he *could* simply let himself roll down. If the rest of the path was like it had been, it was only ten more kilometres down and he could let gravity do the work for him.

So off he went, a little dangerously without being able to pedal, but it worked just fine. Paul looked far ahead. The bus was still up there. Lightening his grip on the handbrakes somewhat, the bike sped up, coasting downward faster and faster. The path followed the shape of the mountainside and now turned again.

All of the sudden, a wide pick-up truck appeared at the curve. Paul's hands pressed the brakes as hard as he could, heart leaping into his throat. But, it was no use. The tension in the right handbrake was gone – it had broken in the fall and now Paul couldn't stop.

The truck driver smoked a cigarette and drove with one hand as loud music blared from his truck radio. The man knew this road so well, he didn't usually need to pay much attention. He shifted the engine into second gear. Paul began to panic - *really* panic now.

Heart slamming out-of-control in his chest, he had to make a decision and fast – he could either crash into the pick-up, slam into the mountain wall or roll off over the edge. "*Damn it all to hell*," he cried out in his head. None of those choices would end well. But, at the last second, the truck driver saw this poor young man on his bike, coming toward his pick-up at an alarming rate. The man hit his brakes – hard. He watched as the young man lost control. As a quick reflex the driver spun the steering wheel towards the side of the road to give the biker more space. Too little, too late.

As if in slow motion, the man watched as the poor young man released the handlebar, the front wheel of the bike flipping, and flew forward through the air. The biker held his hands over his head in protection and a short but gut-wrenching yell reverberated all around.

Both the young man and his bike flew straight off the edge and disappeared into the darkness below. Gaping for a moment at where the young man had disappeared, the driver then shivered from the horror of it. But, he soon shook it off and quickly hit the gas. There was no way he'd be held responsible for the death of a foreigner. And for that very reason, he decided not to tell anyone about what had just happened and continued on his way.

WAKE-UP

BRUCE WAS PISSED off. He and Thomas had adapted their sleeping schedule because of him, yet Paul was nowhere to be seen on Skype and they'd already waited for two hours. Although it rang, Paul didn't answer his phone either. What was he doing over there?

Bruce thought bitterly, *"He's probably hanging around with his teacher girlfriend and getting some 'private lessons'."* The fact was that they needed Paul's input - badly. Thomas was showing more patience with the situation, and smiled after watching the RC-racer kitchen video. That newbie girl was right on target. Heaving a sigh, Bruce decided to start reviewing the software changes Paul had suggested. In his email he kept referring to the reworked racer software. Bruce knew he had to make a jump, but didn't quite understand what this newbie had done. So he kept on crunching the code.

* * *

Jane walked into the central bus station. It was crowded today because the city hosted its monthly market, making all the platforms packed with booths. Locals had dragged all kinds of products from their villages, anything from heaps of fresh vegetables to squawking chickens in cardboard boxes. She spotted some other travellers lugging huge backpacks, just coming off the night bus.

After a ten-minute wait in the queue for a ticket, Jane decided to grab a latte in one of the cafes. "*Ah, that hits the spot,*" she thought, sipping from the rejuvenating beverage. She looked up and saw that a backpacking couple stood right there. "Excuse us, but you seem like you'd know," the woman, who had an American accent, spoke, "Are there any mountain guesthouses you'd recommend?" Jane put down her cup and smiled.

"Most of them are good," she answered, "Just grab a bus and look around a bit." From there, all three got to talking. The couple seemed really nice, and right around her age, so she invited them to have cup of coffee with her. "And look what happened after doing the Annapurna - I'm still not walking completely normal yet," Jane declared, lifting a pant leg to show the edges of her foot injury.

The young woman, Lisa, gasped, "Holy crap, that looks painful." The guy, named Tom, raised his eyebrows.

"You had the guts to do the Annapurna? I'm impressed," he said. Jane waved off their comments, but her smile was full of pride.

"It wasn't all *that* hard, when you go, just stick to path and follow the stacked stone markers. Then you'll be fine," Jane assured them. She got a nice ego boost, obviously the expert backpacker among the three. Trying to convince the couple to try it out, she added,

"Just relax and don't overthink it, otherwise you'll talk yourself out of a truly beautiful trail." After a few more minutes of chatting, Lisa drained the last of her cappuccino.

"Well, we have to head out, but it was awesome meeting you Jane – and thanks for the trekking tips." Jane smiled as Lisa and Tom stood to head on, though she felt a little sad to lose their company. She'd been feeling a little lonely since leaving Paul. "Nice to meet you guys too, and good luck."

After they'd gone, Jane turned her phone on in order to book a flight. A new message caught her attention – it was from Paul. She felt a wash of emotion at seeing his name. While reading his text, the backs of her eyes began to prickle. It was sweet. Maybe he was right about the low valley and the high mountain belonging together - it was a very romantic metaphor.

Jane studied her phone, wiping a bit of moisture from her eyes, and began to question if she'd made the right decision to up and leave or not. It'd been fun trekking in the mountains with Paul up until her injuries, and him virtually ignoring her. When he'd missed their restaurant date, it had been the last straw.

And it showed Jane that he didn't truly need or even want to be with her. At least that's how it'd felt recently. Closing her eyes, she began to gently rub her temples. Paul was in her head and a storm of emotional conflict raged inside. Had her decision been too quick and impulsive? Was he or was he not the right one for her? "I should call him," she muttered to herself, phone halfway to her ear.

Then she paused. What was she doing? Paul had been totally at fault here. "No, I'm not going to act so hastily. I'll call him once I'm back home, when my head's a little clearer," she told herself. After four hours of endless waiting, Jane went back to the bus platform. She looked around, noticing that other travellers seemed upset about something. What was going on? The man who had sold the ticket to her earlier waved her over. "What's happening?" she asked him.

"You need new ticket – bus trouble." And he went on explaining in a very thick accent, all while taking her old ticket, tearing it in half and handing her a new one. Pointing to the updated departure time and date, Jane saw that it was for tomorrow. Though she hadn't understood everything he'd said, she understood it had something to do with a land slide.

She heard others arguing about the change in schedule, but

she was tired and just wanted to find a place to stay. The city guesthouse next to the bus station was cosy – it would do well for one night. After checking in and putting her bags in a storage locker, Jane wandered into the lobby, warming by the nice fire crackling in a stone fireplace.

"Hey, you following us?" A woman's voice suddenly sounded right next to Jane. She looked up in surprise to see none other than Lisa and Tom – the nice American couple.

"We heard about the land slide and the bus," Tom said, "You stuck here for the night?"

"Yeah," Jane answered with a sigh, though she was happy to have company again.

"Hey," Lisa turned to her, eyes sparkling, "Why don't you join this party tonight, it's going to be just around the corner, and a bunch of backpackers are gonna be there."

"Sounds fun," Jane said, "But I think I need to unwind a little first. Could you come by my room, number eight, and knock right before heading over?"

"Sure," Tom replied with a nod, "Not a problem. We'll get you there, even if we have to drag you," he added teasingly. Jane laughed, then headed for her room, bidding the two goodbye for now. She was exhausted and really did need a rest.

Lying on her bed, she grabbed her phone and looked at the picture Paul had sent her again. Heaving a sigh, she texted him back.

<Let's take some time apart, then get in touch when I'm back home, okay?>

She bit her lip as she pressed send, pushing down a surge of sadness, and even a little guilt. Was this too harsh? Or would he barely bat an eye? Jane shook her head, "Do something else, stop thinking about it over and over," she muttered to herself.

Luckily, the Wi-Fi there was fast, so Jane immersed herself in checking email and social media status of her friends, as well as reading the news. It definitely helped get her mind off of Paul.

However, forty minutes later, Jane's mood had gotten worse as she lay on her bed. With a mix of anger and hope, Jane pulled out her phone again. Her message to Paul had been successfully delivered, but he hadn't replied. Why - was he busy working on the bear problem again and too busy to notice her text?

She sat cross-legged on her bed, head spinning again from this mix of emotion. Her resolve to not call him had weakened. Jane touched his name under her contacts. She wouldn't say sorry – not at all. He was the one who had to apologize to *her*.

Riiing, riiing – it kept going with no answer. That asshole - he was obviously ignoring her on purpose. Well, he could forget it! Just then, a knock sounded on her door. It must be Lisa and Tom. Perfect timing - she needed help getting out of this funk over Paul. Jane opened the door with a welcoming smile.

"Ready to 'get your groove on'?" Lisa asked with a grin.

"Hell yeah," Jane replied, laughing as she held up her injured foot, "But I'll 'groove' on the side with my good foot!" Tom and Lisa smiled.

"No problem," Lisa assured her, "You'll really like the club. We've already been and all the stranded travellers seem to be there. It'll be fun, maybe you'll even meet a cute guy." Lisa gave Jane a cheesy wink for good measure. Jane felt a twist in her stomach.

She hadn't told them about Paul. But, she forced out a laugh. And, who knew, maybe she would find a guy – one that would actually pay attention to her. She fluffed her light brown hair, and left for the party with Tom and Lisa. Jane was really looking forward to meeting new people, she was eager to make new friends.

* * *

Paul slowly opened his eyes and saw thousands of stars shining down on him. *"They are all suns and some of them might be galaxies. I wonder which ones?"* he mused to himself in a half-daze. He was lying on his back in a place that was completely enclosed in darkness. It was also completely unfamiliar.

Sniffing the fresh, cold air, Paul surmised that he was outside. *"Where the hell…"* he began to think to himself. Then, after several long moments, it all came rushing back. A slow panic seized Paul as he saw startling flashes of the oncoming pick-up truck and his bike slipping in his mind.

Paul gave an involuntary shudder at the memory, which then triggered the fact that his back was in severe pain. How long had he been knocked out, lying there? His automatic response was wanting to sit up, but something told him that wouldn't be such a good idea. Besides, he was too tired and it seemed his body was having trouble moving.

He soon became sleepy again and couldn't resist the urge to close his eyes. "Just for a moment," he muttered to himself. As soon as his eyes fell shut, Paul slipped back into a state of unconsciousness. Only when his phone began vibrating inside his pocket did Paul wake back up. He knew sitting was not an option, so he tried to inch his left hand towards his pocket.

But it was useless, he couldn't feel his left hand. Was it even still there? It was too dark to see. Thankfully, his right hand seemed to be working okay, and he slowly moved it into his pocket to search for his phone, which had now stopped buzzing. His fingers felt the crinkly paper of the chocolate bar from Djired, and he realized he was ravenous.

Paul brought the bar up to his mouth, tore open the wrapper with his teeth and devoured the milk-chocolate. His body rushed with new energy. He then reached back with his right hand and pulled out his phone. "*Thank god it's not broken,*" Paul thought as he saw its display like a torch in the darkness. Holding the phone in front of his face, he used his thumb to browse.

But damn it if the "low battery" warning didn't keep interrupting. It went into power saving mode. He gasped to see twenty missed calls - the last was from Jane. With his right hand shaking, Paul pressed the "call back" button and carefully brought the illuminated phone to his ear.

Though he knew she might be mad, he was in a serious situation here, it really couldn't get much worse. He needed Jane's help, and fast. It took some time, but after several very long seeming moments, Paul heard a soft ringing come from the phone's speaker. And it kept ringing. Damn. Where the hell was she? "*Please, please answer,*" he thought desperately, "*My phone's about to die!*"

Just before her voicemail picked up, he heard Jane's voice – she'd answered at last. There was a lot of noise in the background on her end, "Hello - hello?" Her voice crackled through.

"Listen Jane," Paul said urgently, "We can work this out, but…' *click*. The call was disconnected. He had to keep trying, it was his last chance. Dialling again, he heard Jane yelling into her phone.

"Hi Paul, I can't hear a thing. There's bad reception here in the club." Club? Shaking his head, Paul opened his mouth to quickly explain the situation, but she spoke first. "Sorry Paul, you should've made plans with me." It sounded like Jane had been drinking – a lot. She kept talking, not letting him get a word in edgewise. "I'm kinda busy here. Sorry they're about to play my favourite song. Please stop calling me. I'll call you when I'm home." And with that she hung up.

Blinking at the screen, Paul's heart sank. The 'low battery' warning flashed once more, then his phone went black – it was utterly dead. "Just like I'm going to be soon," he mumbled in

despair, "I've no way of contacting anyone now." His head thud-
ded back down on the cold, hard ground. She'd let him down.
Was this really how he was going to die? Was this the end? He
still couldn't even sit up, much less stand, and no one knew
where he was.

A mountain breeze swept through, causing shivers from the
bone-chilling cold. Silent tears rolled down Paul's cheeks. He
drifted into a dark, disturbed kind of half-conscious state. At
some point later, a very distant voice echoed through his ears. He
must be dreaming, or was he in the 'after-life'? All was quiet for
a moment.

Suddenly, he heard it again, this time more clearly, "...on the
charging pillow please" It couldn't be...was that Teddy2 talking?
The next instant, Paul woke up. And he didn't care how idiotic he
sounded calling out to a teddy bear. He cried, "Teddy2 - Teddy2
is that you?" Silence greeted him. Paul tried to half-sit up and
turned his head in the direction of the voice.

He called out again, with every ounce of energy left in him,
"Teddy2!"

"Hi Paul," the bear answered after a moment, "Can you put
me on my charging pillow please?" Paul smiled and laughed all
at once.

"Emergency call please!" Teddy2 responded immediately,

"I'll switch on position detection...no emergency contacts
available here. Please phrase emergency phone number."

Paul didn't have any phone numbers memorized since everything was stored in his phone. Suddenly he remembered the two
bears chatting with each other the other day. With his last ounce
of energy Paul raised his voice once again,

"Emergency call Ada2 please!"

"Emergency sequence initia..." But Teddy2 never finished that
sentence, instead saying, "Please put me on my charging pillo...

Powering off now." Paul closed his eyes, now in utter despair. *Now* he truly knew he didn't have a chance in hell to survive. It was dark, freezing and he really had no way of contacting anyone. His heart sunk to the pit of his stomach.

A strange kind of calm acceptance soon came over Paul. He felt utterly exhausted, but he couldn't feel the coldness anymore. He really couldn't feel anything whatsoever. And so he was ready to die. A deep need for sleep overwhelmed his mind and body. The last thing Paul remembered was the fact that he was falling asleep and he didn't expect to wake up again.

***

Bruce, Thomas and Rafael were all on the group Skype call listening carefully to a newbie racer, '2Fast4U'.

Her name was Therese and she tried to explain it again. "With that jump I simply bypassed the start-up software boot sequence." Thomas scratched his neck as Therese continued. He didn't know much about this particular part of the software. It was more Paul's thing.

Bruce interjected, "You mean you used a tweaked RC car to wake your own car up? Am I getting that right?"

"Yeah," Therese answered softly, "I pushed a new start-up software and after the…" Thomas now cut in,

"You're absolutely sure? And were you able to continue to run it off-line?"

"Yeah, of course I'm sure," the seventeen-year-old girl told him, "That's why I put the video of my kitchen test drive on-line."

"Holy crap," Thomas declared, "This means that, in theory at least, we can upgrade the bears' software."

"That's right," Therese said, "But only when you're in close range. By the way – I also noticed a wrong pointer and…" Just then, they were all interrupted by a bunch of noise coming into the conference call. Apparently Rafael had disabled his mute while driving.

"Guys, do I understand that we can somehow wake up the bears?" he asked.

"Yes," Bruce told him, "We can push special new software locally to the bears and upgrade them."

"And," Thomas jumped in, "We can use the bears to upgrade each other. If we upgrade a few bears, they can upgrade other bears which can upgrade others and so on and so forth. It'll develop exponentially."

"That's not a good idea," Bruce interjected, "We can't ask the bear's owners to upgrade each other's bears."

"Yes we can," Rafael argued, "This is great – it sounds like a hibernation wake-up."

"What do you mean?" Thomas asked, cocking his head in confusion.

"If we tell the kids that they're able to help other children with their upgraded bears," Rafael explained, "That's the solution right there."

"You mean…?" Thomas prompted.

"Yup," Rafael answered with confidence, "I mean we organize a worldwide bear wake-up from hibernation and let children play with each other in the process. We can use the retail chains to initiate the roll-out."

"The only problem is that, well," Bruce said sceptically, "You see, the bears burp after an upgrade."

"Not a problem at all," Rafael laughed, "We can explain that, hmm…oh I know, we tell them that's what bears do after hibernation."

"Hello world," Thomas said jokingly in a low sleepy voice after burping, "Has spring arrived?" Everybody laughed. Therese felt a proud glow at being able to help the team.

"Listen guys," Rafael added, "You continue to chat while

I call Maria to see how we can use this hibernation wake-up method. In the meantime, you guys do a careful double-check and verify that this is actually possible."

"Relax Rafael," Thomas smiled, "It's technically feasible - we've seen the video."

"Okay then," Rafael said, "We only have to organise, explain and execute. Well done everyone."

"Please support these guys with everything you need," Bruce said, "Prepare a demo or something and make it work. This is amazing, we're preparing a worldwide hibernation wake-up!" Bruce was especially thrilled because he'd been feeling responsible for all the problems.

"If we can upgrade them," Bruce added, "And get them to behave better, we might be able to convince the mobile operators to re-activate the bear's connectivity again. Thomas and Therese, can you both come over and work on a solution with us – please?"

"That's not possible," Therese answered softly, "My parents simply won't let me leave during school – sorry."

***

"So I think this is how we should go forward," Maria heard Rafael say over the phone as she sat in her dad's house, "I still trust this guy Maria. You know, we might still have a chance."

"But Rafael," she responded, "Does this mean we have to involve all of our retailers? A few days ago you called them grey, dusty, old economy guys."

"That's true," Rafael answered with a smirk, "I did, but we have to forget about that. We need all of them. And listen, if they want people coming to their stores to fix each bear, then we'll do it." Maria was silent for several beats, considering the options. But there were basically no alternatives and she commended

Rafael on his cleverness. A surge of excited hope swelled up inside as she told him,

"You're right, Rafael. This is the only way and I say we go for it!"

"That's the spirit," Rafael enthused, "I'm glad to hear you're on board Maria. I'll take the next plane and ensure that nobody leaves that Nepalese mountain before we have everything operational. Let's name this endeavour the 'hibernation wake-up'."

"Whatever you want to call it Rafael," Maria said with a laugh. She trusted him to pull this off.

Rafael added, "Let's wait and see how far the boys can get with the code. Can you check with FLQ-electronics and inform KMO-Telecom?"

"Absolutely," she said, though she cringed a bit at the thought of talking to Mr. Lee again. He'd been so pissed the last time she'd talked to him, but at least he hadn't gone through with the claim.

"And I'll initiate on my side and silently prepare the marketing aspect."

A blush of renewed excitement and hope crept across Maria's face – they could still salvage the bear project. Rafael wasn't really all as bad as she used to think. She went back into the living room and declared, "Dad, wait 'til you hear what we're up to!"

UNITE

THE NEXT THING Paul knew was that something bright and hot was shining on his face. It was the morning sun beaming down on his body as he lay there on a bed of small rocks, which he'd apparently been on all night. How had he not died? Shivering from the cold, Paul also felt an urgent thirst in his throat. His lips felt like cardboard, and he couldn't move his very swollen left hand.

Looking to the side, he saw the bike just a few meters away, its front wheel bent. He glanced down at his phone that now lay loosely in his right hand – still dead. And Teddy2 lay face down, still not responding to him, his batteries also dead. As he lay there, completely helpless, Paul heard a car passing by here and there in the distance. When he heard them, he tried calling out for help. No answer.

After a while, Paul managed to push his aching, stiff body into a semi-sitting position, pins and needles shooting everywhere in his body. After waking his body up a little more, Paul got himself to stand, though his back and joints sent jolts of pain through his body. But, when he feebly tried to walk, the loose rocks didn't allow him to climb. It was too steep and too slippery.

With a frustrated sigh, he laid down on his stomach this time, planning to try and crawl inch by inch back up to the road. While he was slowly and very painfully proceeding upwards, Paul heard a car screeching to a halt. "Paul…Paul are you there?" Holy shit! Somebody was calling him - someone had found him!

Heart beating out of his chest, he stood up but instantly fell down again. Adrenaline pumped through his body, he'd never felt so awake - so *alive* in his entire life. Paul yelled up with everything he had "Here! I'm here!"

"There," he heard a voice shout, "Over there. Paul, don't move, okay? We'll come and get you! *Don't move!*"

"Okay," Paul called out, nearly weeping for joy as a stream of gravelly stones tumbled down near him. "I'm here! Follow my voice - I'm right here!" And all of the sudden Paul saw Adam standing right in front of him. Adam looked him directly in the eye, frowning with concern.

"You must've had a tremendously difficult night." Paul felt the urge to cry, but was simply too tired. Then, Miriam appeared, quickly checking his injuries.

"Nothing too serious," she smiled, "You're one lucky guy." Paul couldn't agree more, he'd never felt such relief and pure happiness. He'd been rescued, He wasn't sure how, but his friends had found him. And he couldn't stop thanking them, over and over. Even though he'd been giving it his best shot to crawl back up, he never would've made it to the main road on his own.

Between Adam and Miriam, Paul was dragged back to their car. And there she was, in the back of the pick-up, now sitting right next to him – Jane. They just sat there staring at each other for several moments, not needing words. The depth of emotion that flitted through their eyes said it all.

Then, in the blink of an eye, they were kissing. Even as Adam and Miriam got back in to the front seats and drove down the road, they kept kissing – passionately. As if it was their last hour together. And it *had* almost been Paul's last hour. Jane eventually pulled back, gently stroking his almost four-day old stubble. She looked deeply into his eyes, her own filled with tears.

"Paul, I…I'm so sorry. For everything – I never should've left so abruptly. And it took me a while, but I finally understood Teddy2's message."

"Please don't apologize," Paul assured her, his eyes tearing up as well, "It was all my fault - I was such an idiot and I'm sorry. I'd realized how stupid I'd been, and was biking to catch up to your bus. But this truck came, and the path was too narrow - I slipped." Jane gave him a quick, emotional kiss and pulled back.

"Thank you," she said softly, "I can't believe you actually tried to chase after my bus on a bike!"

"That was pretty foolish too," Paul grinned, "But I had to stop you from leaving. Jane, you saved me. If you hadn't figured out Teddy2's message, I…I would still be…" But Jane just smiled and silenced him with a kiss. Then, she gently lay him down in the backseat, brushing the ruffled hair off his forehead.

"It's okay now," she whispered, "Everything is, well, more than okay now."

After helping him drink some of Miriam's water, Jane held Paul's head in her lap, letting him rest for the remainder of the trip back to the guesthouse. Djired was already preparing a second hammock just for Paul, after hearing the news of his injuries. As Jane helped him out of the truck and into the room, Paul winced quietly at the pain in his ribs.

And when Jane tried to help him take off his clothes in the bathroom, the pants stuck to the wound on his knee. "Stop," he cautioned, "When you take them off, the wound will probably start bleeding again." Jane nodded and was prepared for this as she grabbed a pair of scissors she'd brought just in case.

"Don't worry," she told him, "We'll buy some at the shop

down the road." Jane finished cutting the pants and shirt away and was now washing his injuries with warm water. As the soothing water ran down his back, Paul felt a strong happiness – he was here with Jane and alive. Adam came in, handed him athletic pants and a fancy colour-printed shirt with a local beer brand logo on the front. Paul raised an eyebrow.

"What kind of shit is this?" he asked.

"It's not that bad actually," Adam grinned, "And the bottle is in the fridge and waiting to be poured."

Ten minutes later they were all down eating some delicious spaghetti and meatballs made by Djired and drinking ice cold beers to match Paul's new stylish shirt. Jane looked at Paul and told him, "I asked, but the doctor isn't in the village today." Paul took a long draught of his bottle before saying,

"I think I'm fine, I don't need a local butcher."

"Don't exaggerate so much," she said with a laugh as she walked over to the map on the wall, "And try to act like a real man Paul van Dijk. A few hours ago you were crying, remember?" She kept studying the map even as she spoke.

"No I don't remember," he teased. As Jane passed by, Paul playfully tapped her bottom and said, "I think we need to clean our room - and you know, funny thing – one of the local practices is to close the curtains when you clean a room."

"Forget it Paul," Jane teased back, "Your ribs need rest for at least six weeks."

"Six weeks?" he protested. She looked at him, still with a playful smile on her lips.

"At least six - that's what they say," she insisted.

"Okay, if that helps," Paul replied, "I promise I won't clean or cook for the coming six weeks." Jane responded with a gentle whack on the back of his head with a rolled up magazine and smiled.

"That's not what I meant, and you know it," she exclaimed.

Paul laughed and tried to escape from the table with his beer bottle in hand, almost falling over as he went.

* * *

Maria counted down fifteen minutes on her watch and redialled the French phone number. She waited and heard the ringing on the other end. The newbie's parents were surprised when they spoke with Maria.

They'd seen their daughter playing with a remote controlled car and her dad had wondered if she wasn't perhaps getting too old for that kind of childish thing.

He hadn't understood why Therese was so excited when her car suddenly drove through the kitchen and crashed into the wall. Maria used a somewhat impatient tone as she explained to Therese's dad, once again,

"We've used the same technology in the problematic UN-bears as is used in the RC-racers. Your daughter has found a solution and we want to implement this into our bears as soon as possible. We need Therese's help sir. If she could fly to Hong Kong and join the development team for a week that would be great…Yes, we'll cover all expenses."

"But, you see there's a problem," her dad explained, "My daughter has school, and besides she's never left France before." Maria held back an irritated sigh and answered,

"We're willing to offer Therese, you and your wife a flight to Hong Kong, and will pay for you all to stay in a nice hotel. Make a small family holiday of it." This was almost too much for Therese's dad, Phillipe, had to work in the same mediocre office job his entire life. They'd never had the money for these kinds of holidays. Now, suddenly they were given the opportunity to go to Asia for a week – and all for free? It was difficult to grasp.

When it finally sunk in, Phillipe began to get excited and tried to persuade his wife. "Listen honey, it has to do with those

UN-bears. Our Therese has presumably found a clever solution. Why don't we give her this opportunity? I'm sure we can explain it to her school." Therese's mom, Catherine, shook her head.

"Therese needs to go to school - I won't let her lose her focus this year. Don't you remember the beginning of the semester, when we promised the teacher to fully support Therese in her studies? She's so bright, but spends more time sitting in front of her computer than on homework. This year Therese has the chance to reach the level for going to university. I won't let toy teddy bears interfere with our plans."

Of course, her husband had also been upset over half a year ago when the police had explained that their daughter had broken into other people's computers. Although she hadn't damaged anything, Therese had to promise to not do it ever again. If she did, they'd prosecute her. Both Phillipe and Catherine had been surprised, but after a serious talk with Therese, she promised to stop all hacking attempts.

"*And now,*" Phillipe thought with pride, "*Our daughter has the chance to help somebody – a whole lot of people actually - by using her computer.*" However Catherine wouldn't budge, not even with the prospect of a free holiday. Maria decided to give the two time, waited fifteen minutes, and called them back, this time with Catherine answering.

"No, I won't allow it," she held firm, "Therese won't leave this city and has to focus on her schoolwork." Then Catherine listened attentively to Maria for several minutes. Phillipe saw his wife listening and nodding, then she spoke.

"Okay," Catherine finally said with a growing smile, "That sounds good…yes…okay thank you we'll discuss that later on." She ended the call and turned towards Phillipe with a very wide smile across her face. "Can you believe it?" she told her husband, "They're coming over here to talk about it. I guess they're desperate."

"Wonderful," Phillipe said, grinning from ear to ear, "And will she also get paid?"

"Yes," Catherine beamed, "They'll prepare a contract with quite a nice amount."

"Catherine," Phillipe said, putting his hands in the air in excitement, "This is fantastic, our Therese can save the bears with her computer. She's the doctor in the house!"

* * *

The noise of a helicopter hovering over the village filled Paul and Jane's ears as they slowly woke up. He mumbled, "There must be an accident up the mountain." They'd both slept very well and decided to stay in the hammocks.

"My bones are in agony," Paul groaned. Jane's eyes still remained closed as she sleepily replied,

"You guys are always exaggerating – so dramatic." Then she opened her eyes and tilted her head. "It sounds like it's landing to pick up the doctor," she commented, "I hope whoever it is turns out okay."

Paul had fully woken up now and browsed through his messages while he smiled softly to himself - the guys had found a solution to push new firmware into one of the bears. "Clever," he muttered, impressed.

After replying with a 'thumbs-up' symbol, Paul activated the airplane mode and looked at Jane. "How are you doing, honey?" They were now holding each other's hands as they slowly swung in their side-by-side hammocks.

"I'm fine," she responded, then joked with a squeeze of his hand, "But you made me miss my flight." Paul turned his head to look into her bright green eyes.

"You really want to leave this place huh?" he asked. She was silent for a few moments.

"You know," she finally answered, "After I slid down the mountain path, I just wanted to go home straight away. I've been having nightmares about sliding into dark chasms ever since." "Actually," Paul said, "We're both having that same nightmare now."

"Yeah," Jane gave him a sympathetic look, "Yours must be even worse since you were alone. So, I say let's go home and get the bears working, recover a bit and then go to a warm white-sands paradise island without mountains. And with room service." Paul coughed in surprise, then chuckled.

"I'm in," he declared, "I never want to go on a holiday without swim trunks again – *ever*."

At that moment Adam came in and gave them both high fives in greeting. "Did I hear something about mountain trekking in swim trunks? I'm not sure if that's a good idea. They expect snow for the next few days up here."

Jane exchanged a pointed look with Paul and said, "What on earth are we doing? Let's get out of here!" Before Paul or Adam could respond, Djired came in leaving the door open behind him.

"Yes, here they are sir," he said looking at someone behind him.

"Hello young backpackers! Are you stranded?" A man's voice boomed out. Paul and Jane exchanged a puzzled look - they recognized that voice. They both turned to look at the door from their hammocks,

"Ishmael," Jane cried out, "Sorry… Rafael. What the hell - I mean it's good to see you, but what are you doing here?"

Paul mutely stared as Rafael Silva walked in with two backpacks, a blue and a red one. He'd actually done it, like he'd promised a few days ago – the backpacks were for Miriam and Adam. This guy was astonishing. Rafael smiled widely.

"Today I'm your taxi service – it's back to civilisation for you both." Rafael told the two. Jane still couldn't quite believe her eyes as she blinked at him.

"Hey," she suddenly asked, "Who's he?" She pointed to a man dressed in a pilot uniform behind Rafael.

"This is Dave, the chopper guy," Rafael said. Dave took his sunglasses off and tapped his forehead.

"Good morning. We have to hurry because the weather is changing."

"You're picking *us* up?" Jane asked as her jaw dropped, "We're leaving right now?"

"Yup," Rafael nodded with a grin, "That's the plan Paul and I discussed a few days ago." Before a shocked Jane could say anything Dave added,

"We have to leave within five to ten minutes." Rafael threw the red and blue backpacks to Adam who caught them easily.

"These are yours," Rafael told him.

Jane arched an eyebrow at Paul. "Why didn't you tell me about all of this? I wouldn't have had to take the bus." Paul looked from Rafael to Jane and almost whispered as if in awe,

"I never dreamed he'd actually do it," admitted Paul.

"Well," Jane added wryly, "If he's crazy enough to put money on our heads, he's crazy enough to pick us up and hover us down." Paul started coughing again which hurt his ribs.

"Give us ten minutes Dave," Paul told the chopper guy. Within minutes they'd grabbed their belongings and were saying goodbye to Miriam and Adam, everyone quickly hugging, exchanging emails and well-wishes.

Paul went to pay Djired down at the front desk. "Thanks for letting me use your computer and bike. You're lucky that I only crashed the bike and not the computer." He joked.

Djired chuckled, then said with a smile, "That is $80, to get another bike please." After obliging him and saying goodbye, Paul walked with Jane to the helicopter that was parked on an empty field close to the village. They smiled at the sight of some children who were walking around it, cautiuosly touching the sitting copter.

Once Dave, Paul, Jane and Rafael were in and the doors had clicked shut, everyone tightened their safety buckles and put on their headsets. Dave started the engine, glancing worriedly at the darkening clouds that moved towards them from the other side of the mountain. The snow was coming soon.

The helicopter generated a lot of dusty wind and slowly rose up. When it was about 100 feet above the ground, Dave turned its nose towards the valley. Children waved up at them as Paul and Jane waved back. One of them was carrying Teddy2 which Paul had given the child just before leaving.

Then Jane, Paul and Rafael let out a collective gasp as they flew over the canyon, now 1000 meters below. Paul pressed Jane's hand and shouted through the headset microphone, "I'm not liking this altitude!" She shouted back reassuringly,

"Don't worry silly, just don't look down."

LET'S DANCE

NIKOLE'S EYES WELLED up. The newspapers had sent a clear message that, "Politicians started the chain reaction network outages." She felt terrible after reading:

"According to the spokesman of one of the mobile operators they were forced to implement roaming guidelines which created a chain reaction of network outages in the EU-region. "We couldn't do anything about it. Our network was able to handle the traffic, but as soon the others went down, our network automatically took over all the traffic.

It was simply too much to handle and it got out of control. This is what we've always said. Governments should not interfere with market players like us. We, commercial mobile network operators - we know what our customers want: high quality and high speed mobile network connectivity. Just give us the frequency spectrum and we do the rest."

We tried to get in touch with both local and European authorities on the issue, but the spokesman stated that 'the series of events is still under investigation.'"

As Nikole's eyes teared up, you could practically see the steam coming out of Theo's ears as he slammed his flat hand on the table in his office. "Nikole, you've made a mess of it. Why didn't you test this properly before rolling it out? We've the public and GSMA at our throats. This certainly doesn't help us during the negotiations of the upcoming frequency spectrum allocations. You simply washed money down the drain Nikole!"

Her tears quickly dried up and Nikole felt an indigent anger in place of her humiliation. She looked him straight in the eye, her face pale with conviction,

"Now you listen to me Theo," she told him in a low but firm voice, "I can imagine that this frustrates you. But instead of trying to be the 'technology-pusher' of the network vendors, I ask you to look at this carefully. Network robustness is something we've discussed numerous times, but you've always waved it away and wanted to leave it to market players. Last time we spoke about emRoaming was on a stage where you happily gave me flowers. You know, it wasn't us that crashed the networks Theo."

He stared silently as Nikole spoke, both impressed and calmed by her words. She added, "How far should we go as a government? If we push national roaming is that enough? Or perhaps we should own our own networks and offer wholesale services. But, that's ridiculous isn't it?"

"You're right," Theo said after a moment, "But I also believe that critical functions shouldn't rely on 'best effort' networks. I mean train, police, and ambulance communication as well as emergency signalling systems for earthquakes, tsunamis and things like that."

"Interesting ideas," Nikole smiled, "Though we don't have tsunamis here. But seriously, in the meantime we're depending on the commercial networks and, well, presumably children's teddy bears were able to take them down, Theo."

"This is simple statistics Nikole," he said with an eyebrow quirked, "This situation will never happen to us again I promise you." He paused, then pointed at her. "And if I survive this politically, you're going to help me achieve that Nikole."

* * *

It was a few days later, Friday evening, when Catherine, Therese and her RC-racing car all waited in a café close to their home in a suburb of Paris - waiting for them to arrive. Catherine felt a bit nervous as the front door opened. Her daughter instantly recognized the Dutch guy, who stumbled a bit and was accompanied by a dark-haired man in his forties.

They all grabbed some coffee, settled at a large round table and the older man, named Rafael, began. "Thanks for taking this time for us. It's good to meet you both - my name's Rafael Silva, from Idrel Toys in Atlanta and this is my friend Paul from Amsterdam."

"Nice to meet you too," Therese's mom smiled, "I'm Catherine and this is my daughter Therese. So, what exactly is it that you want with us – or more specifically, with my daughter?"

"It looks like we need some guidance from your daughter on an issue with our bears," Rafael said, "As Maria explained a little on the phone, these bears seem to behave the same as RC-Racers and Therese was able to get her car moving again. We saw the video she'd posted." Rafael glanced at Paul and continued, "Paul, can you explain a bit what the issue is?"

Paul went on, mostly addressing Therese since it was technical stuff, and told how he'd written the software and he was sure the solution lay deep down in the code. Therese put her car on the table and said, "It took me some time, but below the line it was quite easy to get it working." Paul was about to ask something but Rafael put his hand up to silence him.

"We're impressed by your work my dear. None of our employees or friends were able to fix it. My colleague Maria told me that you're very busy with school." Here Rafael gave a knowing glance at Catherine, then continued, "School is very important and should have you highest attention."

However, Therese wasn't really listening and proceeded to

open her laptop to search for some files. "Here," she said, "Let me search for the example. Sorry, I don't have it here with me, but it's a library file in which I inserted a hard coded jump."

"What do you mean?" Paul asked, curiosity piqued now, "Are you saying you've...?"

"Well," Therese explained, "When I was able to put the radio chip from my spare test car in test-mode, I could push a test-command to the car. So, I simply pushed a jump-command to bypass the default start-up procedure." Paul thought for a moment, then nodded as he fully grasped what she was saying.

"That's impressive Therese," he told her, "It sounds extremely promising. I didn't dive that deep to be honest, just took the standard libraries from the chipset manufacturer. I'd love to see more." Therese was about to tell him more about what she'd found, but Rafael interrupted their tech conversation.

"Sorry, this techy talk is too difficult for Catherine and me to follow." He gave Catherine a playful wink and continued, "Therese, it looks like you can give us a lot of help in solving our bear problem, and maybe with any future challenges our company faces." Catherine beamed with pride at the strong influence her daughter's findings had on these two men.

"Why don't you both come to our house tomorrow morning for coffee at around ten?" Catherine asked them eagerly. Rafael and Paul agreed, and after a bit more chit-chat, they ended their meeting. It seemed that newbie '2Fast4U' had just found a way to get on the good side of her parents, teachers and even the police by doing this noble project during her summer holiday.

* * *

"Please allow me to explain Mr. Lee," Maria said on the phone as she sat in her Atlanta office, "This isn't for Idrel or any of its partners, but for the children abroad who don't have access to learning materials. We have the learning tools, the systems and everything, and the only thing we need is to get the mobile connections to the bears properly up and running. You're the only one in the world who's able to help us with that."

Mr. Lee was silent for a while. Then he explained, "I'm definitely willing to assist, Ms. Drel, but you have to understand that we can't afford any more disturbances or outages in our network. We're still trying to restore our necessary system functions. If you give the bears access to our network right now, they'd go right down."

"I very much understand your situation," Maria said calmly but firmly, not letting herself be intimidated by this man who'd once threatened a claim against Idrel, "But our team actually found a solution, and I promise the bears will behave decently."

Mr. Lee didn't want to just say 'no' outright, so he politely pushed back by saying, "Ms. Drel, perhaps it's a good idea to certify your bears? I'm sure we have some people in our organisation who can assist your team on this, or at least get you in touch with IoT specialists."

Maria wasn't so easily dissuaded, and continued her persuasive pitch. "In three weeks I'll be in Korea along with Anthony, the director of the United Nations Children's Fund which is running the African bear-learning programme we're supporting along with Scry, the pop-star in your country. Do you know him?"

Mr. Lee knew both Scry and the Unicef-CEO, Anthony, very well. He'd been on stage with them during a TV show. But, Maria didn't wait for his answer and simply forged ahead, "It would be great if we could meet soon - in three weeks. Let's see how much progress the various teams have made with their work at that point in time."

A few months ago Maria never would've spoken with such authority to a company leader, but all the pop-star related attention she'd had to deal with in the last few months had boosted her level of confidence to new heights.

Mr. Lee was just happy he didn't have to commit to anything during the call and agreed to make some time available to meet with Maria. After hanging up, she quickly walked to Rafael's office. He gave her a little smile as she walked in and said, "Maria, what brings you to the sales floor? Are we behind with the figures?"

She closed the door, took a chair and looked at him with a serious expression. "Rafael listen, for Idrel it's now or never." He arched an eyebrow questioningly at her.

"What do you mean?" Rafael asked. She took a deep breath and plunged ahead.

"I want you to convince the mobile operators to allow the bears to use their networks again."

"Hmm," Rafael said as he thought about it, then replied, "That's like asking a beekeeper to entertain a few hundred bears on his meadow full of bee-hives and honey," Rafael smirked at his own analogy and continued, "I thought we agreed at the board meeting last week that from now on we'd only support local bear-to-bear functions. We skipped the upsell of content didn't we?"

Maria leaned forward in earnest and said, "Rafael, you were right from the beginning, I admit it. We should jump on top of this IoT opportunity." She leaned so close, he could smell her floral perfume and could see that she was absolutely convinced. Before he could respond, she added,

"This IoT innovation didn't only change my world, but also Idrel's identity. With help from the UN we still have potential to change the world and provide hundreds of thousands of children access to learning programmes. Nobody has ever had this capability before – this is the first time in human history. It's an amazing opportunity which we simply can't allow to slip away just because of a single board meeting with conservative members!"

"Maria," Rafael grinned, "Do I actually hear you saying that you want to bypass the advisory board?" She nodded with utter conviction.

"Looking back Rafael,' Maria said, "That meeting with the advisory board last week was about nothing. They haven't got a clue. During the discussion we had, all plans involving our toys-of-the-future faded away in a minute. I refuse to give up that quickly. I'm a different person now. And, as we speak the FLQ-electronics team is implementing the solution that the RC car hacker discovered. You and I know that if we bring the right people to the meeting and show the right things, Mr. Lee will be swayed."

She then said in a low voice, "I'm already chasing our Unicef contact to support us on this." Maria sat up straight again and finished in a regular voice, "We have Idrel Teddy bears distributed throughout the world in mass, but the only thing they're doing now is saying 'hello' or burping. I can't leave them like this. Rafael, it's up to us - you and I. We have the power within our grasp and we need to turn around the world. Are you in?"

* * *

Everything seemed to be normal again. Nikole was in her Brussels office with a steaming mug of coffee that morning. Theo was travelling and had forwarded an email to her, though she wasn't sure she could handle yet another email regarding those damn bears. With a weary sigh, she quickly scanned the long message sent by some guy from Idrel Toys named Rafael Silva. She only started to read carefully when she got to the middle.

"Pushed by our customers, we're thinking about relaunching the improved and upgraded products as SmartBears. Together with our stake holders (United Nations Unicef programme, producer FLQ and mobile operators) we're preparing this bear-relaunch programme.

Although our organisations don't have a direct relation, we share the same goals - to safeguard that we, and all of our partners, take the appropriate steps and precautions, I would appreciate if we could have a short informal discussion to ensure that European mobile operators are prepared for this. I want to emphasize our interest and…"

It continued on for a while, but Nikole stopped reading – it was clear to her that this was the manufacturer of the Teddy bears. "Unbelievable! Those idiots are planning to relaunch the bears," she muttered to herself. What would this mean for the European networks? Idrel's commercial intensions were obviously more important for them than safeguarding the networks which society depended on.

Nikole immediately called Theo, but all she received was the automated, 'In a meeting' message. Before she even knew what she was doing, Nikole dialled the US phone number which was at the end of Rafael's email. He was polite and open for discussion, which made Nikole relax a little. It was quite the coincidence that Rafael Silva happened to be in Belgium visiting a distributor at the moment. She found herself accepting his suggestion to meet for lunch the following day in Brussels.

The next day Nikole and her colleague Bjorn were waiting in the café Place de Londres, when a man in a well-tailored suit entered the place. Nikole instantly recognized him from his social media profile picture. After introductions, the waiter took their orders and Rafael got right down to it. "The reason I contacted you is because we've prepared a treatment for our bears." He looked directly at Nikole.

"A treatment - for children's bears?" She chortled. Rafael smiled at Nikole's response. He liked her – she spoke calmly yet with unwavering conviction. The way she seemed to carefully choose her words along with her elegant appearance impressed him.

"I'm serious about this," Rafael replied, "As the leading toy company we've taken responsibility and prepared a worldwide software roll-out." She played with the spoon in her cappuccino.

"The operators will never allow your bears to use their networks again Mr. Silva," she told him simply, "Are you aware how much damage you've caused?"

"As a company," Rafael persisted, "We never sought to make a profit with this project, only doing it for the common good. We just want to support the UN and offer lessons to children in third world countries. However," He paused, shifted in his chair then went on, "To be honest, we never expected so many people would order these bears. Looking back, it was too big for us - too many orders and zero time to run a pilot, which is apparently quite necessary with this technology."

"You mean," Bjorn asked, "You make no profit on any of this?" Rafael nodded and let out a breath before saying,

"Nope, nothing at all." Nikole took this time to browse the menu as she questioned without looking up,

"So, in that case, what's your hidden agenda Mr. Silva?"

"We don't have any hidden agenda Ms. Solon," Rafael told her. When she lifted her gaze to meet his, she could tell he was being sincere, but she didn't want him to know. She'd also decided to let him pay the bill.

"So what does Idrel want from us then, Rafael?" Nikole asked.

"That's right, what *do* you want?" Bjorn echoed as he poured some water from the fancy glass bottle. Rafael took a plastic bag from the floor and handed Nikole a package, then looked at Bjorn.

"Sorry, I only have one sample available."

Nikole arched a delicately shaped eyebrow and teased, "Well, I like presents. You're not trying to bribe me are you?" Rafael gave Bjorn a wink and answered,

"When I get the chance I will – but, no, I'm just joking." Nikole bit back a smile.

"What is it?" she asked as she unwrapped the parcel. A moment later she placed a teddy bear in the middle of the table leaning him against the bottle of water: "Well, I know what this is – they're quite cute in person."

"It's the only sample in Europe that's received the 'hibernation wake-up' treatment," Rafael answered, "We're looking for a launching operator. In the US they're still discussing claims and are too afraid to touch it."

Gazing pensively at the adorable bear, Nikole realized she liked that Rafael needed something from her – it made her feel powerful to be in this position. Rafael added, "The first operator will either be Asian or European."

Nikole's mind buzzed. Connectivity would make the difference between a normal bear and a SmartBear, and she knew what public opinion was - everybody wanted their smartphones to be able to control absolutely anything and everything these days. It would be good for Theo, herself and last but not least, good for Europe if they strode forward as a continent ready to support the SmartBears.

"I'm not sure if I can do anything for you Rafael," she looked from the teddy to Rafael, noting what deep brown eyes he had, "We're taking care of frequency spectrum and aren't being paid by citizens to spend time on teddy bears." Then Nikole glanced at her watch and said, "I don't mean to be rude, Rafael, but Bjorn and I need to go back."

Though Rafael knew she'd help him at this point, he acted desperate just for show. "Maybe you could at least try and ask them to have a look at it? I mean, you've got all the contacts. We're just simple toy makers." She took the bear and stood up with a half-smile.

"Duty is calling and we need to go. But, I'll call around and let you know."

"That would be very kind," Rafael nodded gratefully, "If you succeed I'll get you on stage with a pop-star."

"I'll hold you to that Rafael," Nikkole said with a laugh, "Shall I ask for the bill?" As Nikole had predicted, Rafael insisted on taking care of it and so they all shook hands and said goodbye.

The soft fur of Europe's first SmartBear felt nice in Nikole's hands as she and Bjorn walked back to their office. Yes, she'd help him.

UNO, DOS, TRES

A FEW DAYS later, Nikole stepped out of the taxi and paid the driver as Bjorn lit a cigarette then turned toward her. "So, what do you expect from me during this meeting?" A light breeze blew hair into her face and she quickly smoothed down her short brown hair.

"I simply expect clever questions, nothing more, nothing less." She shrugged.

The meeting had a nice open atmosphere as Tawfeek and Steve explained how the bears had caused an overload of the mobile networks in a way the operators had never dealt with before. Tawfeek patted Francis' shoulder with pride. "However, this hero here responded quickly. We were the first operator within the EU-zone to recover and withstand the attack of these 'horror bears'." Francis' cheeks reddened as he said,

"These networks are getting so complex that, for us as experts, we simply can't know everything, and neither can the suppliers. They've got experts on all subsystems, and I see ourselves more as integration experts who facilitate the product management and financial colleagues who want to have seamless invoicing systems working. For the long term..." Here Francis paused, looked at Tawfeek, then continued,

"For the long term I expect that we'll be able to operate using 'network-as-a-service' and run it as a cloud service."

"But," Bjorn said, "That means that we would end up with, let's say five networks worldwide, operated by vendors, right?"

"That's a good question," Francis started, but Nikole interrupted by taking a teddy bear out of her bag. Francis gave a short laugh and joked, "Clear the area! Here we have one of our little troublemakers."

***

That afternoon, Francis took the sample SmartBear to the back of his office area where the old network testing equipment sat. To his excitement, Tawfeek had agreed to 'play around' with this little guy that Nikole had left. So, Francis took the very ordinary looking bear from its charging pillow, turned it around and moved some fur aside to expose plastic housing sewn into the body.

Next to an old-fashioned SIM-card slot was a sticker with a handwritten note: "Message me before you test - paul@idreltoys.com" Francis sighed, waning to get on with the test. "I'll email him later." He proceeded to activate the network traces of the test system, slid a test SIM into the bear and watched as nothing happened.

"It's not working," Francis mumbled in disappointment after five minutes. He put the bear back on its charging pillow and decided to take a coffee break. As soon as he re-entered the area with a steaming cup of dark roast, Francis thought he heard a voice. Peering around, he saw nobody else in the room – all was dead silent except for the soft hum of some computers.

Taking the bear from its station, he shook it and a loud voice spoke, almost causing Francis to knock over his coffee. "Hello, let me be your teddy bear! What's your name?"

After recovering, a mischievous grin spread over Francis' face and he told the bear, "Nasier, my name is Nasier."

A few seconds later the bear responded, "Oh, that's a nice name, Nasier. My name is Ada. Can you put me on my charging pillow Nasier? I need to get some rest and energy before we continue to chat." Francis laughed. His colleague would have a fun surprise during his shift.

***

It was Saturday morning when Paul and Jane had a long skype chat, both wanting to be together again as soon as possible. Jane had decided that their dramatic, life-threatening experiences should be viewed as a test for their relationship – a test that they'd both passed with flying colours. She was more convinced than ever that they were soul-mates.

Paul was at Bruce's place now, but had already booked his flight to come be with her in two weeks, and Jane was full of anticipation. In the meantime, she was thankful to be back home. She didn't mind a nice hike here and there, but the adventurous mountain trek that they barely survived in Nepal was too much. Jane now sat on her bed in Seoul browsing through magazines, relaxing before heading out to meet with some friends.

As Jane looked through a gossip magazine she saw a picture of that Korean pop-star, Scry. "Oh shit," she muttered to herself, suddenly remembering, "I promised Paul I'd check out the Bear-IoT-platform." Tossing the magazine aside, she opened her laptop.

After a minute of scrolling through the platform, she still didn't see anything especially strange or notable. There were about thirty test bears in use and all of them seemed to be doing fine. But just as she was about to close her laptop, Jane noticed that SmartBear#3 had registered for the first time. She clicked the icon to learn more about the owner and found his name to be Nasier, somewhere in Europe.

Apparently this Nasier fellow hadn't responded to the introduction programme and so his bear was in the default 'Ada' mode. She quickly typed a request to Ada to ask if there was anybody around. Nobody answered Ada's question. Jane squinted as she read more information on this bear. It hadn't moved since it was activated and was on its charging pillow, but where exactly was this bear - an office, a home?

Her finger hovered over the mouse-pad, the cursor on the 'take-a-remote-photo' button, but she wasn't sure if she should go that far. Taking a picture would give her more information about the bear's environment, but it would go against Idrel's privacy guidelines. "It's probably being tested by an operator anyway," she told herself, deciding not to take the pic.

Instead Jane texted Paul asking what to do with this unused operator-test-bear and then headed into the shower. Her ankle and foot were almost fully recovered now and she decided that she deserved a new outfit. "I'll hit up the city tomorrow and shop around," she thought with a smile as the warm water ran down her face.

After she'd dressed and dried her hair, Jane had to hurry to meet her friends. Paul hadn't responded yet, and she decided to offer Nasier the Spanish learning module through the platform. That would at least generate some traffic, which was what mobile operators wanted to test, right?

***

Tuesday morning Francis and Nasier were in a meeting room waiting for their purchasing colleague to come and discuss some additional licenses they needed to buy. Nasier swivelled in his chair to face Francis and said, "Uno, dos, tres, déjame ser tu oso de peluche!"

Francis looked at Nasier like he'd lost his mind and asked, "What the hell's wrong with you?"

Nasier's expression remained serious as he continued, "Yo soy Nasier, cómo estás?" Then he broke into laughter and said, "That was a neat little joke you pulled with the bear Francis. How did you know we were planning a trip to Spain this summer?"

"Sorry," Francis blinked in surprise, "I had no idea. And what does the bear-joke have to do with Spanish?"

"Well," Nasier explained, "Since your bear, Ada, is teaching me Spanish, it has everything to do with it." Francis furrowed his brow.

"But it's a test bear and dead when I left it. Is she working now?"

"We had a great time during my shift – me and Ada," Nasier replied enthusiastically, "She taught me some Spanish."

"You're joking," Francis said, eyes widening and a smile growing on his face, "I only connected it to the test network and…" But he was cut off by the sound of his phone buzzing. It was their purchasing colleague calling to say he was stuck in a major traffic jam and asked to postpone the meeting.

After hanging up, Francis looked at Nasier. "He can't make our meeting, so shall we have a look at the bear?" Nasier nodded eagerly.

"Bueno," he said and with that, they rushed to Ada.

* * *

A few thousand kilometres away Paul and Jane were texting.

<u mean eubear#3 is active?>

<<yeah, but no user answer, I asked Ada – no help. I pushed Spanish lesson. Is ok?>>

<prfct. Plz don't touch now. They r prob looking at the ntwrk load. Will have a look too!>

<<thnx, and miss u ☺ x>>

<miss u 2!:) x>

<<btw – the user didn't email. Will just ask Ada to ask them to share findings. Ok?>>

<ok, x>

ON STAGE

BACK IN THE operator's office, Francis looked at the bear's log history file, then he and Nasier discussed the network behaviour and signalling in detail. Ada was behaving well, even better than an average smartphone app. During the night they saw she'd been active as well, probably loading data or updates.

"I've never seen a mobile device like this before - Ada's behaving perfectly. Let's let the test run for a week or so and see if she stays like that." Just then, the bear's microphone and standby functions detected a noise increase and she woke up. Waiting until she was sure she'd correctly recognized Nasier's voice, she surprised both of them saying,

"Hello Nasier, cómo estás?"

"Está bien!" Nasier answered with a smile. Ada went on,

"Nasier, can you do me a favour and email my maker? You can find his email address on the sticker of my back. He wants to know if I'm behaving." Francis' mouth dropped in astonishment as Nasier responded,

"Okay, Ada. I will."

"Thanks," Ada said, "I'm going to sleep again now. Bye!"

A stunned Nasier and Francis both said, "Bye Ada." Once Francis collected his swirling thoughts, he looked at Nasier.

"It's amazing," Francis declared, "I'll send this 'maker' all the log files we have." Nasier had grabbed Ada from her pillow.

"Can I take her home to show my kids?" he pleaded. Francis took Ada from him and turned her around to look for the email address.

"First let's give her a normal SIM-card okay?" he told Nasier.

"You want to give her access to the normal production network already?" Nasier asked with a frown.

"One single bear can't harm much, right?" Francis shrugged,

"Let's give it a try, and you can surprise your kids this weekend."

* * *

Mr. Lee was alone and sitting behind his desk on the 21st floor of the Seoul Headquarters' office. He watched the video taken with a smartphone on his laptop, yet again, while leaning back in his chair. The footage was a bit shaky as it showed some children playing with this new SmartBear, which suddenly began to talk. "Como estas?"

"Muy bien!" the kids gleefully replied with a giggle.

"Very good," the bear continued, "Well done! Let's continue. Please say: uno, dos, tres!"

"Uno, dos, tres!" the kids repeated excitedly.

"Muy bien," the teddy bear praised them. Then the view changed to show a smiling man who said,

"Sorry Francis, but the kids won't give Ada back. She's part of the family now. If you want her you'll have to come and get her. But, I think she's doing fine." The video ended.

Mr. Lee read Maria's accompanying e-mail again, "*As you can see the SmartBears are perfect. They were tested by a European operator that we gave samples to so they could investigate the emRoaming function they're required to support. Now that we've resolved the issue with our 'hibernation wake-up' software upgrade, this operator is so eager that they're pushing us to produce SmartBears for them."*

He paused to digest this information and continued re-reading, *"We can modify our production to give them the bears they want, but as strategic partners I would appreciate if we can discuss possibilities with you as our global service provider. I suggest we exchange ideas next week during an informal meeting. I'm travelling with my friend Anthony from Unicef to support his appearance on a charity auction being broadcast on TV. It's a popular TV-show where several big popstars will perform. Please let me know if you want to join us, and, if it's okay with you, I'll also bring Anthony to our meeting."*

It was all going so quickly, Mr. Lee could hardly wrap his head around everything. He'd received the confirmation from his chief of technology that a patch in the core of the mobile network would prevent any future signalling storms. No matter what kind of IoT-device it was, they could withstand it. He'd also looked at the SmartBear's network traces given by Maria's colleague Paul, and verified it with experts from his network supplier.

The bear's behaviour and resulting network traces all looked good with apparently no reason to delay the SmartBear relaunch. "Perhaps it's best if I do a pilot, just to be safe," Mr. Lee muttered to himself, though that wasn't really necessary. A knock on the door drew him from his thoughts. It was his administrative assistant announcing that Ms. Drel and the UN-representative were waiting in the board room.

When Mr. Lee came into the board room, he found Maria and Anthony gazing out the large window at the nice view of Seoul. "Welcome my friends," Mr. Lee shook both of their hands. Maria began with an apology,

"Sorry about the mess our bears have made."

"We can't blame you guys," Mr. Lee said with an understanding smile, "You were the first to try out a massive amount of IoT applications."

"It's true," Maria agreed, "We had to produce so much and were completely focussed on getting the bears shipped before Christmas. We didn't foresee their software generating so much trouble. You're very kind, but I'm truly sorry for causing this."

Here Anthony jumped in, "To be honest, it was our mistake Mr. Lee. The UN marketing team pushed this bear campaign. On behalf of the whole team, I'd like to ask you to forgive us."

Mr. Lee smiled and accepted the apologies, then said, "All networks, including ours, were apparently not ready for this. If it hadn't been your bears, it would've been caused sooner or later by another IoT application. So, please don't take the blame personally. We've all learned a lot and Maria…" Mr. Lee turned to look at her and said, "Don't worry, we won't proceed with any claims."

"Thank you so much," Maria said, letting out a quiet breath of relief. Mr. Lee nodded and continued,

"Our network vendors provided solid solutions and ensured that this will never happen again."

"Mr. Lee," Maria smiled, "That's very good to hear." She then proceeded to open a bag, unwrapped two identical bears and put them on the table.

"I do already have one at home you know." Mr. Lee gestured to the bears. Maria shook her head and pointed to the bear on the left.

"This one's different. It's received the 'hibernation wake-up' software and has a mobile connection with our central IoT SmartBear back-end system. That contains stuff like lessons and stories, and once a bear has gotten the hibernation wake-up treatment, it has access to that platform. But it won't work without your help." Mr. Lee looked at the bear on the left with a new respect.

"How does this hibernation wake-up work?" Mr. Lee asked. Maria thought for a moment, then looked at him.

"Don't laugh at me, okay?" she said.

"Ms Drel," Mr. Lee said with a smirk, "This is serious. I

promise I won't laugh." Suppressing her own smile, Maria had Anthony stand up and step next to the table.

"We need some space for this," she explained. After she'd given Anthony the SmartBear Maria told him, "Please keep it facing upwards against your body." She took the regular bear and looked thoughtfully down at her shoes for a moment. Then she took them off. "We can't have an accident just because of my heels."

Mr. Lee was now thoroughly intrigued as he watched Maria position herself in front of Anthony who was still holding the SmartBear. In a sudden motion, she moved her teddy bear three times up and down, turned 360 degrees and shook the bear three times. Then she firmly pushed the bear against Anthony's SmartBear in a kind of bear hug.

"SmartBear wake up please," she said loudly. Mr. Lee thought she must be making a joke, but held back his laugh. Maria and Anthony stayed put and kept silently holding the bears together, almost like they were dancing. She whispered to Mr. Lee, "It will take about fifteen seconds and then he'll wake up."

Sure enough, Anthony's SmartBear spoke, "SmartBear wake-up successful. You can take him home now. Please give my friend a few hours to wake up." Maria put on her shoes again and they all sat down.

"You see," she explained, "The bear's software has now been upgraded and works according to all the guidelines. It won't cause network trouble anymore. We now have two SmartBears in the room. The first one has already sent the identity of the upgraded bear to our central IoT Bear platform" Mr. Lee rubbed his chin, impressed.

"And," Maria went on, "I can forward the related mobile network subscriber details of the upgraded bear to you, ensuring that you only grant SmartBears access to the mobile networks."

"Upgrades through 'dances-with-bears.'?" Mr. Lee finally asked, "Amazing."

"That's right," Maria said with a little laugh, "It works seamlessly. We've tested it with a European operator who wants to roll this out in a few months. What should I do?" The silence buzzed with anticipation as Mr. Lee mulled everything over, all three of them gazing out at the Seoul skyline.

Mr. Lee finally broke the silence. "Please let us support you with your global hibernation wake-up and leave the connectivity to us. I'm sure if we take the right measures and test it during a pilot project, we can handle this for you guys."

Maria beamed at him. "That's wonderful to hear! Thank you for your trust."

* * *

Maria and Anthony sat in a TV studio room with a producer, two spokesmen from Idrel and Anthony. They were all about to go on a prime-time Korean show to explain what had happened with the bears, the mobile phone networks and talk about possible future plans.

During the show they'd keep track of how many social media spin-offs each participating member of the audience got, and whoever generated the most spin-offs would be declared the winner. It was a pity Scry couldn't attend since he'd initiated all of this. But, yet again, he needed to rest and recover away from the public eye.

Though Scry wasn't at the show, his songwriter was there to tell the audience how he'd come up with all the lyrics for the hit Christmas pop song. Also, Scry's manager and the producer had prepared a pre-recorded video message from Scry himself that would air during the show. The popular boy band, DuoDynos, however would be present and had attracted tons of media-attention and fans as well.

As the spokesmen sat in the room, waiting to go on, they came to a decision. "Okay, so it's agreed, no mentioning of the outages on-air," one of them said, "Let's focus on the money we're raising for projects helping children in need." Everyone, including Maria and Anthony smiled and nodded. The show had just started and they had to wait back-stage for about half an hour.

As the make-up artist put the finishing touches on everyone, Maria felt a wave of excited jitters wash through her. She started telling everyone in the room about their future plans. "And all the children have to do is a little dance with their SmartBears, and they can turn their friend's regular teddy bears into a SmartBear."

Maria's eyes gleamed as she added, "A SmartBear offers simple lessons like counting, teaching the alphabet and practical hygiene tips." Everyone was impressed and, of course, agreed to keep it secret.

Just then the sound of cheers and applause erupted from fans out in the audience – they could hear it even in the backstage lobby. DuoDynos had started to play and the audience was going through the roof. The stage coordinator popped his head in the room. "Just, to let you know, looking at the audience's reaction we expect a long 'we-want-more' chant and they'll probably do an encore. It might take an additional fifteen minutes before you go on stage."

"Fine, with me," Maria answered with a smile. They continued to chat and Scry's manager walked off to answer a phone call. A few minutes later, Scry's manager came back, phone in hand and face flushed.

"Listen," he told the room, "That was Scry. He wants to perform and he's on his way! Where's the co-producer?" With that, he ran to the control room. Everyone started buzzing - with the country's most popular artists in one show, the audience would go mad.

Minutes later when Scry had arrived, the make-up artist noticed he looked extra pale, so they tried to add colour in his cheeks and hide his dark under-eye circles. It was five minutes to show-time, and everyone had on their microphone headsets, ready and waiting in the lobby. Scry walked up to Anthony and Maria and shook their hands.

"Very nice to see you again," he smiled, then explained in his usual high-pitched voice, "I heard that DuoDynos was coming and simply couldn't sit back and watch without being here. I feel responsible for the bears."

Maria gave him a thankful smile. Scry's manager briefed the pop-star about the SmartBear plan, making sure he knew to emphasize the positive news and explain the campaign results – and to, under no circumstances, mention the SmartBear upgrade plan. Scry agreed to hand-out the social media teddy bear sales winner. Just then, the stage manager came in and guided Scry back-stage to prepare.

***

"My dear friends," Scry's squeaky voice addressed the eagerly listening audience, "I'd like to ask you to give a big hand for two special friends. Please welcome them directly from the UN headquarters in New York and teddy bear headquarters in Atlanta - Maria and Anthony!" As Maria and Anthony walked on stage, Scry made his famous V-shape, peace symbol.

Maria blinked in the spotlight, almost blinded by it at first, and the burst of applause caused her pulse to race like crazy. "Thank you," she said, kissing Scry on the cheek. The well-known presenter, Chung-Hee now took over.

"Thank you Scry for bringing your friends with you. Tell me Maria, what have you been doing these last few months?" He put the microphone near Maria's mouth.

"First," she answered, "Thank you all for coming to the show, you're support means a lot. So, in the last few months, we basically worked 24-7 to produce and ship teddy bears to all corners of the world. I want to give Scry here my gratitude for helping get the word out on these bears initially. Thank you." She beamed at him and the audience went wild.

Everyone could see Scry was starting to get emotional, as always, and the fans began chanting, "Scry! Scry! Scry!" Chung-Hee calmed the audience down, then went over to Anthony, "So, tell me more about what you're doing with the funds?"

While Anthony gave an overview, a video of children playing in Africa was shown on the large screen - now they could go to schools, receive medicine and much more. It was all good news and Anthony asked the audience to applaud for every person who'd bought a bear. They went crazy, the noise reverberating off the stage.

Chung-Hee again silenced them, this time by holding up an envelope which he handed over to Scry. Maria, Anthony and Chung-Hee sat in three comfy chairs on stage, behind Scry. Now Scry had the entire spotlight. "Thank you my friends. As you might know I have had difficult times. Please don't believe what the press is saying. I just want to help everybody."

A short applause sounded and he continued, "I also want to let you know that I'm not finished yet. I'm happy to announce that I'm working on a new album." The audience erupted into whistles and excited shouts along with clapping, again with some chants of,

"Scry! Scry! Scry!"

Although he hadn't discussed the announcement of a new album with his manager, Scry felt excited and urged on by the audience, so he went on, "My friends working in the shadow." Here he turned to nod at Maria and Anthony behind him, then faced the crowd again. "They're also working on a new project – the hibernation wake-up of your beautiful bears." Maria took in a sharp breath – what the hell was he doing? But no one intervened as Scry continued,

"After an upgrade, the teddy bears will be able to teach. Please give a warm round of applause for my friends Anthony and Maria who work so hard!" Much of the crowd had bears themselves, and over the burst of applause, they shouted, "Upgrade! Upgrade! Upgrade!"

Maria felt like she couldn't breathe. Scry had gone against their agreement and announced the hibernation wake-up plan. Hundreds of thousands of people were watching this show, how could he do this? Her eyes began welling up with tears as she frantically tried to think of a way to stop this disaster. Yet, what could she do? Anthony leaned towards her and said, "Did you tell him he could announce this?" Maria shook her head and answered in a hoarse whisper,

"Not at all - this is ridiculous. He's messing things up, yet again." Her blood began to heat up with anger, and then the spotlight aimed directly at her, making her blink from its glare. Through the brightness, Maria could see Scry approaching her and heard him ask,

"Maria, please come and share a few words?" Without having to think more than a moment, she knew what to do, and whispered her plan to Scry. As she walked with him to the front of the stage, the Korean pop-star spoke into his microphone.

"Of course we need to be careful, Maria just told me she simply needs a pilot." He looked out into the crowd and put his hand in the air. "I'm sure we can solve this together! Is there a pilot in the audience? Is there a pilot who can fly the bears to Africa?"

Maria thought she was going mad. This idiot thought she was using the term 'pilot' to refer to a person able to fly a plane to Africa with bears. Maria of course referred to running a pilot project, but she realized this couldn't stopped now. Some people in the crowd screamed, "Yes here! I'll be the pilot – over here!" Scry jumped up, pulsing with adrenaline. "Please come forward, we need you," he cried. A spotlight swung to a young man who slowly came forward. Meanwhile Chung-Hee had realized that Scry was overcome by emotion from all the attention and took over.

"Speaking of teddy bears and pilots," he said, "Scry, tell me, who has generated the most social media sales spin-offs?" Oh right, Scry had almost forgotten. He now opened the envelope in his hand.

"The winner is…" Scry read the note, "Hye Kim!" An ecstatic scream sounded and a second spotlight swung into the audience. Slowly and with happy tears streaming down her cheeks, the winning teenage girl, Hye, came forward. She lined up on stage with Scry, Maria, Anthony, the pilot and Chung-Hee came over and gave her flowers.

"Congratulations Hye," the host said, "You've generated a total of 860 additional teddy bear sales, well done!" Tears of happiness streaming from his face, Scry knelt next to Hye and kissed her hand. The audience roared with excitement and Chung-Hee walked over to Anthony.

"This is all wonderful news. Anthony, can you please let us know when the children in Africa will be able to get lessons from their upgraded bears?"

Anthony looked a little uncomfortable but replied, "As soon as we can safely do it, though I can't tell you an exact date. Perhaps Maria can tell you more?" He gave Maria a subtle pleading look but Chung-Hee walked to the front of the stage where the pilot from the audience stood.

Chung-Hee silenced the audience and asked, "Please tell us, how long does it take to fly to Africa if we take a safe route?"

"Including the preparation we can fly there in forty-eight hours, then it will take another twelve hours to get all the way there," the man, who was apparently a real pilot, explained.

"Well that's all excellent news," Chung-Hee said, then walked to Maria. "Maria, this hibernation wake-up sounds amazing. How were you able to arrange it?" Maria knew she had to choose her words carefully.

"Well, we have many colleagues who are working on the toys of the future, and this is only the beginning." Chung-Hee was running out of time and didn't let her continue.

"That's awesome news Maria, please give our teddy bear friends their well-earned applause!" During the overwhelming applause, background music for Scry's song began to play and he took centre stage to sing.

Maria and Anthony were guided backstage and, after entering the lobby, Maria turned her pale face to the Idrel spokesman and started to cry. She'd just announced the hibernation wake-up plan to the entire world.

GIRL POWER

MARIA WATCHED MR. Lee's eleven-year-old daughter come out into the garden where she and Mr. Lee sat. Maria had been shocked when he'd invited her over to discuss the disastrous 'Scry' situation. But here she was and his clearly shy daughter came over and introduced herself as Eun.

"Eun, can you bring the bears please?" her dad asked. Maria was surprised that they had any bears at all, but he explained, "We were one of the first." He asked his daughter: "Have you ever heard of 'dances-with-bears.'?"

"No," Eun spoke softly as she shook her head, "Only that old movie, 'Dances with Wolves."

"This one is different," he told her, "We can make your bear friendlier if you want. Do you want a friendly bear?"

"Yes, please," Eun answered politely, though she wasn't really sure what her dad meant. He smiled, then faced Maria.

"Maria, can you please dance with the bear?" he asked. Maria understood now. She gently instructed the girl,

"Please hold it like this and pretend you're a statute, don't move, okay Eun?" Eun looked a bit nervous but did what Maria asked. Then, when Maria carried out the 'dancing' upgrade procedure, Eun's surprised expression turned into an amused smile.

When it was done her dad patted Eun's shoulder. "Thank you, sweetie - it's all done." Eun bended politely towards Maria, smile on her face, and quickly walked away with her upgraded bear which was now a SmartBear.

Maria looked at Mr. Lee and said, "If you let me, I'll forward the bear's mobile network subscriber details to you. With this you can enable the SmartBear to use mobile internet connectivity and have access to all content."

"Will it be safe?" Mr. Lee asked, one eyebrow quirked.

"Absolutely safe," Maria said as a smile grew on her face, "The SmartBears won't cause any trouble."

* * *

Although she was in a meeting with Tawfeek and both their spokesmen, Nikole walked out of the meeting room and answered the call. Rafael sounded insistent on the other end, "…and we, as Idrel, are a new distribution channel for them, you see?"

"Sounds great Rafael," Nikole replied, "But tell me, what exactly are you going to distribute for them?"

While driving, Rafael used his hands-free device as he answered, "The content of course. All the children's audio books, can you picture that? As Idrel, we never foresaw that we had the possibility to become a major distributor for audiobooks! You know, this publisher had already prepared audiobooks for phones. For young kids, there were no proper child-proof audio book players. They've been looking for devices all over the world and want to team up with us and our bears."

As Nikole listened to his exciting news, she walked to the coffee machine. "Well done Rafael, sounds like you're enjoying yourself, and your company's moving ahead."

"It's not bad at all," Rafael enthused, "Kind of great actually. The reason I called you is that I have a ticket for you." She selected cappuccino on the coffee machine and curled a piece of her hair with an index finger while waiting.

"A ticket?" Her pulse began to pick up.

"Yeah," he said with a smile in his voice, "A ticket for the SmartBear hibernation wake-up event in Paris. It's organised by one of our TV-channel partners. Kids can bring their bears with them and upgrade each other. It's a massive event and there will be pop-stars, famous artists and so on. You can bring friends with you if you want."

"Sounds fun," Nikole grinned, "But my bear is already upgraded into a SmartBear." He disregarded her last remark and plunged ahead,

"Listen, they expect you to come over and be in the show as one of the guests."

"Me?" she asked, "Appear on a popular TV-show?"

"Yup," he laughed, "I promised to get you on stage, didn't I?"

"Hmm, I'm not sure" she answered, "But I'll think about it."

"I'm sure you can squeeze it into your schedule," Rafael persisted, "And I also need a little help from you. Do you remember this hacker girl who helped us out?"

"Right," Nikole said, "Therese - I remember. But hold on, can we chat about this later? I've got to go back to the operator guys here. We're preparing some press stuff."

"Wait, just give me a few seconds. This girl is also attending with her parents and the producer just asked me if I could get you to agree to appear along with her. You know girl-power and so on. Is that okay?" Of course Rafael knew that when it came to girl-power, Nikole couldn't refuse.

"No problem, Rafael," she finally agreed, "Send me the details okay? I need to go back to my operator meeting now."

"Thanks Nikole," he said, relieved, "And please tell your European operator friends that we're happy to give a free audiobook to each kid that upgrades their own bear. We just want to encourage kids to turn their bears into SmartBears, and get them ready to receive content."

And with that they ended the call and Nikole returned to Tawfeek who was in a discussion with the spokesman. Tawfeek summarized, "But that means that we're not the first one at all. We're far behind the Asian operators." The spokesman dropped his head.

"Sorry, I can't do anything about it. These are the facts." Nikole quickly understood and interjected, "Listen, did you know that you're the first operator worldwide who's able to give free audio fairy-tale content to kids?"

"Are we indeed?" Tawfeek raised an eyebrow.

"Yes," she nodded, "After the hibernation wake-up others will follow, but I'm sure you can be the first with free fairy tales."

"That would be great," he beamed, "Who told you this?"

"My personal contact within Idrel just a few seconds ago," she answered proudly. "I can forward you Rafael Silva's contact details if you like."

"Yeah, that would be perfect," Tawfeek said, "There can only be one 'first'."

***

"So Maria," Wendy from Idrel's marketing team said, "If I may, you have it technically working and expect to have the SmartBear tested on Monday and you want to discuss with us how to do hibernation wake-up with the bears throughout the world. Then start on Thursday - three days from now?"

Maria confirmed with a short, "Yes." Wendy looked around the hotel lobby from Paul to Jane to Rafael then to Bruce who were all at the meeting. She was flabbergasted.

"Well" Wendy hedged, "Normally we have to make plans, agree with sales and so on. I mean…" Maria firmly interrupted,

"Listen Wendy, we have to act fast and I take all the responsibility personally. I want you to prepare a simple plan of approach – a method of telling or even showing people how to perform this hibernation wake-up procedure."

"Okay," Wendy replied softly, still in a daze.

"Or," Maria added, "Do you want me to dance and post a video myself with the hibernation wake-up routine? I can ask Scry to share it with his fans. I guess that will go viral."

"No, no, please allow us," Wendy spoke with a note of panic,

"We'll prepare a decent viral action plan. Please allow us."

Next, Bruce went on to explain that they needed to have at least ten SmartBears in each continent, given to ten students. "These students," he said, "Would receive fully paid flights and make a tour around Idrel retail chains where they'll wake-up bears. Kids can take their own bears with them and visit a shop to upgrade for free."

"And from there," Paul added, "Those new SmartBears can upgrade their friend's and family member's bears. SmartBear growth will be exponential."

"Okay," Wendy said, "Do we have enough SmartBears on standby in each continent to start this student roll-out?"

"In Asia, it's no problem," Bruce replied, "We have enough at our place."

"Same in the US," Maria said.

"What about Europe?" Wendy asked, "I only see one here on my screen." Everybody thought quietly for several moments.

"I know somebody who has a garage of twenty bears," Paul said with a wide grin, "We can call him right away and I can guarantee his cooperation."

"Where? Who is it?" Wendy and Maria asked at once.

"My brother Chris," Paul replied, "Close to Amsterdam."

"Okay, that's' great," Bruce said. "We can send an FLQ guy to his place right now with a bear and let him dance in his garage. That'll work."

"Sounds good," Maria said, "Let's keep our group in contact and aim for Monday at 1 pm, Seoul-time to start the hibernation wake-up."

"One more thing," Bruce held up a finger, "Do you want me to arrange the students and SmartBears now or…?"

"Yes," Maria answered, "Select the students and book their flights, but please ensure that nothing will happen or be communicated without approval from Wendy. We've seen things going viral before. We need to stay in control this time."

THE FUTURE

THE FLQ PRODUCTION guy had convinced Bruce to go over-the-top. "We have to do the best for our customer."

"You're right," Bruce agreed, "Then we know for sure they'll distribute the right software."

On Sunday morning three men in black suits strolled through the central hall of Shanghai Pudong International Airport, about to check in. Each had two hard suitcases which contained five SmartBears each. There was no room for clothes or toothbrushes, which they'd have to buy at their destinations of Amsterdam, Sydney and Johannesburg.

"Fuck!" Rafael slammed a fist on the table in his office twenty minutes later. The suitcases of bears weren't allowed to go on the plane to Amsterdam— too suspicious. And now it looked like Europe would be the last continent to do the SmartBear upgrade after Rafael had promised Solon they'd be the first.

"In that case," Maria told the upset Rafael over the phone, "You have a problem, but that's not an issue is it. I mean your EU-contacts aren't buying a single bear are they? Don't worry, you can call the distributors on Monday."

Rafael still wasn't satisfied with the situation and called Paul. After the poor young man had woken up, Rafael asked, "Can't we do this upgrade remotely? I mean over the air or something?"

Paul was still half-asleep, but he answered in earnest, "No, absolutely not. We either need to bring the bear from the operator lab to Chris or we simply need to fly in there."

"Paul, listen," Rafael said, "Would Therese be able to upgrade a bear?"

"Yeah of course, but she doesn't have a bear and she won't be able to fly to Amsterdam. She's got to go to school on Monday."

"Let me handle this. Give me your brother's phone number and get back to sleep. I'll handle this."

* * *

Jane and Scry almost burst into tears from laughing. "Yes, this is how the dance goes," Jane explained in a TV-studio in Seoul. Scry was willing to assist with the viral video they had to make on.

Sunday. He'd demanded that his little nephew could also be in the video. The two of them danced again, made the famous UN-finger shapes and pushed two bears to each other.

"Bear sex, sex!" Scry cried.

"Cut!" the director yelled and stopped recording. "Sorry, Scry, we can't have that in. This is for kids, remember?"

Scry bent his head, "Sorry, you're right."

"Just say dance-dance if you want, okay?" Jane smiled.

"Okay," Scry nodded, "Give it another go." The shoot continued and Scry demonstrated how to do the hibernation wake-up dance. "And after this upgrade, the bears can teach you how to count and, can also help children in need in Africa." The camera man noticed Scry's lip trembling and zoomed in on his eyes.

Yes - a small tear appeared and rolled down his cheek. This was great, exactly what they wanted. Scry continued, "Go and wake-up the bears of all your friends!" The producer was happy and Jane grinned - this was what they needed to go viral.

* * *

Valentina held Marco close to her. She had just nursed him and was trying to get him to burp. Once he did, she walked to their large garage with her new little son. "Let's see what daddy is up to," Valentina whispered in Marco's ear. Chris hadn't slept for almost two days as he prepared the boxes.

Before he'd flown to Therese in Paris, he had put all 20 bears on their charging pillow in the garage. Now he had to do the hibernation wake-up dance to turn them into SmartBears. Valentina offered to help as well, but Chris wouldn't hear of it. And after an hour he was tired of dancing, but he'd finally finished the upgrades.

There was only one problem. According to Paul's email, he had to ensure that all the bears, including the first bear upgraded by Therese, were in range of a mobile phone network. He'd packed all the bears into the boxes again and put them in a pony trailer he'd recently bought for the pony Valentina insisted their new-born son have.

As Chris drove the bears up, Valentina sat in the back of their new four wheel car with Marco. His beautiful baby boy always seemed to get excited when they went up the hill. It was the place where Chris had tried to contact the nurse when Valentina was about to give birth.

On top of the hill Chris dis-engaged the pony trailer from the car. He'd leave it here tonight and the next day a student with a rental car would pick it up and drive to various locations in Europe.

While he unclamped the trailer's tongue and positioned the jack to park the trailer, he suddenly heard a continuous stream of burps coming from inside the trailer.

Chris smiled - it was like his brother Paul had told him. The bears had found the mobile network and were ready to go.

* * *

Spring had arrived. Grams glanced up from the stroller where Marco slept and looked at the children that ran through the sunny garden in her flat's complex. "What are they doing with those teddy bears Chris? I can't see it properly because I lost a bit of my eyesight." One of the kids pushed a bear into another one and they all played that they went to sleep and lay down in the grass.

"They're sharing fairy tales." Chris explained.

"Well," Grams said, "I'm loving every minute when I watch them play - their freedom. They make me feel so alive. It's truly amazing, those toys of the future Paul told me about. I wonder how the world will look in the years to come. Can you describe to me the world you foresee?"

Chris looked from his Grams over to Marco's round, peaceful face. "I don't know exactly," he replied, "But it feels good and I guess we simply say 'hello to the future'."

* * *

"Ahoy there, sailor," Jane said into her phone as she waited with some friends at a trendy French restaurant in downtown Amsterdam. It was a month after they'd launched the SmartBears and she and Paul had planned an early farewell dinner before taking off on their next adventure – hopefully one that was free of bears, massive arguments and painful injuries.

Jane and Paul had arranged a week-long sailing trip around the Mediterranean, starting in Trieste, Italy. They'd been going strong for the last few months – no big fights, and Paul had been careful to make time for Jane and not be constantly attached to his computer or smartphone. He didn't want a repeat of the Nepal fiasco, and definitely didn't want to repeat his Kat break-up experience.

However, Paul was already fifteen minutes late to dinner and Jane felt a little doubt deep inside. "Babe, I'm so sorry," Paul answered, "I got held up – do you mind if maybe I skip this one out?" Jane heard the words, but couldn't fully process them – her brain felt like it'd frozen and her heart dropped into her stomach. Could he be serious? Were they at this place – this dreadfully awful place – in their relationship again?

The two of them were supposed to fly out and sail around one of the most gorgeous areas in the world for a week, and he was pulling this stunt again. "I...Paul," she stammered into her phone, "Are you serious? I thought..." Jane's words were cut off as one of her friends nudged her in the arm with a smile and gestured towards the restaurant's entrance.

A mixture of disbelief, affection and annoyance washed through Jane as she saw Paul walking towards their table with a mischievous grin on his face, dark hair disheveled as usual. She stood and gave his arm a good shove, though she couldn't keep the smile off of her face. "You devil you – I was about to...you scared me."

Paul put his arms around her waist and stole a quick kiss before saying, "I know. It was kind of darker humour I guess, but I couldn't resist. And sorry I made you wait." Jane stepped back and shook her head, the left side of her mouth tilting up.

"Fine," she relented, "I guess I'm kinda used to it now anyway – just don't ever make me wait too long, okay?" Paul's expression turned more serious and he locked his gaze on her vivid green eyes.

"Never," he said simply.

* * *

The shimmering deep blue water rippled in a stiff breeze as the old-fashioned clipper ship sailed away from Trieste and towards Croatia's coast. Paul and Jane stood at the bow of the sailboat, taking a break from their crew duties.

They'd found an older couple who owned this boat and always

took on crew in order to both teach them sailing skills and give an exciting tour of the Mediterranean. The cost was pretty low since all those on-board were partially working for their below-deck rooms and food.

As the two of them stood there, the sound of a pinging phone made them both glance down at Paul's coat pocket. He pulled it out, seeing a text from Rafael as well as an email from Mr. Drel. For a moment, Paul considered responding, but he'd promised to keep work at minimum to zero for the entire week, so he and Jane could finally have a screen-free, and hopefully stress-free, vacation.

Without a second glance, Paul slipped the phone back into his pocket and pushed any thought of work or SmartBears to the side. Jane leaned over to kiss him on the cheek. "Thanks honey," she said in a low voice, eyes shimmering along with the evening sunlight that bounced off the water.

And they sailed off into the molten sun, focused only on each other and the thrilling adventure ahead.

— ● —

RESOURCES

GSMA IOT CLP.03 ANNEX A

Annex A of the GSMA IoT Guidelines "GSMA IOT CLP.03" contains reports from mobile operators who have faced severe network issues caused by IoT devices. It was the trigger for writing this book.

MUSIC

Some dialogs are inspired by the following songs:

Katy Perry *(Wide Awake)*, Corcovado Frequency *(Connect)*, Daft Punk *(Giorgio by Moroder)*, Imogen Heap *(Telemiscommunications)*, Thugli *(Run This)*, Deadmau5 *(Maths – Botnek Remix)*, Röyksopp *(I Had This Thing)*, Lady Gaga *(Telephone)*, Dua Lipa *(Be the One)*, Gary Clark Jr. *(You Saved Me)*, Tove Lo *(Talking Body)*, Dynamic Duo *(AEAO)*, The Shapeshifters *(Lola's Theme-radio edit)*, Empire of the Sun *(Alive)*.

Search for the playlist: "book disrupted when iot"

ACKNOWLEDGMENTS

During the last few years, we have put quite a number of traditional teddy bears on tables during IoT workshops. It helps participants to open their minds and start creative brainstorming for IoT-use cases, business benefits and beneficiaries.

The actual story popped into my head while reading the IoT GSMA Guidelines which contain a list of "networks almost going down events" described from a mobile operator's point of view.

Although some readers might think they recognize situations or persons, all names and scenarios in the story are randomly taken and any similarity to reality is simply coincidental.

I would like to thank many friends working in the IoT and mobile network industry and working at various Dutch and European governmental organisations.

Special thanks goes to Arjan de Heer, Lucien de Konink, Michel Tiessens, and Ward van Wanrooij who shared their ideas on mobile network behaviour and open-source software strategy.

I would like to thank my IOTC360 partner, Gilles Robichon, who encouraged me to proceed with this amazing project.

I have deep respect for my US writing partner, Charlotte

Hipolito. Charlotte was able to make the characters come to life. She was a great help during the whole writing process, re-ordering the story-lines, and speeding up the pace.

Many thanks to the reader panel members for their honest and open feedback: Stijn en Bart van Boxmeer, Ann Connolly, Vincent Everts, Bart Faber, Svetlana Grant, Annika Heerekop, Kristine Keesey, Maxime Oosterhof, Jan Prins, Dave (chopper pilot!) Rietveld, Machteld Lindenkamp, Manfred Roosenstein, Afke Schaart, and Ulla Sokka.

Last, but not least, I would like to thank my wife Simone and my children for their patience and you, the reader, for reading this story.

Whether the story about a SmartBear plays nowadays or in the future, one thing is for sure: the future starts today.

Robert J. Heerekop

The Hague, November 2016

TABLE OF CONTENTS

PART 3 - THE LESSONS